POOL

Robin Beaudette

Robin Beaudette

L & L Dreamspell

Spring, Texas

Cover and Interior Design by L & L Dreamspell

This is a work of fiction, and is produced from the author's imagination. People, places and things mentioned in this novel are used in a fictional manner.

ISBN: 978-1-60318-122-8

Library of Congress Control Number: 2009926361

Visit us on the web at www.lldreamspell.com

Published by L & L Dreamspell
Printed in the United States of America

Enormous thanks to:

Michaeline Della Fera
Lorraine Lordi
"The Queen"
and the Eminent Writers Group
who helped me hatch my first plot.
Lieutenant John Scippa
My loyal family and friends who have been supportive
readers and an inspiration.
Cherri Galbiati
Hollis Police Department
Mischievous Fairies
Mom and Dad
Theresa Tucker and Amy Zapp
Cindy Davis, the Fiction Doctor
L&L Dreamspell for the opportunity
And Steve, Jonathan and Eric,
Mugsy, Steggs, and especially, Porka.

One

Ice pushed at the sides of the pool like an iceberg. The thick crust spread across the top, but underneath the frigid water remained slow and loose. Only the very top of the water of in-ground pools actually freezes. The freeform design of the cement hole allows for the unique curves that mirror a deformed, bloated kidney. The decking around the area is barren of any decoration. All outdoor furniture is stored away. The new high-tech cover is green mesh, much like a large trampoline, and is harnessed to the concrete with cables. Water seeps through, but leaves and debris do not. Neither do elephants, according to the advertisements.

Most pools in the Northeast are closed by the end of September. Even with heaters, autumn is an endless battle. The lines are drained, equipment turned off in time to brace for harsh winters. The pool is neatly dormant. The remains of a body scattered on the bottom will remain undisturbed until the warm sun returns. Right now three feet of snow sink into the green cover. The tomb sleeps.

Six months earlier...

Kyle Mercer recited her list of errands: grocery store, dry cleaner, and the vet's office to pick up eye medicine for Maggie, the family dog, the only other "girl" in the house. Kyle picked her out of a litter of rambunctious, chocolate, little heads chewing each other. Her buddy. Kyle rocked her to sleep as a pup, in a blanket, and now rarely left her side without giving the canine an explanation. And a milk bone.

"Will the excitement never end?" If she hurried she'd be home in time to start dinner. With one motion, she grabbed her keys and patted the Lab, who sat dutifully by the door. Maggie's big brown eyes widened. She'd listen to any complaints if she could go for a ride in the car.

"Come on, Maggie. Let's go." Kyle opened the door and headed for the car. Maggie got there first, as usual, tail wagging. Just as Kyle lifted the handle, the dog snapped her head toward the woods, pointed her tail and growled. One hand reaching for the collar, Kyle turned her attention in that direction. She scanned the edge of the back yard along the grass line and then moved her eyes into the dense trees. With several acres of untouched greenery behind the house, it was a haven for animals small and not so small. On more than one occasion, deer, porcupine and wild turkey emerged. Maggie's interest today was probably focused on something in the rodent family.

"I don't have time for chasing squirrels today." Kyle gripped Maggie's collar and dragged her into the back of the silver late model Explorer. The dog groaned and barked. "Lie down! Or you're going to find your way back to obedience class."

Squatting low, a young male watched as the sparkling clean SUV drove away. He stood and leaned against a thick pine tree; the rough bark stuck into his back. His dark clothes melted into the background. Military boots squashed the mud under his feet. Days of record rain for New Hampshire had put him behind schedule. He pulled out a pack of Marlboro cigarettes and lit one up with his Bic lighter. Putting the lighter away, he reached for his small notepad and noted:

12 *Bowen St yellow house*
brown dog, Maggie, responds to commands

He also scratched in the day and time. He looked around, crushed his cigarette into the small pile of butts and retraced his steps, but first kicked some leaves over the pile of litter. From the slight elevation, the pool and patio were completely exposed. He fixed his gaze, studying the scene. A dog door on the back of the house led out to the fenced-in area around the pool, and a far gate that opened to the forest. Neat rows of split wood sat piled in an intersecting stack outside the fence. A large axe shined in the sunlight. He smirked. Why don't they just leave me a key? He turned to the woods and moved on.

Behind the wheel, Kyle flinched at the little techno song coming from the cellphone. Even after months, its ring still startled her. She could never find it to shut it up. The music had a harsh tone, but she had no idea how to change it, having missed the technological revolution. Her husband, Jason, and son, Jeffrey, touted the endless abilities of the little black communicator. "We survived okay for years without them."

Unfortunately, her family of two men did not. Information was kept, stored, formatted and DVR'd. The urgency of that was the most irritating. One second you're alone with your thoughts, dull as they may be, the next, someone is expecting a response. "Hello?"

"It's me," came her husband Jason's voice. "Hey, have Jeffrey call me later, after he's checked the mail. Oh, and I saw Mulhorn; he's expecting us Saturday night at that reception."

"Thanks, Jay. I'm fine. And how is your day?" Kyle groaned.

"Give me a break, Ky."

"Do we really have to go Saturday? Dr. and Mrs. Drone are two of the slowest speaking, uninteresting people in the world. I'd rather clean a closet than be stuck with them all night."

"He's the head of the department. We have to go. Have Jeffrey call me. I'll be in surgery until at least four. I'll be late tonight. Bye." Click.

"What am I going to wear?" Kyle spoke into the dead line.

He wouldn't care or understand anyway. Everything fit him.

He could still wear the same tux he wore to their wedding nineteen years ago. Other than the few gray hairs that dared peek over his ears, he didn't look his age. Each morning, he found time to run either outdoors or on the treadmill. Alternative workouts included mountain biking, tennis and kayaking. The evidence sat in a small pile on their bathroom tile floor. On more than one occasion, Kyle stepped into the sweat-soaked clothes on her way to the toilet. She often left them for him to pick up, but couldn't stand seeing them there all day. He promised daily to "get to them." And seldom did.

"Next time I have a school committee function for the town, I'm making him go!" Kyle said to the canine and let out a breath. Her confidant, always the patient listener, dropped her ears when Kyle finished. Her husband's profession as a surgeon consumed their lives. Her job was support staff, which most of the time was fine.

A stop at the dry cleaners yielded no help with clothing options for Saturday. Her clothes all seemed ancient. After a few hours of running, she pulled the SUV up the long, inclined driveway past the thick private line of trees. The lawn needed one more mowing before the first frost arrived. The recent rain had pushed the grass up another inch. Fresh, creamy yellow paint adorned the acorn style house. The many peaks and levels reminded Kyle of the first time she saw *The House of Seven Gables*. The home was bigger than they needed; Jason and Kyle expected to have more children. Jason, the oldest of six, thought that was a nice round number. Kyle, being an only child, felt half of that would be more manageable. But after years of trying, it became clear that more children were not meant to be. Jeffrey was now eighteen and applying to colleges, fleeing the nest. These days Kyle's mind rarely wandered to babies.

Two

Brendan Reed leaned backward in his buttery soft, black leather chair. It smelled like a new car. Sleek, with the comfort level of something that should garner the name, La-Z-Boy. He could sleep in this chair and might need to on occasion. It was just what he requested. After making Junior Partner, he met with the firm's interior designer about his *space*. That was in late July. Two months later, the airhead designer with purple glasses still did not have it completed. He took nothing from his old office on the second floor. It was all junk. Being moved to a higher floor was literally "a step up." The main entrance to the firm was on the second floor with all of the daily business that it brought. Once some punk delivery boy, with piercings, and earphones swinging around his neck, wandered into the office and asked him to sign for something. What the hell! He had done his gopher time. After finishing Law School, he clerked for State reps, schlepped lunches, chauffeured mistresses and even pretended not to care when one of the married state officials cornered him one night and squeezed the front of his pants. One of the good old boys' in a jungle with mahogany doors instead of trees.

Brendan finally saw some light when he landed the job here, a rare opportunity in a firm filled with descendants of prominent families. He was their attempt at diversity, a white guy with no family money. Brendan grew up in central Massachusetts, in a stagnant mill town whose claim to fame was that it had the most registered gun owners and bars in the state; and currently closing in on a record for the most pizza parlors too. The most progressive action a resident could take was to get out. So with his secrets, his family and financial aid, he pushed his way through college and law school. His loans were almost paid off and his family far away. His younger brother was in and out of the House of Correction, just like his father. His mom worked various little jobs to retain the trailer size home. Last he heard she was working as a chambermaid at a truck stop motel. No real accomplishments, good or bad.

Brendan put the hours in...and in. His new paralegal, Melanie, was competent but more importantly, showed the respect he deserved. She didn't bother him with unimportant tasks. She did, however, keep up with office news and looked great. She was a keeper, at least for now.

Brendan glanced out his oversized window, proud of the coveted location. Unlike many of the other partners, he was on the "right" side of the building, looking out onto Congress Street, not some back alley. Getting this view meant almost as much as the increased salary. Early September? What a dreary day. Cool and rainy, a lousy day to go out, but he left the suit jacket over the back of the chair and pulled on his black trench coat. He inspected the micro-fiber garment, pleased it looked as good as the day he bought it a month ago.

"My cell's on," he reported to Mel without stopping, and stepped into the elevator. He exited the building on the Congress Street side. Avoiding puddles, he made his way across the street to "Jean-Paul's Fine Men's Clothing Since 1962". He entered, shook off his coat and hung it on one of the many brass hooks to the left. The interior boasted deep mahogany wood tables and built-in shelves with brass accents. Rose and tan granite tiles adorned the floor. Soft piano music filled the air and crystal light fixtures sparkled. Dust never made it to this floor. Jean-Paul's establishment had an unspoken dress code.

Bright summer colors hanging on a window display popped out at him: lime, orange and yellow. Weekend wear. He moved to a row of linen jackets he'd considered buying before. They were now on sale. A thin salesman in crisp clothes, with a pencil mustache and a waist no bigger than 30 inches, said, "Hello" and nothing more. A couple of other men browsed.

Was he too early? He had a meeting in forty-five minutes and couldn't hang around forever. Brendan meandered around the racks searching for something other than clothes. Then he saw her, standing high on a stool…Kate. Long lean legs, smooth, blonde hair, and a perky ass. He'd watched her for months. Today, she wore a soft blue shirt and black pants that, if not for Lycra, would fall from her narrow hips. Her thick hair fell flat against her back in a blunt-cut line.

He dropped his jewelry in his pocket and smoothed the sides of his hair back. "Hi."

"Hi." Her face warmed to a smile.

"What have you got there?" He motioned to the clothing in her hand.

"Oh…these just came in…silk tee's. They're nice for fall. I was just trying to pin one up on display." Kate climbed down, and with her hand pushed her hair back over her head. She tucked the back of her shirt in, trying to hide a tiny rose tattoo with a stem spiraling downwards into her thong. Standing inches away, she inhaled the tailored smell of his designer aftershave that came along with him on every visit.

"Maybe I'll try one. What color do you think?" Brendan flashed a smile.

"You're a medium…" She held up a light blue shirt. "It goes with your," she paused looking back at the blue eyed, fair haired man, "coloring."

"I'll try it." He took the garment from her hands and said, "Hey, you look like you got some sun," referring to freckles sprinkled over her nose and sun burnt cheeks.

"I went to the Cape with a couple of friends for the weekend. We saw the sun on Saturday. The rest of the time it poured. But we had fun. This weather's unbelievable, huh?"

"Well, good for you. It was just plain crap around here all weekend. Do you have a place on the Cape?"

"No, my family does…in Chatham, but they never use it."

He entered the dressing room and tossed the overpriced t-shirt on the shelf. He had a collection at home, among the vast wardrobe he had built up with careful choices and the ability to maintain his off-the-rack size 38. His long and lean physique served him well over the years. The biggest payoff was when he was offered cash to model some clothes at a Boston hotel event during law school. He remembered asking, "You want to pay me to walk around and smile?" He'd agreed to try it once. Though one had to avoid the obvious gay element, it had one important payoff: watching young, lanky girls wearing only panties getting their hair coiffed. Better than any bar, it proved to be a consistent source of entertainment. It was where he met his wife.

Brendan emerged from the dressing room a changed man.

"Well," Kate circled inspecting the shirt. She stalled behind him, pulling a bit at the hem. A sharp current ran through his spine jump-starting the litany of short fantasies in which Kate starred.

"It really doesn't do anything for you."

Brendan smirked. "I thought you got paid on commission."

"You wouldn't be a repeat customer, Mr. Reed, if I didn't tell the truth."

Brendan loved the concept of truth, but it was merely a summation of what one perceived as facts, but he loved those who voluntarily subscribed.

They caught each other's eyes. Kate looked away first, glancing down to his commitment-free fingers. She pulled up the back of her shirt; making sure her artwork was visible. She was glad to have it, despite hearing her mother's words, disgusted by the "tramp stamp."

"Kate, I told you, call me Brendan, please."

"There's a rule here…Brendan." She smiled.

"I don't do rules. Besides, the customer's always right!" he responded.

After some other small-talk about the weather, this rain kind of making everyone crazy, Brendan made his way to his coat, wondering if it was too soon. Even with the careful calculations, usually the first shot was the only one.

As the married attorney spoke, Kate looked over his shoulder. "Oh, sorry. The son's in charge today. He's so creepy. Every time I look at him he's rubbing that sorry excuse of a mustache. He's gross. And it's just the two of us 'til closing time. My skin's always crawling by then. I try to get out of here as soon as I can, but he always finds things to keep me."

"Tell him you have plans to meet a friend for drinks."

"Who?"

"Me."

The rain rolled off Brendan on his way back to the office. Head held high, he walked with a skip in his step. Just as he reached the lobby, his cell phone rang. Caller ID wiped the smile from his face and he let out a huff.

"Hi. It's me."

"Hey, Sarah, I'm pretty busy; can I call you later?"

"I just wanted to remind you, we have that reception on Saturday night at the hospital. Do you need anything taken to the dry cleaners?"

"No, just the regular stuff. Gotta go, I'm already running behind. Don't wait up."

"Okay. I'll take the late aerobics class. Don't work too hard. Bye."

At his floor, he noticed a commotion at his office door. "Mel?"

"Hi, Brendan, the rest of your furniture is here. It's beautiful. The designer's here, too, arranging. I told her to hurry. She should be finished soon." Mel's hands swung, pleading her case.

He stepped into his office. New prints graced the walls. Fabric and wood chairs sat across from a deep brown leather couch;

an earth toned wool area rug stretched out under the furniture. Many of the partners had couches in their offices already. They, and the full-service restroom on this floor, came in handy on late nights. The restroom, called the "spa," was stocked with towels and all the essentials, open areas with sinks, four private showers and toilets. Rumor had it that the firm once had a nearby apartment for late nights and guests. However, it had apparently been used for more play than work, so "old man Hessman" got rid of it. He hadn't got any for years, so he didn't want anyone else having any fun.

Gathering folders and his laptop, Brendan started off to the conference room. "Mel, one hour!" he ordered, handing her his soaked coat. With that she turned and eyed the designer.

Three

Six thirty-four p.m. Kyle tugged at her plum dress. It clung a bit more than ever before.

Jason called to her from downstairs. "Hey, Kyle how much longer?"

"Be right down," she yelled back. Her shoulder length, straight brown hair was held back securely by a shiny barrette. A single strand of graduated pearls hung from her neck, a gift from Jason for her thirtieth birthday. Another evening she'd spent alone, waiting for him in a restaurant. Finally he'd arrived, as always, exhausted, out of breath and distracted. It came with the territory. But he was not on call tonight. The necklace swung back and forth as she darted across the room. Black clutch bag in hand, she slid her feet into her black strappy sandals and took a deep breath.

"Jason, will you run some of the names by me again?" Kyle asked as she wrestled will the seatbelt, trying not to wrinkle her dress too much.

He ticked off the names of the CEO, the Board Members, Physicians and other staff that would be in attendance.

"I'll never remember all of the names."

"Oh yes, Sam Heffron is another. He'll be there."

"How long do we have to stay?"

"You'll be fine. Think positive."

"I'm positive all right," she mumbled, tugging once more at her dress.

The reception already buzzed with activity. A bright young architect had outdone himself. The east side of the Beaudsarts Building had been extended with an enormous addition. The new surgical wing had state of the art equipment, computers, big screens, everything but portholes to beam you to another universe.

With much effort, a large reception area had been transformed into a glamorous gathering space. Silver and gold balloons covered the high ceiling, their long ribbons dangling. A small fountain erupted water from its center. Large glass vases with tall irises adorned the sides of the room but the Stargazer lilies in the table arrangements won out and scented the air. A few small tables and chairs were scattered around while a single harpist in the corner plucked quiet sounds that floated throughout the high space. The whoosh/pop of uncorking champagne interrupted the low chatter.

A sea of black dresses, dark suits and tall glasses clustered beneath the shimmering balloons. An occasional light dress peeked out from amongst the waves. A rebel.

"Time to go swimming." Avoid the sharks. She hoped to find her way to Ann Marie Donahue, another doctor's wife with whom she found safe harbor during previous events. Kyle looked around with her head high, and sneezed. Heads turned. She felt as if a spotlight just hit her, highlighting every wrinkle and imperfection in "high definition" in front of a panel of judges.

"Great. My allergies are acting up. I'll be right back. I've got to get some tissues."

"I'll get you a glass of wine," Jason said as he stepped off into the sea of bodies. He was a strong swimmer. He was tall, so he'd get plenty of air.

Kyle made a quick exit. She reached the room marked LADIES and stocked up on tissues. She put on more lipstick and shrugged her shoulders. Good enough. Her nose was already red. Her sinuses would be combating those flowers all night. She stepped back out and combed the faces. After a few moments, she spotted Jason next to the temporary bar. Two 20-something women cornered him. He smiled and chatted, while his head bobbed up and around. Kyle laughed to herself. She knew he'd never even remember their names. She had been with him for more than twenty years and at times he barely remembered hers. They must be the same young administrative assistants who arranged the Christmas party. No spouses. Jason had always refused to go to the holiday gatherings. Kyle didn't care, knowing that most staff and nurses either loved him or hated him. Lately, it had been more of the latter. Marriage security.

She smoothed and tugged at her dress one last time. She braved the waves and rode the surf, moving through the crowd. There would be wine at the end of the journey. Jason looked over and caught her gaze.

"This is my wife, Kyle," he said to the two women as he handed across a glass. Without mentioning their names, he said, "They work in billing." The women exchanged greetings and smiles.

"Would you excuse us? We haven't said hello to Dr. Mulhorn yet," Jason said and led Kyle away.

Oh, yippee, thought Kyle. Dr. Drone.

"So are you looking forward to your trip next summer?" Dr. Mulhorn asked. Kyle tried to answer without staring at his thick, mountainous eyebrows that reminded her of wooly caterpillars. The gray accent hairs looked like snow. She wondered if they affected his vision. He was a brilliant man who never managed to relinquish a monotone delivery. He could be saying either that you had a fatal illness or had just hit the lottery. It would all sound the same.

"Yes, I'm excited. And won't it be terrific to get out of all of this rain?" Kyle said. "I've never been to Rome. We have already started making plans. Jeffrey wasn't sure he wanted to spend six weeks in Rome, but we made him an offer he couldn't refuse." As Kyle spoke, another couple joined them.

Dr. Mulhorn did the honors. "Jason and Kyle Mercer, this is Brendan and Sarah Reed. Brendan is an attorney from Angus

Hessman's firm. Brendan has generously agreed to fill the legal advisory post to the Board. Angus was with us for years, but he's scaling back. I believe the Reeds live in Hollis, also."

While they all shook hands, Kyle admired the handsome couple. Brendan was at least six foot, not much shorter than Jason, and slim, with a kind of boyish smile. His blond hair and blue eyes gave him an all-American look, like the star quarterback. Sarah had a tall, slender body that filled out her calf length black dress. She had beautiful, thick dark hair and big eyes held up by strong cheekbones. Kyle found her stunning and wondered if she had ever been paid to wear clothes.

The circle widened, and Kyle found herself on the sideline next to Sarah. Kyle looked up to make eye contact. "I love your dress."

"Oh, thanks," Sarah said. "I got a great deal on it at Saks in Dallas when we were visiting my parents. Did I hear you're going to Rome next summer?"

"Yes, some big conference with surgeons from all over the world. An old professor from medical school got Jason interested. It will be an adventure. There are eleven US docs attending."

"Well, I'm jealous. I've never been. And the food!" Looking at Sarah, Kyle didn't think she indulged much.

They talked about Hollis and some people they knew in common. Being a big horse town, they both knew owners. The Della Fera's just purchased a new horse, Clara. They expect her to be a champion. The conversation drifted to the depressing weather. Brendan listened to the larger group talk, but he also kept an ear on Sarah.

"So you're already making plans for next summer. Will you have someone look in on the house?" she inquired.

"It's the less obvious things that will get me. I took care of the mail and we won't bother opening the pool this year; no big loss considering the weather. But I think of something new each day. I've contacted the cable and the electric companies, and we've worked out the service. I'm sure I'm going to forget something.

Hopefully my mom will catch it. She's going to check the house from time to time."

Kyle noticed the grace with which Sarah held herself, swinging her weight onto one slight hip, manicured fingers holding the wine glass like an accessory. Her thick lips were outlined in a line of mauve; her gentle motions seemed fluid.

The bottom of the glass stared back at Kyle. People had come and gone, but she and Jason were still in the company of Dr. Drone. Her feet ached and she held back yawns. She could only think of her cat, Pumpkin, curled up on her bed, getting a head start.

Upon finally returning home, Kyle stripped off her pantyhose—the great constrictors—even before the dress. In less than five minutes, she'd washed clean, donned a cotton nightgown and had her book open. Pumpkin found a spot next to her and settled in. The nightly ritual. The cat poked her head up when Jason emerged from the bathroom and climbed into bed.

"See, that wasn't so bad," he said.

"It was fine."

"You worry too much." Jason reached over and pulled her book away with a smirk on his face. He tossed it to the wood floor.

"Hey, I was reading that."

"You can read tomorrow night while I'm on call." He turned off the light. In the process, he displaced the feline. Pumpkin fled.

Four

A little bleep went off on the screen. Brendan watched the flash as he listened to his client review his position for the fourth time. He could repeat it all he wanted; it wouldn't change the facts. His company was partially responsible for the failure of some kidney patients not receiving proper or complete dialysis. Yes, the hospital staff should have monitored the entire process, but these were still his machines. Mr. Parker was someone he dealt with only because he could pay. The second he got behind, he was history.

"Mr. Parker," Brendan interrupted, "I will look at it again, but I really don't think we have any other strategies. At this point, we really can only limit your company's liability. You're going to take a hit. I'll ask for a second opinion here and get back to you. I'll have Mel call you about an appointment next week." Brendan hung up and his hands raced to his keyboard.

The icon told him he had an IM. Few people had this address, and his wife wasn't one of them. A smile jumped to his face when he read the sender's name; "KATwTOYS".

"Love to get together tonite...dinner and DESSERT...know you're busy, but need some fun. Respond ASAP."

His fingers worked fast. "Hi, K, love dinner/will def save room for dessert... might even want my dessert first! C U @ 6, but I have to work later. B." Send. He sat back in his leather chair, still smelling new, and marveled at the computer age. Letting his fingers do the walking, private and efficient. A knock at the door swung his attention back to work. He let out a deep breath and stuffed Kate's image to the back of his mind.

Mel entered. "I've got everything together for the Parker case. I'm sorry to put him through again. He said he forgot to tell you something important." Mel knew the answer from Brendan's glance to the ceiling.

"Its okay, Mel. Would you call him tomorrow and set up a meeting for next week? Just an hour. I'll charge him for another five hours to tell him the same thing I did today. Maybe then he'll accept it."

"You have a meeting with Angus at 4:00. If you're all set, I'll be leaving before you get through. I start my law classes tonight."

Brendan shook his head affirmatively. "The calls are covered?" He knew Mel would take care of it before she left for her class. She'd started taking Law classes at night. At this rate, she would take the bar when Brendan was retiring. But, the more she knew, the better for him. She took care of so many details now, he'd forgotten how do them himself.

The day seemed to drag by, Brendan was eager to leave. As if looking out from a cage, he spent long periods staring out the window, planning his evening's extra circular activities. He revisited every curve of Kate's tight body, lingering on a vision of her firm breasts, trying to pick a place to start...and finish. He was out the door when the time came.

He parked his navy Jeep, still with that new car smell, at the first spot he could find, but still had to walk several blocks. He brushed off his clothes, removed and untied his silk tie. He hung it around his collar, evenly hanging down on the front of his shirt. He walked fast compared to the other weary travelers in the muggy air. His jacket swung over his shoulder, held by one hand, just like a Ralph Lauren ad. The still somewhat crisp white shirt folded up at the cuffs and his Italian leather shoes melted onto the steamy pavement. The weathered brick building loomed ahead, smaller than most on the street, with much less traffic in and out.

In the alcove, he pushed the button next to 2B. There were only three floors, with two apartments on each floor. He waited a minute and then pushed the button again. No response. The sweat on his forehead thickened. He considered using his cell phone, but dropped it back in his pocket. With caller ID, Kate would then have his number, which he still wanted to avoid. He pressed again and held the button down. An annoying buzz hissed.

"Hello?" Kate's voice answered.

"Hey, it's me. I'm outside."

"Sorry. I was in the shower. You're early."

The door buzzed and Brendan passed through. He took the stairs instead of the dated elevator. Kate was at the apartment door when he reached the landing on the second floor. She gave a quick glance to the other apartment. Seeing no sign of life, she let the door swing open, revealing herself in a thin robe, wet hair, and a big smile. Brendan was behind the closed door in an instant.

"If you're ever waiting again, use the back door. It's usually unlocked," Kate instructed.

His appetite was ravenous. Within seconds, her robe was on the floor revealing her firm body and long limbs. Her wet hair dripped down her back. The cool air in the air-conditioned apartment dried Brendan's skin. Kate unbuttoned his shirt and ran her tongue down his chest, with her hands framing her work. Brendan let out a loud moan when she dropped to her knees and unzipped his pants. Eager to get down to business, he eased her up to a more comfortable location.

On their way to the bedroom, the only other room besides the bathroom, Kate darted away to turn off the stove. She met Brendan in the bedroom and watched as he removed his pants and folded them over a chair. His body looked different than that of guys her age, 24, but not much. He was slender with some mass about his shoulders and some wrinkles crept from around his eyes. The two joined in the fluffy, queen size bed and were quick to entangle. Despite the cool air, sweat formed on Brendan's forehead again.

Kate snuggled up close and asked Brendan if he was hungry for food now. In agreement that it was time for sustenance, he pulled on his pants, leaving his shirt unbuttoned and open. He stretched his neck from side to side. His watch read 8:07. If he kept to the schedule, he'd be home by ten.

When he reached the small, too bright, canary yellow kitchen, like a cave on Prozac, Kate had retrieved her pink robe. "WOW! That's some color!"

"I picked it out myself. Isn't it great?" Kate fussed with the table set with two plates of chicken. She spooned out pilaf.

"Just a little. I'm really not that hungry," he said. A previous meal proved Kate a mediocre cook. No matter, she had other talents. She handed across a bottle of the same Boston Ale he ordered at the bar the first night they met after work. He smiled as he cracked open the now staple in her frig. "You always pay so much attention to detail?" He laughed.

"Only with things that interest me," Kate said.

After dinner, they left their plates on the table and sat on the couch. Kate put both her hands on his chest and pushed his shirt away. Her hands pressed hard on his skin, rubbing against his nipples. She kissed his chest and as she spoke her hot breath hit his skin. "I know you have to leave soon. Will you let me know when you can stay the night?"

"I've still got work left to do, Kate," Brendan said as she continued nuzzling.

"Brendan." She sat back and met his eyes. "I know you work a lot, but I also know you must go home somewhere to someone. And I know I'm not supposed to be asking any questions. This is just fun. That's all I want, too. But…be honest with me…you're married, aren't you?" she said with flush cheeks.

"Kate, look…I told you, I am in no position to start anything serious. Isn't that enough? I'm trying real hard to be honest." He leaned back, moving his hands from her to the back of the couch.

"I'm sorry. It's just that I'd like to see you more often. And

I think it would be easier for me if I understood..." Her speech trailed off. She hung her head.

"Okay. But just remember, you wanted to know." Brendan paused and looked at the ceiling. Just what he wanted to have, a relationship talk with a twenty-something. Every time this started, it only meant problems with future liaisons and he didn't expect Kate to be any different. He delved into his speech, feeling all the enjoyment being sucked out of the evening. "Technically, I am still married. My wife and I are trying to work out something quietly. I didn't want to split up when I was up for partnership. I need her to want this to end smoothly. It's going to take time. If she gets mad and hires an attorney, I'm toast. They'll go after the financial records of the firm and she'll hit me up for future profits. I might as well quit." He shook his head, and rubbed his eyes. He glanced at his watch. "I've already told you too much. I really shouldn't be getting into this. And, you can't tell anyone about me. ANYONE. If she ever found out, she'd blow her stack. She's got nothing to lose. Kate, promise me."

Kate reached up and put her arms around him, making sure her breasts rubbed up against him. She pressed her cheek against his face and whispered, "I promise, not a word. I understand. This must be very hard on you." She settled in with her head on his shoulder.

Brendan looked at his watch.

A short time later, he was in his Jeep cruising home.

Within a few days, the man was drawn back for another visit.

"Wow! You're in a good mood. What's up?" Brendan smiled.

"I'm just happy to see you. I've been lonely." Kate sighed as he entered the apartment. She reached around him and kissed his neck. She pulled up at his white shirt and smoothed her hands under it, against the smooth skin on his back. Brendan responded likewise, running his hands up the back of her thin strapped tank and then pulling down the straps. The black cotton/spandex top settled around her ribs. His hands grasped her firm breasts. His lips smothered her neck, pounding out his hot breath. Soon, the skin of their upper bare bodies pressed hard against each other. They raced to the bedroom.

Later, Kate lay quiet and still, her head resting on his shoulder. Brendan dozed off. Kate didn't say a word. She had promised herself. He hated talking. While he slept, she watched his chest rise and fall. For some reason, he was even more attractive sleeping. With his eyes shut tight and twitching, it was apparent he was in a deep sleep, exhaustion due to the stress of a demanding professional position and an unhappy marriage. He would be angry if she didn't wake him, but she wanted him to stay the night, the whole night. His wife could sleep alone for once. A message had to be delivered.

Damn it! She had to pee. After waiting as long as she could, she let herself out of the tangle of arms, legs and sheets. Glancing back from the bathroom, she let out a breath. Brendan hadn't moved, but let out an adorable light snore. However, just as she was about to shut the door, she noticed his pants lying on the chair, unguarded. She looked at him again. No movement. She reached in the back pocket and pulled out a thin, black wallet. It felt smooth in her hand like the skin on his chest.

Behind a closed door, she inspected the contents. His license read, *Brendan Reed, 34 Dove Road, Hollis, New Hampshire.* He was smiling in the picture. There were a couple of receipts: Staples and Home Depot. Nothing exciting. A rainbow of credit cards and $84.00. With her inspection over, she put everything back in place without a sound and returned the wallet. She did her business, checked her face and brushed her hair. She slipped back into bed, admiring the bare chest that rose and fell in a slow rhythm. She edged closer and closer, until she fit snugly against him. A soft, warm heat radiated from the man in her bed. Her man. He was not some immature idiot like the boys she was used to. He had enough drive and focus to take care of both of them. She rested her hand on his hipbone and closed her eyes. His scent lingered among her sheets. She would not change them for some time. She wished for a way to save this night forever.

Five

The SUV glided along. Kyle squinted, even with her sunglasses on. The weather cooperated and gave them a nice day. September in New Hampshire was beautiful. She sang "Hello, It's Me" back to Todd Rungren as she drove along the quiet street with her window open. One of the many songs she knew by heart, from back when singles were purchased on 45s. Turning onto Palmer Ave, she spotted the blue lights in her rear view mirror. Darn. She had almost made it home. She pulled over to the side and waited for the cruiser to stop behind her. It raced up fast, like she just robbed a bank. Her window already down, she started pillaging through her purse. She had just caught a glimpse of the uniform, when the officer leaned into the vehicle and kissed her on the cheek.

"I thought that was you." The face of Lieutenant Matt Shea beamed. Kyle moved her head back an inch and then focused on the face. His freckles were all in the same place, although his carrot colored hairline was higher and his eyes were red with some darkness under them. Even so, it was the same Matt she had ridden her bike with at the age of ten; the same guy she played kickball with, and who later helped her through the treachery of dating. The same guy who went home with her after school one day for a snack and found her father dead from a self-inflicted gunshot wound. Somehow, even at that age, Matt seemed to know what to do. Having lost his father years before from a heart attack, he knew how hard it was on a teenager. He would be the man in her life, her blood brother.

"What are you doing in Hollis?" Kyle asked. "We usually don't require the State Police."

"My buddy, Nick—your chief—asked for help filling in some gaps until he gets the two new hires approved. It's all routine, but after what happened, they want to take their time." One corner of his mouth turned up. He was referring to the "small misunderstanding" as quoted by the selectmen in the paper: one police officer blackmailing another, allegedly over an affair. Both officers were immediately let go.

"Are you giving me a ticket? Or can I take you to lunch?" Kyle smiled.

"The only one speeding was me. Let me check in and I'll see if I can take a break." Getting the OK, he followed her to the small restaurant in the center of town that boasted a big red rooster and home cooked food on its sign.

"So how is the good doctor?" Matt asked before taking a big bite of sandwich. He sat across from Kyle at one of the many little wooden tables. Rooster figurines lined a shelf along the ceiling. Heads turned to get a look at the unfamiliar uniform.

"He's fine." Kyle shrugged. "Working a lot, as always." She dug into her salad. "How's Kristen?" The entire restaurant smelled of hardy aromas from the small kitchen. A tray of overstuffed homemade blueberry muffins cooled up high on a display case with swirls of steam escaping.

"Great...did you know she's pregnant?" Matt's eyes gleamed as he stuffed what seemed like only his second bite into his mouth and finished his roasted turkey with stuffing and cranberry sauce on wheat.

"Again? Matt, How old is Gracie?"

"Two. Jack is four and Neil is five."

"Kristen's got to be exhausted. She's a saint. Four kids under six, do you think that's enough?"

One side of Matt's mouth turned up with a smirk. "I'll take as many as I can get. They're the best. You know."

"I know. But if you weren't so good with them, I'd tell Kristen to get her head examined."

"Hey, we got a late start. We're just moving fast." Kyle didn't hear his last few words, as her eyes jumped to a dark haired, uniformed police officer that strode across the small restaurant toward them.

Kyle pointed over Matt's shoulder. "I think someone is looking for you."

Matt turned and shot up from his chair. Then, he put out his hand and a big smile came over his face. "Hey Kyle. This is Lieutenant David Linscot. He's one of your new policemen. I recommended him. I was still an instructor when he came through the academy."

He invited David to sit down. "Oh, Dave, this is Kyle." He smiled at his old friend.

"Nice to meet you, Kyle," David said. "I don't mean to rush you. They told me at the station you were here. I just wanted to say hi and to thank you for your recommendation in person. It helped."

"My pleasure. You're going to be a great fit for this town."

Kyle sat back as the two men in uniform spoke to each other. David looked younger than she and Matt. Maybe thirty-ish. A standard crew cut made his dark brown hair stand up at attention. He had a long face with strong jaw line and deep, dark eyes set off by fair skin. His cheekbones were either Greek or Italian. It would not be hard to remember his name, Kyle thought: David, as in Michelangelo's work of art!

A few minutes later, the three made their way outside. David was the first to leave. "It was nice to meet you." He gave her a courteous smile.

"Aren't you going to tell him we're old friends?" Kyle asked after he left. "You know what he must be thinking. All of you 'uniforms' are suspicious by nature."

Matt laughed. "I'll set him straight later. It doesn't matter though. I know him well. He wouldn't ask and he wouldn't tell."

"In your dreams." Kyle smiled as she reached up. Matt was only four inches taller than she, but it seemed like ten. She put her arms around him and gave him a big hug, and felt the thickness of his vest inside of his shirt. It was a heavy reminder of the serious side of his work that he was so at ease with. "Be careful, Matt. Call me next time you're in town, instead of pulling me over."

"You know me. I'll do my best!"

As Kyle drove home, she passed a lanky young man wearing gray sweats and a zip front sweatshirt. He looked dressed for a jog, but was walking. Who was she to judge? The quick glance stayed with her, though. Something was out of place, but she couldn't put her finger on it. Just a feeling deep in her gut.

When Kyle's car passed, he darted into the woods, trudging with his heavy black boots. In a short time, he got to one of his new spots that had been well cultivated. He lit a Marlboro and flipped through his small black notebook. He glanced down to a beat up black plastic wristwatch. Today was Thursday. She should be leaving any time. He waited. He watched.

Ten minutes passed. He ran his fingers in a tapping motion on his thigh. It occurred to him that she might have already left. There's a first time for everything. She could also be home for some reason. He'd have to venture closer to find out.

He maneuvered through the trees and brush until he reached the edge of the thick grass sprawling through the back yard. Flowers provided contrast amongst the dense beds that defined the area. The smell of fresh mulch filled the air. Landscaping. It was a flag for him. If you spent this much on dirt and grass, what did you have inside your house?

From his vantage point, he heard no sounds and saw no movement. Knowing there was no dog allowed him to creep up close. The large glass windows that framed the rear of the house made surveillance effortless. The keypad for the alarm flashed green. Unarmed. He peered into the garage through a window and saw no cars, so he stepped up onto the back deck, then took a final look in all directions. He crouched under a window, open only an inch, and untied his boots, which were almost hidden beneath the baggy sweatpants. He stepped out of his footwear and placed them together against the house. He popped the screen out and laid it flat on the deck. With a gentle push, he opened the casement window and stepped down into the family room. Before he moved, he pulled the window back down to all but an inch. Since this was his first time inside this house, he paused a moment to take in the surroundings. The family room was huge, with a stone fireplace that reached up to the high ceiling. There was plenty of furniture, but it took up only some of the massive space. Glossy wood flooring sprawled on from room to room while colorful rugs centered each area. His stocking feet whispered past the large television and stereo, passed the various electronic devices on a large wooden desk, which was rather messy, and headed upstairs. Lots and lots of good stuff.

Like a silent breeze, he found his way down the hall to a large bedroom. The dense room had thick, heavy furniture and a high ceiling. A king-size, unmade bed sat in the center. A fair amount of clothes were tossed over the ball of blankets. Woman's shoes littered the floor. Someone, who was small and liked black clothing, had some trouble getting dressed this morning. He opened the simple, wide oriental box on the dresser. Pearls and gems lay inside, vulnerable. He chose one of the diamond earring studs and then closed the case. He popped it into the vacant single hole in his ear lobe.

With the gem secured, he wasted no in getting back to the window and slipping out of it with ease. He then replaced the screen. From the woods, he stopped and inspected the house and yard. All looked untouched. The best way not to get caught was never to have the crime reported. The lone earring would be presumed lost. Insurance would cover a replacement. No harm. No foul.

Six

Kyle strained to hear the news from the small flat television as she stirred the pots on the stove: Jeffrey's mashed potatoes, Jason's beets, and her sautéed Brussels sprouts. This, along with the Tilapia Piccata, was their favorite. Everyone would be home tonight for dinner, which was a rare occurrence. Kyle set the large, rectangular kitchen island for three. Pumpkin brushed against her legs, causing her to trip. She caught herself on the handle of the refrigerator and then reached down to pick up the needy kitty.

"Do you want me or the fish?" Kyle asked.

The cat purred. She wanted both.

Kyle put Pumpkin down next to her on the island. "If you walk around, you're gone." She warned. The cat didn't move, until she heard the dog come closer. Then the feline leaned over the edge and stared at the brown canine. Maggie's eyes fixed on her nemesis. A slight hiss came from Pumpkin. The uncivil war raged. "Maggie, not you, too." Kyle smiled at the feline's big eyes, so Maggie took a few steps back and lay down. She didn't think there was much chance of her getting invited up onto the island.

Kyle finished cutting up the apples, which were the first of the season from the orchard in town. Soon, the house smelled of fruit and cinnamon, warm apple crisp.

The scent pulled Jeffrey from the computer and he circled around the food. When the phone rang, he and Kyle looked at each other. She reached for the receiver, "I wonder who this is... Hello?" Jason was on the other end.

"Kyle, I'm tied up here and it's going to be awhile. I'm sorry. I'll call back in an hour or so."

"Jason, before you hang up, Jeffrey's dying to tell you something. I don't want to make him wait any longer," Kyle said and handed the phone to the young clone of her husband.

"Dad, I got a call from the Lacrosse coach from B.C. It looks good. But remember if I get into Bates, I'm going there." Jeffrey beamed.

Kyle fed the hungry teenager. The long fingers, with the aid of a fork, shoveled the food in at racetrack pace. His dark, thick hair framed a clear, fresh face highlighted with hazel eyes. She had been looking in those hazel eyes for years, but this pair did not show signs of wear.

"Jeffrey, we just want you to make a good decision for your entire life, not just for now." Kyle and Jason on many occasions clearly spelled out their concerns about their son following his girlfriend to college.

"I told the little guy, it's my decision." Though Jeffrey was only about a half inch taller than his father, he frequently pointed out the difference. Lindsay, his girlfriend, was a priority. Lindsay was a sweet, bright girl with a future but they wanted Jeffrey to have the same great experience that they had at Boston College.

After dinner, the evening flew by fast. Kyle was almost asleep when Jason came upstairs. Jeffrey had given up waiting and gone to bed at ten. He had a lacrosse game tomorrow and needed the rest. Jason smiled at Pumpkin who was stretched out next to Kyle on the king sized bed on top of a deep fluffy, white comforter. "That cat's got a tough life," he smirked. "She's on the bed more than me." When he sat down on his side, the cat rose, slowly of course, and rubbed against Jason's back. He spoke to Kyle as he patted the purring, tan feline. "I don't want Jeffery making an important decision based on a girlfriend."

"He's seventeen…and Lindsay is wonderful. We were only a year older when we met. There's really not a whole lot we can do." Kyle yawned and Pumpkin pranced back to her. She was sure to be the center of attention. "Besides, I worry that we are too much for him sometimes. We've poured all our energy onto this kid. I'm afraid once he leaves the house he'll never want to come back. Don't you think it must be hard to be our kid?"

Jason rolled his eyes at her. Kyle, more awake now, rested on one elbow and watched him get undressed. His body was resilient to age. From his belly button down, his abdomen was tapered and tight. She pulled the covers up a bit higher over her.

"We'll see," Jason said. "Hey, I'm on call tonight, so I'm going to get something to eat and sleep in the spare room. Goodnight."

Kyle heard his pager go off as he went downstairs. She reached over and cradled Pumpkin next to her. She turned off the light and hoped for sleep, but knew there was only a slight chance. For the last year or so, she slept in pieces.

She tossed several times, moved pillows around and dozed a bit. But her thoughts about Jeffrey raced in her mind. It was hard to give everything to just one child. But, even with ten children, the last one leaves at some point. Jeffrey had been weaning his mother for years. Each year, he needed her less and less.

The clock's red letters stood sharp and alert. Kyle reached for Pumpkin, who let out a jolted coo. After a few minutes of petting, she retreated from her favorite spot on the bed to her seldom-used cat bed in the corner. She was only so needy at 2:39 in the morning. Kyle decided getting out from under the covers was a good idea. A slight chill in the air met her skin. She wrapped herself in her favorite blue fleece robe. It would soon be time to turn the heat on. She made her way downstairs.

The kitchen was silent with shadows stretching across the fruit bowl to the toaster. The tile floor felt cool to her bare feet. Kyle flipped on a light and retrieved the cranberry juice from the refrigerator. It was always a good time to prevent a urinary tract infection. She sat down and began scanning the newspaper. There were a couple of regular columnists she really enjoyed. Both were women.

Kyle's heart jumped through her throat when she heard the thud from the garage. Still, she sat in the chair. Her blood-streaked eyes fixed on the doorknob; no bark from the dog. When the knob turned, Kyle edged back in her seat. A sound came from her throat, but it wasn't more than a grunt. She held her breath and watched as the door swung open. Both hands pressed against her chest, trying to keep her heart in.

"Oh my God...you scared me," she gasped as she looked at Jason. "I didn't hear you leave. I thought you were asleep."

"I never went to bed. I got paged while I was eating. You're up again? You're sure jumpy!" He unloaded his pager, phone and keys on to the counter. "You should be in bed," he said with a weary voice.

"If you'd give me something, maybe I could sleep. Can't you even get me one Ambien?"

"Call your doctor...in the morning," Jason snapped. He turned off the lights, herding Kyle with his arm, and walked her upstairs. As she crawled under the covers, he sat on the edge of the bed, in full bedside mode. "Your problem is that you think too much," he said and patted her leg.

"Well, maybe you don't think enough!" Kyle retorted.

Jason shook his head and rubbed his eyes. He was more than tired. "Wow, you sound rational. Go to sleep. Sleep in late." Then he got up, stopped and turned around. He paused, then his tired, hazel eyes shot at her. "You can figure out what's wrong and deal with it now, or deal with it later."

He shut the door to the dark room on his way out. Kyle summoned Pumpkin, but the warm cat did not move. Kyle lay alone on her back with her eyes forced shut. She was more awake now than most people were at ten a.m. It was getting worse, she realized. At this rate, she'd just pass out for a couple days and catch up on sleep that way. But when would she hit that point? And how would she be functioning? She turned on her bedside light and opened up a magazine. She considered working on the school budget for the new addition, but she thought it might keep her awake so she read recipes instead: exotic creations that she'd never prepare.

The doorbell jarred Kyle from a deep sleep. The dog barked like aliens had just invaded. Kyle's head remained crushed into the pillow, blocking out the light that seeped in through her window. A familiar heaviness weighted down her right arm. Pumpkin. The bell rang again. She pushed herself out of bed, imagining a pulley helping her up. She had the robe around her when she got to the door. Recognizing Bill, the pool guy, she let him in.

"Good morning. Catching a few extra winks?" Bill grinned. Kyle ran her hand over her head and felt many uneven surfaces.

Luckily, Bill wasn't a slave to fashion in his well-worn blue jeans and blue uniform shirt. A cigarette sat tucked behind his ear. After years smoking he quit, but kept the spare behind his ear to take a whiff of once and a while. "We've finished closing the pool. I have a note here to talk to you." Kyle opened her eyes wider.

"Oh, yes." He followed her into the kitchen, along with attack dog Maggie, happy to see the familiar face. Bill put down his stack of work orders in front of him and he sat in the kitchen.

"You okay? You look like me after my bowling night," Bill said. His coarse hands rubbed stubble on his face.

"I'm fine." Kyle said. "I just didn't sleep well. Anyway, about the pool…we're not going to open it next summer. We'll be away and won't be back until mid-August."

"Oh… now that note makes sense, well, the only thing though…in June we really should pull the cover off, clean out some of the build-up and add more chemicals. With the hot sun, the bacteria will grow fast." Bill wrote some notes on the paper.

"We'll have to charge you for the clean-up and chemicals, but it won't be too much."

"That's fine. Just let us know what we owe you." After he left, Kyle stumbled into the bathroom and took a look at herself. Even Bill didn't deserve this vision. She found her way to the shower, tripping over Jason's workout clothes. She yawned. The days were running into each other.

The air changed during the afternoon from warm to crisp. Heavy rains in August had nourished the trees, which now displayed bold fall colors. Kyle was raking leaves when Jeffrey came home from school. Kyle's face brightened; she hugged him when he greeted her in the back yard. "How was school?"

"Fine. When's Dad coming home?"

"He's on call, so your guess is as good as mine."

"I'm going over to Lindsay's. I won't be home until after dinner. Okay?" Kyle didn't argue. She told him to tell Lindsay hi. He smiled and was off. When did all this happen? Just yesterday, they were sitting on the carpet, playing Lego's. Jeffery used to fall asleep wrapped in his blanket, watching Pooh. Now, the only pooh he watched was the crap in R-rated movies, featuring overpaid, immature young males.

Kyle dumped her leaves into the woods. Something moved. Probably a squirrel. She looked around but didn't see anything. Maggie, inside the fence, barked and growled, pleading with her eyes to get out. Kyle pulled her gray sweater closed. It was chilly and she was tired. She leaned the rake against the fence and left it there.

From the woods, he watched her enter the house. His cover of leaves fell around him. He stood stiff, afraid she might notice him. She didn't look happy today, not until her son came home. She was nice, he decided. He inspected the yard with mounds of fresh mulch and a lush, clipped lawn; it resembled a picture out of a woman's magazine his mom sometimes bought home to their apartment. Mums provided speckled color in clusters around the yard. She must have planted more today. Even the edge of the woods looked clean. Hidden behind the trees, he listened to the quiet. He recalled the peaceful tone with which she spoke to her son, like she respected him. For over a half hour, he sat in the quiet.

Seven

Jason glanced down at the clock in the car: 12:11. These late nights were adding up. He sped along the long, narrow, country roads. The lack of streetlights blanketed the roads in a thick, cool darkness. Old, heavy pine limbs hung over the road casting gloomy shadows onto the pavement. The car lights reflected on the few visible tree trunks. He rubbed his eyes and yawned. His white shirt had long lost its crispness; his tie hung loosened around his neck. Wrinkles streaked his slacks. Having Saturday and Sunday off would bring a welcome break. It had been a long week and he felt guilty for spending so little time with Kyle. He vowed to take her to dinner at a nearby inn she loved. It sometimes seemed as though he had two lives and so much going on in both. Family and the hospital, each demanding and satisfying in different ways. Nothing like he had imagined while in his residency. He let out another long yawn. His weary foot pushed the pedal and the car sped along. His hand reached into the cup holder and felt around for gum to cover the wine on his breath. His popped a piece of gum into his mouth.

A sudden jolt knocked Jason to the edge of his seat. His foot jammed on the brakes. He felt the immediate impact and heard the crunch, but in the thickness of the night, he only caught a glimpse of a car he sideswiped. He managed to hang onto the steering wheel, despite the jolt. There were no lights, but a car edged into the road off the shoulder, as he had come around the corner. He pulled over in front of the darkened vehicle and got out.

His car, still running, cast some light onto the dark mass behind him. He made out a small black car. A young woman sat behind the wheel of the still-running vehicle, without any lights on. The front quarter of the driver's side showed body damage. Jason rubbed his head. The week wasn't over yet. He knocked on the window. She put on only her parking lights and opened her window an inch. He spoke into the opening.

"Are you okay? Are you hurt?" Jason saw her eyes, red and swollen. She was crying.

"I'm fine. I didn't see you. I just pulled over to find something." She pushed her long blonde hair out of her face. "It's my fault, really. I'll just go. You're fine, right?"

Jason rubbed his head. She'd pulled over to find something in the dark? "Look, I couldn't see you. This is a pretty dark spot for a black car. Why didn't you have your lights on?" He waited. She didn't answer. "We have to exchange licenses, and insurance. Just a second, I'll get some paper."

He went back to his car, reached in and searched for something to write with. He was still bent over when he saw the blue lights flashing into the car. This week was definitely not over. "Great," Jason said.

Flashlight in hand, the policeman looked into the car and spoke with the young woman. Jason approached. The policeman asked where Jason was coming from. He explained that he was heading home from the hospital and had not seen the car. The officer took both their licenses back to the cruiser. Jason focused on the passenger who remained in her vehicle.

"Here is all my information. Here's a paper and pen. Would you write down yours?" She took the pad and wrote without a word.

"Can I leave now? I really have to go," the girl said with her big eyes staring up at Jason. The patrolman approached them.

"Okay, if you've both exchanged information, you can go. Ms. Thompson, are you sure you're okay? You look upset." Jason wanted to explain that she was in this condition when he got here, but refrained from any unnecessary conversation.

"I'm fine," was all she said and then drove away.

The blue lights continued to flash into Jason's car as he pre-pared to leave. He looked down at the paper: Kathleen Thomp-son, 117 Hartnet Street, Boston, Massachusetts. He wondered what she had been doing pulled over in the dark, at midnight, on the corner of Pierce Lane.

Lt. Linscot watched as both cars drove away. He logged in the information, adding question marks at the end. He rubbed his head and looked around. The road was settled now, except for the cruiser's blue lights that intruded into the homes nearby.

Sarah moaned in the dark room. Brendan's breath hastened. Slowly, he moved off her and fell onto his back. His breathing slowed.

"Well, what's gotten into you? You've been acting like a teen-ager lately," Sarah said gulping some air.

"Are you complaining? You didn't sound like you were com-plaining." In the darkness, he reached over and feathered his hand over his wife's breasts and stomach. "You look wonderful, you know. You stay in great shape." Sarah returned the caress-ing and stroked the side of his face, feeling the tingle from his hands on her skin.

"I love you," Brendan said.

"I love you, too," Sarah said. They drifted off.

Lights flashed through windows. "Brendan, what's that?" Sarah staggered out of bed, rubbed her eyes and wrapped herself in her robe. Brendan joined her at the window and peered out, pressing his naked, warm body against her.

"It's nothing...must be an accident around the corner. The police are there. They'll take care of it. Let's go to bed." He kissed Sarah on the forehead. She removed her robe, picked up a thin strapped, pink nightgown and started to put it on. Brendan took the pink garment from her and tossed it on the wood floor.

Eight

Brendan studied the computer screen perched on his new desk. He scrolled down the list. Four this morning alone. How long would it take for Kate to get the message that he was not answering? He deleted all four without reading them. It had been over a month. He told her then that he would be swamped at work for a while. He didn't want to make this a habit, a responsibility. Sex was supposed to be fun. The liaison lost much of its appeal when she began asking questions. Just like the last one.

Mel walked in as Brendan stared at his laptop, motionless. "Something wrong?" Brendan looked up and flashed Mel a big smile. His shiny white row of perfect teeth sparkled.

"Nothing I can't handle," he quipped. "What's up, Mel?" He folded his hands behind his head as if he didn't have a care in the world.

"The 'elders' are looking for all of the University Hospital contracts. I told Shelly they would be ready tomorrow as promised, but they want to look at whatever's done. I couldn't put them off." Mel stood, ready for orders.

"Shelly. Jesus, how old is that prune? She's such a bitch. Hey, do you think she's doing the old man?" Mel smiled and laughed with a hand over her mouth. Shelly was old man Hessman's *assistant*. She pre-dated everyone, it seemed, even the building and most pterodactyls. Despite her age, she guarded the old man like one of her flying lineage. He didn't take a call or see anyone without her approving it first. She tightened her grip when Hessman's wife died a few years back.

The most popular rumors regarding the prehistoric matriarch were that she never married and she had worked for Angus since her twenties. She was Angus' first and only assistant. In fact, he hired her after he left law school and Angus saw to it that her influence and command grew with the evolution of the firm. She knew everything and said little. Nothing she asked for was a request. Year round she wore turtlenecks and gray wool skirts, which hung on her frail frame. Her face resembled a dehydrated lizard with thick wine-color lipstick. Rare glimpses of her smiling were only caught when she was speaking with Angus. Librarians trembled in her presence.

Brendan sat back in his tall, black leather chair.

"Well…" He tilted his chin up to the ceiling and rubbed his throat with the back of a hand. "Give them what I have done. That should keep them busy for a while. I still need to check a couple of items on the other two. We're still on for eight a.m. tomorrow with the big guns, right? The clients will be in at ten?"

"Yes, Friday, eight sharp! Shelly has sent three emails to confirm. Everyone is in tomorrow. I'll be here at 7:00. Do you want me to grab you anything for lunch while I'm out?" Mel stood, pen and pad waiting.

"No, thanks. I feel like stretching my legs. We'll do our final check on those last two contracts this afternoon." He watched as Mel left his office. She had her light brown hair pulled back in a bun, short pieces sticking out like hay. Her blouse was a silky taupe, tucked into a high-waist long black skirt. Leather boots matching her blouse, wrapped her legs. He imagined her stretched across a large bed, wearing only those boots. His fantasy deflated at thoughts of sexual harassment suits. His first rule: you don't play where you work or, as his dad used to say, 'you don't shit where you eat.'

Rising from his chair, Brendan turned on his cell phone and

dropped it into the pocket of his trench coat. At the elevator, Brendan ran into two other junior partners, clad in black, tailored suits and deep colored silk ties. The only acceptable "peacocking" was within the tie competition. The "uniform" consisted of dark or gray suits, maybe blue, heavily starched white shirts and exceptional ties. Some attorneys had even been known to check the stripes in the insides of the silk accessories. Beau Brummel had nothing on these guys.

"Good afternoon, counselors," Brendan smiled, sans teeth. Both men, Jared and Connor, were senior to him, but held the same title. Jared's sharp mind moved him up the ladder fast. It was such a shock, considering he had graduated from Harvard law. Hessman loved him. He moved into the unofficial "management grooming program."

"Hi, Brendan, going to lunch? We're headed for Maxine's. Want to join us for appetizers?" Jared turned up one corner of his mouth. Jared liked martinis. Maxine's made great martinis. Brendan grew a slow smile: appetizers on Thursday?

"Why not? I could use a proper lunch." Brendan asked if they were celebrating anything. They said they'd find something.

The three men exited the elevator to the lobby smiling and exchanging gentle chatter. Noise on the mezzanine level drowned their copasetic tones. Streams of suits and briefcases flowed over the smooth, worn marble floor. Easing through the crowd, the three fell into line and merged into an exiting lane. Just before they reached the revolving doors, the smile fell from Brendan's face. His stomach turned. He stretched and angled his neck to confirm what his eyes showed him. His brain refused the image. His eyes struggled, refocusing through the interrupted view from people shuffling in front of him. There, on a cold, gray granite bench, sat Kate.

Brendan stumbled over his own feet and then stopped. Clearing his throat, he reached deep to find words. He managed to push some over the growing lump in his throat.

"Hey," his said, clearing his throat, "I forgot my cell. I'll meet up with you guys later." He patted them on their backs, turned, and headed toward the elevators before they had a chance to respond. His present state of shock would be clear to these trained evaluators. He mulled around, until they crossed through the turning doors. He swallowed hard, several times. His heart picked up the pace and his head felt hot. Letting out a deep breath, he adjusted his tie. He started walking, and then slowed himself down. His feet hit the ground hard and he nudged people out of his way. The endless streams now moved like grazing cattle.

When he reached the bench, Brendan grabbed Kate's arm without a word. His teeth shined and his mouth formed a smile.

"Brendan, what a surprise!" Kate's smile faded when Brendan didn't respond. He held tight and pressed to the doors, pulling Kate along. He exited far left through the stationary door. He moved both of them through the sidewalk traffic as fast as he could, pulling her like baggage. "Brendan…wait, wait. I'm not going to just take off… I'm meeting someone. I HAVE PLANS!" She shook her arm loose and folded them in front of her, planting her feet. She wore all black with a silk scarf around her neck that looked as if it melted violet ice. Her shiny hair fell flat. Her lips were moist with a covering of a matte finish in pale lavender.

"Look, Kate… What are you doing here? You're meeting someone…right." His heavy, cross voice drove through her. He leaned in close.

Kate felt his hot breath hit her skin. She took a step back, then another. "I am meeting some people, Brendan. I don't know what you're so upset about. Did I cramp your style or something? What are *you* doing here? Did you get my messages? Did you read any?" Kate glared into his eyes awaiting a response.

"LOOK, KATE. I don't know what you're up to, but it stops now," Brendan ordered.

Kate smiled.

"We need to talk," he said.

"Sure, we can talk. I'll get in touch and we can make plans,"

Kate said in a mocking, little girl tone.

"No, Kate, now!" Red faced, he reached in to his pocket and pulled out his cell phone.

"Mel, it's me…something has come up. You need to cover for me. Review those contracts, and I'll get to them later. Do you understand?" He set the phone on vibrate and dropped it back into his pocket. "Come on." He dug his fingers deeper into her arm and led the way.

"So where are we going?" Kate asked as she turned and looked at Brendan standing beside the year-old Jeep. She had only been in the vehicle a couple of times. Most of their rendezvous had been in her apartment, primarily horizontal. She sunk into the soft, black leather. "Brendan, where are we going? I have a right to know."

"Your apartment. J-just wait." Brendan almost said more, then stopped. What would he say when Jared or Connor asked why he had not returned? That was much simpler than the explanation of Kate's identity, if anybody saw her. Keep it simple, keep it short. Maybe she was his wife's screwed up cousin that he didn't want to talk about. Simple, or say nothing at all. He tapped his fingers over the steering wheel, working his way through the traffic. Calm down, you can handle this. Calm down. First appeal to her for understanding…your wife. See if you can reach her that way.

How the hell did she find out where he worked? He had been so careful. He must have made a mistake. Kate must have followed him.

If Sarah even suspected she'd go through the roof. That prenup would kill him. He wouldn't get a penny. She'd run back to her family. Her grandfather had been a founding investor in the largest oil company in the country. Her father had been listed in Forbes Magazine last year. She was an only child. She wanted nothing to do with oil, but wanted to move back to Texas and have Brendan learn the family business. Her father did not entirely embrace this idea, which was why it hadn't happened yet.

He presented obstacles as to why it was not a good time for Brendan to become involved with the business. He remembered the day her dad pushed the pre-nup and a pen in front of him. "You got no problem with this, right son?"

Brendan's hands squeezed the steering wheel. Then he loosened his grip, took a deep breath, and rotated his head to stretch his neck. He needed to calm down and think. He did not want to make the situation worse. All he had wanted was a little fun. Kate knew he was married. She knew. What a bitch. Why couldn't women just enjoy something for what it was, and not make it into a lifelong prison? They just couldn't leave a good thing alone. The sex was great, but all this shit…like he had time for it.

The thick traffic presented itself as a further block to eat up more of his time. It was as if every vehicle in the greater Boston area had converged and sat in his way. His travel seemed to drop to a trickle. Brendan weaved to avoid as much as possible. As he got closer to Kate's apartment, the squeezing of the steering wheel returned. Now, he just needed to find a parking space.

"There's probably a spot behind the building at this time of day," Kate offered with a smirk. She reached into her black shoulder bag for her keys, careful not to rummage the contents with force.

Brendan took her suggestion and eased behind the building. As he pulled into a spot, he noticed a small black car next to him. He gave the vehicle plenty of room. From the look of the scrapes along one side, it didn't look like people were too careful around here. He shut off the motor and pulled up the collar of his trench coat. He kept his head down. In silence, the two walked to the plain metal door in the center of the back of the building. Kate pushed it open and they passed through unnoticed.

Inside her apartment, Kate threw her keys and purse on the counter. "Do you want something to drink?" Before he could answer, she stomped away saying she needed to make a call. He heard her telling someone that something had come up, she wasn't coming, and that she'd call later.

Brendan found it to be a solid performance.

"So, did you read my last message? Is that why you're here?" Kate sat on the couch, running her hands through her long blonde hair. She kicked off her buckled boots and pulled her black clad legs up.

"Kate, look…we've had fun together…" Brendan felt the tension rise in his neck. "And you know I've enjoyed it. I just don't think right now it's good for either of us. I'm nuts at work and Sarah…" He bit down on his tongue. *God dammit!* He gave her Sarah's name. That was stupid. "My wife is giving me a hard time. I am going to be dealing with this divorce for a long time. Months, maybe even years." Brendan watched Kate's face for clues. He was unprepared for her answer.

"How stupid do you think I am? You haven't even asked your wife for a divorce. I bet…I bet you don't even want a divorce. You just want to screw around, don't you?" Kate snapped. Before Brendan could tell her to keep her voice down, she shot up from the couch. Brendan watched her jerky movements. "Do you want a drink? I need something."

"I'll take soda, if you've got any." Brendan sat back and tried to appear comfortable. This would take awhile.

In her small neon kitchenette, off the main living area of the apartment, Kate retrieved two cans of Pepsi, ice and filled two clear glasses up to their blue rims. The bubbles erupted over the ice, pushing air to the top. The pressure released itself. She wasn't sure she could do this. It was sooner than she had anticipated. She wasn't sure she'd ever succeed in getting him back to her apartment. It seemed like a good idea before… But, if she was going to do it, now on a Thursday afternoon, was as good a time as any. She walked back into the living area, retrieved her purse and announced she needed an Advil. She brought it back to the kitchen with her.

Brendan sat as still as he could on the couch assessing that Kate probably had her period. What a mess.

She fished her right hand through the black leather sack.

When she could not identify some items, she pulled things out, dumping them on the counter. She pushed the clutter out of the way, careful not to let anything fall to the floor. Her hands became frantic. She didn't have all day. Her fingers identified the object and she pulled out the small container. Her eyes penetrated the glass and fixed on the clear liquid inside the small vial with a black top. She felt the strength of it burning in her hand. He deserved this. She was only another stop for him. She wasn't the first but she might be the last, or at least different. She wanted to hurt him and leave a mark. Her hand trembled and the liquid crashed against the sides of the vial. She closed her hand around the container and shut her eyes. Now or never. Here goes.

The guy at the party said a quarter of the vial would do the job. But Kate wanted to be sure. She emptied the entire contents into the glass on the left and then stirred it with her index finger. Replacing the cap on the vial, she dropped it into a pan soaking with bubbles in the sink and watched it disappear under the suds and dishes. Letting out a deep breath, she smiled at the relief of her decision. She hadn't even asked him here today. This was just meant to be. She'd deal with the consequences later. She'd make something up. He always did.

When she returned to the living room, Brendan was on his feet. "What took so long? Kate, look, I've left work in the middle of the day. The old man will be breathing down my neck. I've got important meetings tomorrow starting at 8 a.m. and I'm nowhere near ready. We have got to come to some kind of understanding." Pleased with his clear delivery, he sat back down. Kate handed him the glass in her left hand.

Brendan took a sip then set it down on the table in front of him.

Kate held her glass tight with both hands. So, he thought he had a tough day ahead of him tomorrow. He didn't have a clue. She tried not to look at Brendan's glass sitting on the coffee table.

Kate looked away from Brendan. She needed more time. Turning back to him, she grinned and put down her drink away from his. Her hands went to his belt buckle, and without any eye contact, she started unzipping his pants.

He reached down and ceased her progress. "Kate, no. We have to stop. This isn't good for either of us."

Kate smiled at him, freezing her hands on his pants. His hands pressed against hers. "Oh, I think this will be good for both of us," Kate grinned.

"LOOK! You stupid bitch. It's over…can't you get that? It's too much, now. It's over." Brendan's face was red and his body tensed. His hands formed fists when Kate sat up, startled, and removed her hands.

Kate sat back on the couch with her arms folded. She wanted to tell him to drink up. "You think I'm stupid, huh? Well, you're the stupid one. You have no idea who you're dealing with, do you. NO IDEA! But, I know who I'm dealing with. You're Brendan Reed and your wife's name is Sarah." Her voice dropped and she spoke in a deliberate tone. Her words pierced his skin and fueled his blood. "You live at 34 Dove Road, in Hollis, New Hampshire. You have a white house. Last Friday night, for example, you were out with your wife and returned home around eleven."

Brendan's fists shook. His blood pumped faster and faster as Kate continued. "You work at the law firm of Hessman, Coughlin, and Associates. You just made some kind of partnership." She delivered her words like daggers thrust into his body, piercing his flesh, each one causing more harm than the last.

She gave him a smug grin and then finished. "The only thing I don't know is what your wife is going to say to me when I call her and tell her that you've been fucking a twenty-four year old. And the best part…"

His hands moved. They clutched her throat and constricted her air passage. The whole weight of his body pressed on top. The smirk died. She pulled and clawed at his hands. When that didn't work, she thrashed with her legs. Her feet made little contact. She tried to get a couple words out, but no sound came. Brendan pressed on her tender throat with an unrelenting iron grip. He felt the cartilage of her larynx collapse. It seemed like his fingers were going to push through to her spine. Kate's face was now redder than Brendan's. The skin on her face then grew purple and the whites of her eyes filled with blood as the vessels broke.

Thick beads of sweat from Brendan's chin fell onto Kate's bursting face, running over her purple skin. Brendan loosened his grip and let her head fall back to the couch. He starred at her lifeless face. Shit! Shit! He pressed his palms against his forehead. Perspiration welled up from his pores. Sweat stains darkened through his clean, white shirt. His heart raced and his lungs gasped for air. He loosened his tie and tried to take even breaths. What just happened? He couldn't believe he did this...again. He grabbed the soda and emptied the glass.

Nine

Kyle waited at the table. Her watch read 1:20. Twenty minutes was nothing in Annie-time. Annie was her beautiful, red-headed roommate in college, who was now her old friend. After college, Annie had moved back to Manhattan, gotten married and divorced. Her second husband brought her to live north of Boston, closer to Kyle. Annie moved into a new home in Hollis and was looking for husband number three. It would not take long. Since college, a trip to the ladies room—past the men's room—yielded Annie at least two men. Beauty with a supernatural force.

Though Annie loved and enjoyed children, she had none. She considered herself "freelance" and children never seemed to be a good fit. Over the years, though, she had spoiled Jeffery. He referred to her as "the Rock" and it had nothing to do with her wrestling abilities. The nickname was in reference to the sparkling stones that hung from every "port" on Annie. More than once in Kyle's son's life, he threatened to go live with Annie. Since he was potty trained and had a passport, he would be a welcome tagalong to the smiling redhead. She was a unique, creative part of a large company via the internet and the occasional meeting. Her boss gave her freedom and in return she gave the company a hard ten hours a week, if they were lucky. Her visions of weeks as shapes, and days as colors demanded flexibility in her life.

Ten minutes later, a suntanned and freckled Annie Watson glided into the upscale restaurant, which was full of businessmen. Heads turned. Her great big smile lit up the room. She was dressed perfectly for a fall day, in a tight, black and rust sweater dress. Kyle jumped up and Annie greeted her with a welcoming hug.

"So how was Turks?" Kyle asked.

"The best. I love the islands more each time. In fact, I'm close to picking out a condo. I'd like to spend most of the winter there. How's Jeffrey?" Annie's face softened.

"Oh, he's fine. I'm afraid he and Jason will knock heads over choosing a college. He has to figure it out for himself."

"Sure, if Jason lets him," Annie laughed. "How is the eagle scout?" Annie smiled.

"He said to tell the nomad hello. The usual...working a lot. I'm looking forward to our trip to Italy. We should have some time there, without a pager."

"Make sure you get me the exact dates. I want to visit while you're there. I love Rome. I went there on my first honeymoon, remember?"

"How is Larry?" Kyle asked.

"He's doing really well. We email all the time. We had lunch not long ago. He still looks great." Annie lifted her eyebrows for effect.

"Annie, you can't date an ex-husband."

"Says who? Think about the make-up sex!"

"It never ceases to amaze me how you can take half, or all, of these guys' money, and they still love you."

"It's a gift," Annie shrugged.

They ordered and dug into two monstrous salads with marinated pears, goat cheese, beets and chicken. They each sipped a glass of chardonnay. Kyle felt the effects when she got up to leave. "Gee, I only had one glass."

"You always were a lightweight." Annie put her arm around her longtime friend. "Next week, right?" Kyle nodded affirmatively. Whenever possible, they met for lunch weekly.

"I'm around. It's always you who's off on some adventure."

After lunch, Kyle forced herself to the grocery store. With

weighted, plastic bags in tow, she made her way into the kitchen and dropped the bulky groceries on the counter. She dumped her purse and keys down next to them and returned to the garage for another trip, Maggie running ahead of her, tail wagging. As Kyle lifted one of the last bags, the handle stretched, tore, and groceries poured over the driveway.

"Shit...shit!" Kyle looked down at a smashed bottle of balsamic vinegar spreading under broccoli crowns, with thick, sour cream mixing in from another direction. Maggie, startled at first, soon sniffed at the mess, assessing the snack value. Kyle pushed her away and then retrieved paper towels from the kitchen.

Kyle sat on the pavement, picking up small pieces of vinegar-covered glass from behind her car. Maggie started to bark, and then growl. Kyle lifted her head and snapped. "Maggie, knock it off!"

Despite her mistress' tone, the dog charged into the yard, back and rigid tail up, head low. Maggie seemed like another animal. With shards of glass in her hands and the pungent odor of vinegar filling her sinuses, Kyle jumped up. She looked beyond Maggie, swallowed a breath, and stopped breathing. Not far from the edge of the grass, the edge of a black boot stuck out from behind a tree. She froze. When she regained the use of her limbs, she threw down the glass and yelled. "Maggie, COME!"

The dog didn't move. Kyle deepened her voice and commanded the dog again. Maggie whined but finally returned to her master. Kyle gripped Maggie's collar, raced to the door and locked it behind them. After catching her breath she clutched at the phone and dialed 911. "Hello, this is Kyle Mercer. There's someone in my yard...behind a tree." She took a moment and told herself to calm down. This was not a crisis. She was okay.

The dispatcher confirmed her street address and instructed her to stay inside until the police arrived. Kyle stared into the backyard from the window until the cruiser pulled up the driveway. She stepped out into the garage to meet the officer. Now, she felt brave.

"Hi, I'm Officer Stowe. What exactly did you see?"

"A black boot next to a tree. I don't know if he's still there." Kyle realized how silly it sounded. But, she knew what she saw.

"A boot? Okay. I'll take a look around. Why don't you go inside? I'll be right back."

Again from the safety of the back window, she watched the uniformed officer scan the yard and speak into a small radio clipped onto his collar. Another officer joined him before he was through searching. After a few minutes, they both came to the door and followed her into the kitchen. She met their faces, recognizing Lt. David Linscot. Oh great. Matt would hear all about this. "Oh, hi Lieutenant Linscot, I am so sorry to bother you guys. I just didn't know what to do."

"You did exactly the right thing. No one should be on your property without your permission," David Linscot said in a calm tone. He noticed Kyle still shaking and motioned for her to sit down. "We didn't see anyone, but we'd like to take a look around your home."

Kyle's heart fell somewhere down into her stomach. Someone could be or had been in her house? The skin on her arms began to crawl. The other officer went upstairs, while Officer Linscot looked around the first floor, checking doors and windows, looking for anything out of order. Finding nothing, he returned to the kitchen and sat with Kyle.

"It doesn't look like anyone's been in the house. Do you notice anything out of place?" he asked. His voice was still calm and easy.

"I don't know," Kyle scanned the immediate kitchen with her eyes. "I guess everything's okay." She put her hand to her forehead and told herself to calm down. She was in no danger. She was being foolish.

"Hey, it's okay," he said.

Kyle thought he read her mind. "I'm sure it was nothing but someone passing through." She let out a deep breath. "I'm sorry Officer Linscot, this must seem so childish. I was just so shocked to see someone hiding behind a tree. Maggie's been barking a lot lately. I thought it was nothing. Now…"

"Relax." He touched her hand. "You'll be fine. You did the right thing. And call me, David." He reached down and patted Maggie on the head. "Maybe just pay attention to what your attack dog here is trying to tell you."

Maggie stood proud. Where was the cat in all this? Under a bed?

The other officer reappeared and reported the upstairs okay. He asked Kyle if she left in a rush today.

"Yes, I did," Kyle admitted. Then she realized her room looked like a cyclone passed through. She wanted to slide under a chair. Nothing fit this morning. Of course, this couldn't have happened if her house was clean. She could hear her mother telling her to always wear clean underwear and keep her bed made. "I'm sorry about the mess. I believe if someone had been going through our stuff, it would have looked neater."

The uniformed men spoke and the other officer left. David came back and sat at the island. He looked at her and smiled. "Hey, you're doing just fine."

"I can't believe I left the house a mess this morning…of all days!"

"That happens all the time. Don't worry, it's nothing. You should see my house. And I live alone!"

"You're going to tell Matt, aren't you?" Kyle asked.

"Not if you don't want me to," said David.

"It's okay. Did he tell you we are old friends?" Kyle tried to read his face.

"Your relationship with Matt is none of my business. He asked me to keep an eye on the house. When I heard the name…"

"We've been close friends since we were about ten. We used to ride bikes together. He's like a brother, an older brother, sometimes an annoying…" Kyle stopped herself from using some more colorful language. He was in uniform after all.

David smiled.

"Since you were ten? That's a long time." Once Kyle appeared to be settled down, the policeman left, reminding her to call again if she noticed anything else.

Long after David left, his image stayed with her. She recalled his sculpted face, his dark hair and his vital presence. Gentle hands balanced his strong, square shoulders. He told her to call if she saw or heard anything that concerned her. All doors were locked and checked. Even so, every few minutes she glanced out to the back yard. It wasn't dark yet, but all lights in her house were burning. Kyle sat, curled up in a soft chair, recounting the emotional day. She paged Jason.

The black military boots marched through the metal door and into the game hall/ video arcade. Dim lights cast shadows throughout the large gray room. Lights and buzzers screamed from the machines, while small clouds of smoke swirled around the low hanging "Budweiser" fluorescent lamps that lit up the two pool tables. The faded green felt on the playing surfaces looked as if it had lost many battles since the 1940's. Current rap music belted out from a boom box planked on top of a broken jukebox. Moldy beer smells from the "ancient" rug rose up and filled the room with a mix of odors. This was the "teen" side.

The teen in the black boots continued straight through the room, with an occasional nod to a familiar face. He pulled a door open, which held the over twenty-one half of the establishment. The joke was calling it the legal side. Being after two in the afternoon, the bar stools were full. This crowd was so regular the stools were assigned via previous altercations. Men and some women idled. Beer bottles and the occasional shot glass lined the Formica bar capped with a chrome edge. Booths with cushions of aged maroon vinyl lined the wall behind the narrow path across from the bar. The teen leaned in at an opening at one end of the bar. The large, dark skinned bartender looked his way. "Hey, Jack's back." The words rolled the off his tongue.

"Hey, Leeford, how's it going?"

"It's a fine day for Leeford. Everyday is a fine day for Leeford. What are you drinkin'?"

"Just a Coke. Mac around?" Jack asked.

"Of course." Leeford pushed a tall glass of soda at the young man he called Jack. He picked up a cell phone/radio and announced Jack's presence to Mac on the other end. Jack seated himself at the closest booth. Mac exited the door behind the bar, which was difficult to see with cases of bud bottles stacked up high around it camouflaging the office door. He motioned to Jack to come in.

Jack entered the small room and sat in the usual chair in front of Mac's desk. Painted gray cinderblock walls were peeling. A dusty, fluorescent overhead light was the only source of illumination. There were no windows. Mac took his seat and moved some of the piles of boxes and zip-loc bags to the far side of his desktop. One of the bags fell to the floor and Jack picked it up. It was full of credit cards. Jack set it back on the desk.

"So, what have you got for me today?" Mac put on his glasses. His hair was silver, what small amount there was. Pale and wrinkled skin surrounded his eyes. The sun had not touched this man's face in years. He was much shorter than Leeford, but not lighter. His big belly protruded through the buttons of a red checked flannel shirt. His teeth were stained yellow. A cigarette burned on the edge of the ashtray. There were stacks of Marlboro cartons in a corner. One lay ripped open. The fresh pack lay next to the ashtray.

Jack reached into the side of his sock and withdrew a small baggie. He handed it across the desk to Mac. "Can I bum a cigarette?" Jack asked.

Mac nodded without taking his eyes off the plastic bag that he was inspecting. "Sure…take a carton, take two." He lifted his arm and pointed to the stash of Marlboros. The young man got up, took one carton and opened up a pack.

"I almost forgot. Where's Pixie? I brought her something." Jack pulled out a can of Fancy Feast from his pocket.

Mac looked up and smiled.

"Just tap the can. She'll come runnin'." Mac handed him a small paper plate. After a couple of taps, the beast appeared. The alley/coon cat looked like a cross between a black bear and tiger…larger than many dogs. The feline reached up and put its paws on Jack's leg. The claws penetrated his jeans. He emptied the can onto the plate and put it on the floor. The cat cleaned the plate and looked up at Jack. He held out his hand and patted the cat. "Pixie sure can put it away," Jack said.

"That's my girl. Jack, these are some nice things here. The watch will move fast. How about 400?"

"Okay." Jack shrugged.

Mac pulled out a stack of bills from his desk drawer and handed the young man a stack of twenties. "You know, you could do better. I have errands…jobs here now and then. If I knew how to reach you. You interested?

"Maybe. I appreciate the offer. Sometime. Not now. I'm good." Jack got up to leave and shook Mac's hand. He picked up his cigarettes and went out the way he came in. He walked alone down the city street, chilled from the wind that lifted the leaves in small tornadoes. He pulled up the collar on his padded jean jacket and then tapped the bills in his pocket.

The rusted Chevy pick-up truck choked and then started, in its dependable fashion. Jack pressed on the pedals of his dad's old vehicle and maneuvered through the late afternoon traffic, which congested the Litchfield City streets. The old mill town, once thriving, now struggled to balance the large number of recent immigrants and few employment opportunities. Large amounts of federal money for low income housing temporarily infused the area with some hope, but now the jobs were gone and the housing full, leaving many to survive on government subsidies. There remained little tax base for the city. Old brick factories vacant, the dust long settled, were constant reminders of a stagnant civilization. Like the polluted river that lined the factory routes, not much moved in or out.

The old truck chugged to a stop in the lot beside a white apartment building. The three floors, with four residences on each, formed the entire unit. This building, along with the other five that lined North Street, had been built during the city's redevelopment phase twenty years ago. A small area of brown grass and dirt held two metal picnic tables chained to a cement weight. The occasional planted tree grew at a stunted pace. At the side of the building, brown dumpsters bulged. An old man gathered leaves and trash and wrestled them into a large green plastic bag. He fought a losing battle with the wind.

The young man with the heavy black boots exited the truck and walked toward the front of the building. "Do you need help, Mr. Felders?"

"No. That's okay. My doctor says I need more exercise. And you know, this place always need some cleaning up. Thanks, Pete." The old man wheezed and returned to his project.

Pete—his real name—bounced up the stairs to the third floor. He turned the knob and entered the apartment. The sharp smell of bleach hit him. Mom was cleaning again. He saw the bucket on the floor with gray rags in it. He took off his boots and stowed them on the small rug by the door. He hung his coat up on a hook.

"Mom...Mom?" He exited the kitchen and entered the small living room.

His mother shut the bedroom door and held her finger to her mouth. "Shhh. I finally got your father in bed. He just had some medicine. He's not doing good. Having a bad day." She adjusted her buttoned, thin, blue cotton shirt, which hung loose. Her brown hair was short and uneven. She cut it herself.

"Oh, sorry...I just wanted to tell you I got paid for that overtime today." Pete pulled out the roll of money and handed his mother three hundred dollars.

"Thanks," his mom said, without looking at her son's face. "I've got to pay the rent today. It's late. How are you doing in school? You still need that diploma, you know."

"It's okay. I'll graduate in June. Don't worry, Ma."

She nodded and then disappeared into the kitchen. Pete heard the pail of bleach and water moving around; the apartment was never clean enough for his mom. Pete walked over, peeled opened the door slightly and looked in on his father. He lay in his bed, covered with gray wool blankets with a faded print of US Army. His wheelchair waited next to the double bed. Pete shut the door, careful not to make a sound. He entered the only other room, besides the bath—his bedroom—which he shared with his older brother, Mike.

As usual, Mike lay on his bed; eyes closed listening to music pouring in from headphones. With tight quarters and thin walls, it was best if self-expression stayed within one's own head. Mike was home during the day, sleeping something off, and gone at night, which gave Pete the room to himself. He pushed his leftover cash deeper in his pocket. He would not hide it until he was alone.

Ten

Brendan made out a muffled voice that sounded as if it were miles away. Words flowed into each other, creating a stream of hopeless noise. He felt fogged by a cold, thick weight. Nothing made sense. Struggling for clarity, he tried to focus, to open his eyes, to move. The far away voice stopped. He yelled for help, hoping for assistance from this paralyzed state, but his plea went unanswered. A blanket of fog swallowed him. He drifted away.

The beleaguered attorney woke to the coldness radiating through him, but he was relieved to feel anything. The fog seemed somewhat lighter, as he again struggled to regain control over his body. After many failed attempts, he got his eyes to open. A haze still filled his vision. Pain shot from his shoulder from something pressing into him. He tried to move. He realized the weight of his problem was beneath him. He jerked back his head, and moved, like a limbless mass of jelly not quite in control. He looked down at Kate's cold and stiff body.

Brendan threw himself off the couch and crashed onto the floor. The sight of the stiff flesh stayed with him even as he turned away. He sunk his head, feeling swollen and ready to burst, into his hands. This was worse than any hangover he had ever had. He uncoiled his memory and replayed events. He should check Kate to see if she was really dead. This thought fleeted from his brain as he recalled the cold hardness of her body.

Brendan sat on the floor to regain sensation and strength throughout his body. His fingers prickled. Blood flowed like a switch flicked on to restart his dormant, suspended system. What happened? Had he been drinking? Pain sparked when he reached back into his memory to decipher past events. He tried to look through the prism, but all the images were distorted. Try as he might, he only remembered coming into the apartment.

Kate's cold body nearby demanded attention. With weak legs, Brendan made it to the bathroom. Ice cold water brought welcome relief to his skin. He dried his face and, holding the sides of the sink, looked at himself in the mirror. The pasty skin color and red sunken eyes startled him.

He relieved himself in the toilet and flushed. He dropped to his knees and proceeded to vomit up Coke, followed by yellow-green bile. His insides emptied out. The heaving continued long afterward. Collapsing over the toilet, dizziness engulfed him. He struggled to maintain consciousness and shivered, unable to warm his body.

Brendan made it back to the living room and wrapped himself in a throw. He stared again at Kate. Erupted blood filled her eyes. He poked her arm. It felt freeze-dried. With one finger, he pushed her eyelids closed then wiped his finger on his slacks. He sat on the edge of the couch. He couldn't remember drinking alcohol, but nothing else explained this.

The bruises on Kate's neck jogged his memory. He starred down at the palms of his hands trying to hold his head together. Images flashed through his mind. Kate's words repeated in his head. Familiar anger welled up. He tried to focus. What the hell had he done?

He noticed the telephone sitting on a nearby table, realizing the rest of the world was nearby. Thoughts rushed him: self-defense, crime of passion? He couldn't imagine any way out of this. Manslaughter and jail time, the loss of his job, Sarah, and his freedom. If Kate had just left him alone, none of this would have happened.

The attorney counseled himself. He tried to focus. For the first time, he was aware that time had passed. The last bits of the day's light peaked in through the window. The clock read 4:40. He had lost hours. First thing, cover his tracks at work. He found his cell in his trench coat and turned it on. It beeped with voicemail. He dialed Mel's direct line. "Mel," he put in a scratchy faint voice.

"Brendan…THANK GOD! Where have you been? Are you okay? I thought something happened. I haven't been able to reach you. Today was awful. I was just about to report that you were missing," Mel reported.

"Yeah, I…" Brendan's dry lips stuck. His tongue felt too big for his mouth and his usual seamless voice had deep ruts in it.

"Are you okay? You sound terrible. I didn't know what to do. You said to cover for you…but everyone is looking for you, and—"

"Who's everyone?"

"EVERYONE! Hessman. Shelly. Your wife."

Brendan couldn't connect the dots, yet. "Something happened, and I just couldn't get back today." Brendan rubbed his aching head. He sat in a room with a corpse.

"Today?" Mel questioned. "Brendan, do you know today is Friday? You haven't been back since yesterday. You know, it's not my business where you've been, but do you have any idea what I've been through here?" Mel pleaded.

Brendan swallowed hard. Friday? He had been out for over 24 hours? Shit. The meetings, the contracts, his workload flashed in his brain.

"Brendan, are you still there?"

He mumbled into the phone.

"I didn't know what to do. I didn't know what the right thing to do was. You said to cover for you so I did. But, when you weren't around this morning and we had those meetings scheduled… I finally told them you called in and you were sick with food poisoning, which was fine. Until your wife called." Mel's voice became thick with emotion.

"And what did you tell her? When did she call?"

"This morning, first thing. I told her I wasn't sure what time you got in this morning, but that your things were all open on your desk. I told her I would have you call, between meetings. But later, when I realized nothing on your desk had been moved since yesterday, I didn't know... Then, I sort of panicked." While Mel explained her list of woes, Brendan began the long process of damage control.

"Okay, first, don't worry about my wife. I will call her. You did fine, Mel. What happened was…" He paused, making sure his concoction was plausible. No story was better than one with holes. "I was mugged. It's a long story, but it really doesn't matter. Let Shelly know I'm better and I'll be in on Monday. And, don't tell them anything else. I don't want them to know you lied. What happened with the hospital contracts meeting? Did it get postponed to Monday?" Brendan was warming up.

Mel took a deep breath. "Shelly told me to take everything to Jared. I went over some things and he handled the meeting with Angus. Everyone was shitty. It was an awful day."

"Damn it." Brendan burst. "Jared. He'll take over."

"Brendan, there was nothing I could do," Mel snapped.

He pulled himself back to task. "I know. You did great, really! Thanks, I owe you. I promise I will make it up to you. Look, talk to Shelly and go home. I'll take care of everything on Monday."

After he hung up, he got Sarah on the phone next. "It's me, Sarah." Brendan pulled his voice together as best he could.

"WHERE ARE YOU? You could have called! I was worried," Sarah yelled.

"It's a long story. I was mugged. I was sort of unconscious."

"Why didn't they call me? Don't you have emergency info in your wallet? Oh my God, if it was stolen….are you okay?" Brendan was relieved that she seemed to be buying his story. "Where are you? I'll be right there."

"I am fine, now. I'll drive myself home. I've got to stop at the office for a couple of things." This would be the hardest point to sell, but he *did* not need her coming into Boston.

"Brendan, I'll come get you. You shouldn't be driving. Which hospital are you in?"

"NO, Sarah! I'm okay. I'll be home later. I have to go. I'll call you if I need you. I will explain everything later." His voice turned stern. With everything he had to deal with, he didn't need this.

"But…."

"I am fine and I will call you later. I have to go. Goodbye." Brendan hung up without letting her finish; an abrupt end that he knew he would pay for later. He turned off the phone and again faced the origination of this chaos.

Brendan crafted a plan to mitigate his exposure. He recalled past and current criminal cases, which he worked on through Bar Association pro bono services. It was good public relations, being committed to justice for all. Police reports, crime scene photos, mistakes and prosecutors words rushed him. The crime scene itself was the most important. It was hard to investigate a crime scene, if you didn't know where it was, and if the body was never found.

Brendan, with stony emotions, went to the kitchen and retrieved yellow gloves, two big white trash bags, glass cleaner and paper towels. With a cold force, he bent her rigid body and stuffed it into the bags, one covering each end. He crushed her down to fit, breaking some ribs and small bones. He closed his eyes in response to the snaps he heard.

He pulled the carnage to the door.

Starting in the bathroom, he washed down the stainless faucet handles, the porcelain sink, the toilet; anything else he thought he might have touched. He threw the paper towels into another trash bag, like a cleaning woman. After wiping the mirror, he opened it, discovering a medicine cabinet filled with a myriad of prescriptions. Some of the names he recognized: Valium, Tagament, and Prozac. Many of the medications listed were foreign to him, and the number of bottles baffling.

In Kate's bedroom, he picked up a small travel bag and jammed it full of an assortment of clothing. He made sure to shut each drawer. He pulled Kate's favorite Gap sweatshirt from the floor and stuffed it in along with the bag of trash. Back in the bathroom, he threw in most of the prescriptions and her toothbrush. Kate was going to be away for the weekend.

On his way back to the living room, Brendan noticed Kate's laptop and purse. Both went into the bulging bag. A light flashed on the answering machine, he remembered the voice earlier. Curiosity got the better of him; with a gloved finger he pushed play.

"Katie… it's Mom, call me as soon as you get this." The sound of another voice echoing the walls sent shivers through every extremity. He had no idea who might stop by. The woman did not sound happy. He erased the message; better for investigators to think she received and disregarded the message. It would help muck up her time of disappearance.

Ready to make an exit, Brendan dragged the bags to the door then inspected the room. Both glasses they used were tossed into the overnight bag. Nothing else jumped out at him. He had wiped down all the prints he could think of. There were no signs of struggle. One thought nagged at him, though. Maybe the apartment was too clean. Even if Kate had cleaned, her fingerprints would again be deposited on some surfaces. No fingerprints at all would be a flag to the police.

His latex covered hands pulled Kate's stiff hand from the garbage bags and pulled the entire bagged carcass around, pressing her lifeless fingers to doorknobs, glass on the end table and other surfaces, which he cleared.

Again, ready to leave, Brendan once more looked over the apartment. He never called her on the phone. He saw no notes around, hopefully everything was contained to her laptop. The only thing he could not be sure of: had she confided in anyone? Finally satisfied he left no clues at the crime scene, he leaned on the wall for several heartbeats. His head throbbed; his stomach ached from the acid, which continued to erode his system. He wanted to get the hell out of there. Adrenaline pumped through his veins.

The peephole offered easy surveillance of the hallway. Not being able to risk two trips, he would have to struggle with both items. Swinging the strap of the travel bag over his shoulder, he tested the weight of the stark white, garbage bags that were now camouflaged by a throw blanket he wrapped his mess in. It would take both hands and he would have to appear unburdened. He flipped up his collar and summoned temporary strength from the adrenaline that whipped through his veins. He turned the lock to ensure it would lock behind him and deposited the yellow gloves into his pocket.

He took a deep breath. And pulled the doorknob shut, wiped it with his jacket sleeve and put his head down. The short flight of stairs strained his exhausted body, but reaching the Jeep without seeing anyone gave him a sense of jubilation. With swift motions, he heaved the bags into his back seat. The darkness in the early November sky cloaked his strained movements; even he was surprised how fast he was. He let the engine warm for only a minute to clear the windows from the patches of frost and then pulled away from the small black vehicle with scratches along one side.

Driving the speed limit, Brendan exited the highway at the first fast food restaurant. He drove through and gulped food; a double burger and bag full of French fries, while he was parked at the most isolated point of the lot. The corner of his eye caught the edge of a white bag. He pushed it back further, preferring as much distance as possible between him and the corpse. In the process, he came face to face with his next dilemma: what to do with the body?

Rain, spitting at first, progressed to a pour. The precipitation closed him off from the outside, mixing the events and emotion into a soup. He spotted a dumpster nearby. No good. She would be discovered too soon. Her body needed to be never found, or discovered only after enough time passed to deteriorate trace evidence…and memories. The first rule of law: delay. He needed time to see if any connection would be made to him. He needed time to think. He just needed some time.

On autopilot from fatigue, Brendan headed north towards home. He grasped each sign and exit in the hope of aid. The Big Dig, long finished now, would have provided all sorts of opportunities. Unable to think of a permanent solution, due to the pressure and his physical condition, he had to at least think of provisional shelter. He had to rid himself of this body or at least store it for a while. A place where no one would search....something not being used...abandoned. Ideas presented themselves for review. Only one stood strong. Dr. Mercer's pool. *No, it's crazy.* But no one bothers with a covered pool. He wrestled with himself, but kept driving.

The Jeep stuck to the speed limit the entire journey, not too fast, not too slow. Answers to policeman's questions were well-rehearsed, even though he hoped they would be unnecessary. The Coke and food eased much of his physical discomfort. The attorney felt stronger with strength and confidence returning. The rain subsided.

Driving past the Mercer's home twice was enough for Brendan to decide it was safe enough to continue up the driveway. Only low lights burned at the front door. The house was dark and secluded from the street by trees and bushes. He sat in his quieted vehicle searching the dark house for any sign of life. No other houses were even visible through the thick woods. Seeing nothing, he took a deep breath and moved fast. *It will have to do for now!* He thought that they might have a dog, so he tossed leftover French fries in his pocket. He pulled free a green bungee cord that wrapped maps and other loose items. The natural and built in privacy of trees and fencing around the pool made the area a fortress of seclusion. A dark colored dog flew out to greet him, tail wagging. The animal sat on command. Brendan threw the food scraps far. The dog followed the food. He hoisted the heavy bagged mess.

Pushing away what seemed a like a foot-deep layer of leaves, Brendan had no trouble loosening the strapped cables, which held the cover taunt. In a split second, he decided to pull Kate's body out of the bags for more destruction of any physical evidence. He slipped the stiff cargo into the deep end and secured her wrist with the green cord to the strap in case he needed to retrieve her, risky as that might be, at a future date. Replacing the cables to their original tightness presented a problem to Brendan's exacerbated muscles. He looked all around, his confidence replaced by growing fear. He fixed his knee, pulled hard and let out a desperate grunt, pulling the cable back in place. It was not as tight, but not obvious to the eye.

Brendan pulled up to his nearby home a little after 8:30 p.m., his head and every muscle unraveled and begging for rest. He soaked up the safe feeling of being home, his eyes teared and he fought back floods. The two-day old clothing was damp with perspiration and rain. Like an unwinding top, his hands shook at the prospect of respite. What a horrible situation. He hoped he could go to bed and wake from this nightmare. He never intended to kill her. It was all a huge mistake, not murder but self-defense. Out of his car, he looked at the trash bags in the back seat. Tomorrow, he thought. He pushed a button on his key ring and locked the Jeep.

Eleven

A cold, drizzly Monday morning, a perfect day to spend butt naked with your legs up in the air. And, as good a day as any for a visit with her gynecologist. Susan Henkley, MD had been friends with the Mercers since she and Jason went through medical school together. Although for different reasons, they both felt comfortable cutting people open. Just the idea of slicing into someone else's flesh gave Kyle the creeps.

Sue had just finished her training and opened her practice when Kyle got pregnant with Jeffrey. Over the next decade, Sue and Kyle spent a lot time of time together, much of it crying, trying to get Kyle pregnant again. "Would you like to take off your shoes before I weigh you?" the young nurse, with no hips, politely asked.

"Sure…can I take off a leg, too?" Kyle laughed. The nurse looked up at her with no expression. "That was a joke," Kyle explained.

"Oh, I see," the nurse said as she recorded Kyle's weight on the chart. "Please follow me." The woman led Kyle to an exam room. "The doctor should be with you shortly." She left Kyle to undress and slip into a paper gown.

Minutes later, Sue tapped on the door. "Hi. It's great to see you." The tall, graceful physician greeted Kyle with a big hug. Her short, light brown hair swept back from her face in a blunt cut. Her brown eyes looked like they had been open too long.

"Hey," Kyle smiled. "How long has your new nurse been out of school? A week?"

"Yeah, she's young," Sue agreed. "She's very bright. We were lucky to get her."

Kyle pondered how bright she could be if she didn't *get* her jokes. "With all of modern technology, isn't there a more efficient way of doing this? A blood test or something?" Kyle winced as Sue put on her gloves.

"Sorry. You'll be the first to know if we come up with a better method. Now scoot down. I'm already running late today. I had a delivery this morning. Can't schedule these babies you know."

Kyle lifted her hips and moved down on the table.

"So, tell me how you've been? How's Jeffrey?" While Sue poked, Kyle updated her on Jeffrey's college search, the pending trip to Rome, and her uninvited guest in her backyard.

"Oh my, I would have been petrified. You don't think he actually got in the house, do you?" Sue peered up at Kyle. "Anything gets me scared."

"No, nothing missing. Jason thinks it was just a kid. I think I've finally relaxed. But, I still find myself looking out the windows a lot, into the woods," Kyle admitted.

Sue finished her work and focused. "Well, if you had to be scared, at least you had officer 'cute stuff' to come save you."

"Yeah, he was sweet. But, you should have seen my house." The women laughed and promised to try and get their husbands all together for dinner soon.

On her way out, Kyle noticed the rain eased up, but the sky remained gray, threatening snow. Kyle craved a great big cup of coffee to warm her up. Her last stop before heading home was the Dunkin' Donuts in the center of town. Even though it was late morning, the small shop still bustled with customers.

Kyle's eyes did not adjust well to the gloomy light. She bumped into a customer coming in and spilled her coffee all over. Before lookoing up, she noticed familiar black shoes and the dark blue pants. Detective Linscot dripped with coffee; it ran down the front of his uniform with puddles by his feet. Kyle gasped. She couldn't find the words.

"Well, good morning to you, too!" He shook himself out a bit.

"I am so sorry. I didn't see…" They both laughed.

"Well, it's definitely Monday," David said.

Moments later, Kyle sat with two fresh coffees at a table. David came out of the men's room and joined her at the table. "Thanks for the coffee."

"It was the least I could do. What a terrible way to start the week. I am so sorry." Kyle sipped coffee watching the young officer tug on his wet shirt, which was soiled from the chest down. Several other patrons turned to glance at the pair.

"Oh, it could be worse. I have other clothes at the station I can change into. I keep them around for such emergencies." He smiled. "I ran out because our coffee is awful." David smiled.

"I would be happy to pay for the cleaning. I wish you'd let me."

"No, really it's okay. How's your backyard? All quiet?"

"Yes. My husband thinks that it was probably a kid. Don't you think?"

"Sure. I wouldn't worry too much about it. But do call us if you see anything else." No words passed for a few moments as they sipped.

"Well, I should get back and put on some dry clothes." They both picked up their cups and walked out together. She waved then drove home with caution, watching her cup. She didn't want to bump into anything else. With a smile, she pictured David taking off a wet uniform revealing a firm chest… and then the young women who must flock to him.

With a fresh shirt, Det. David Linscot sat at his metal desk flipping through pages of reports, all which needed to be reviewed. Every cop complained about the overload of documentation, yet it was the very essence of police work. Computers were now loaded databases for even the smallest detail. "Four corners" doctrine ruled. If it wasn't contained within the four corners of your report, it didn't happen. Attorneys regularly pronounced in court that if it was important enough to testify to, it should be in the report. David, like every other cop, preferred the "hands on" part of the job.

The plain white walls, which long ago lost their luster, were now pale and dull. Two metal chairs with cushions faced the neat piles of folders stacked on the desk. A single clean window directed sunlight onto his back. He drank terrible coffee and chased it with bottled water. His fingers rubbed tired eyes.

"Hey, Ryan," David called to a passing colleague, who poked his head into the office. "You're on thru seven tonight...spend a little extra time in the southern part of town. Keep your eyes open. Let me know if you notice anything."

"Something up?" the young patrolman responded to the new detective.

"I don't know. Insurance claims around there are up."

"Insurance claims?" Officer Ryan Lansing looked perplexed.

"Whenever you file an insurance claim, you need to fill out a complaint to the police department, even if it's not a suspected theft. It helps track fraud. Its mostly small stuff, but the numbers just seem a bit high. It's probably nothing but..."

"Okay, I'll let you know." Ryan said as he left.

David rolled the numbers through his head. Some information was missing. The previous detective had other things on his mind besides recording insurance claims. It was probably just an anomaly. The Chief told him rich people lose things all the time, and this small town was full of wealthy folks. Reported break-ins were down. But, if he wanted to keep an eye on it, all reports would be copied to him.

David closed up the printouts into a large brown file envelope. He secured an elastic around the bundle and dropped it in his bottom drawer.

Kyle crossed his mind. He thought she was sweet and found himself recalling her face, hair…her smile. He thought about Matt, about Kyle's husband, the surgeon. He decided to think about something else.

It was time to go see Jenny, the number one woman in his life, his six-year old niece.

Monday mornings were always hectic in the office. But today would beat all. Brendan arrived at his desk at 5:30 a.m., intentionally beating everyone except security. Even old man Hessman and Shelly would not be in until at least seven.

Enormous amounts of sleep over the weekend brought him back from his visit with the dead. Sarah took great care of him and expressed guilt over jumping to conclusions. He never gave her any reason to not trust him that she knew of, but she felt that he was often just far away.

Brendan recuperated enough to leave the house on Saturday, "for a short drive by himself." He tied up the few loose ends that sat in his vehicle. Contents of the overnight bag, the clothes and the purse were disposed into several different clothing collection bins. He even discarded the clothing he wore Friday night, including his shoes. The Salvation Army probably didn't get many Armani suits. He insisted on vacuuming out his Jeep, even though Sarah asked him to put it off. A large fire on Sunday afternoon to "warm up the house" provided a place to burn identifying contents of Kate's purse while Sarah was out getting foods her husband craved. He would even volunteer to clean out the ashes in the fireplace tonight. Everything was taken care of, with one exception.

A wool-wrapped Shelly marched into Brendan's office at 6:55 a.m., interrupting him. "Good morning, Brendan. You're feeling better?"

Brendan, caught off guard, jumped to his feet and came out from behind his desk. He flashed his pearly smile.

Shelly frowned a little.

"Good as new. I am very sorry about Friday, Shelly. I would like to meet with Angus today and apologize."

"I'll see if he has any time free," she said, folding her arms in front of her. "I will make sure he knows you regret being unavailable on Friday. Are you going to be able to maintain the Hospital account, or should we just let Jared handle it? He did quite a job stepping in last minute."

Brendan tried not to let the steam seep through his ears. Shelly was such a bitch. "I'll be on top of everything. I'll meet with Jared today and thank him for his help." Brendan maintained a pasted smile on his face.

Shelly stared back at him with a long pause. "Very well, I'll inform Angus." Without waiting for any further words, she turned and left.

Brendan felt uneasy with the interchange. He didn't think Mel was a seasoned enough liar to deal with Shelly, the original Terminator.

Mel came in at 7:30, relieved to see Brendan sitting behind his desk. He apologized again. Then they dug back into their work. Brendan waited as long as he could to place his call. Waking this guy wouldn't help, but he needed answers. He closed the door to his office.

"Lars, hi it's Brendan Reed, your attorney."

"Brendan," A sluggish voice answered back. "Do I owe you money or something?"

"Sorry to wake you. No actually, I need your help. Not for me of course, but for a client. I need to advise him on how to deal with a computer problem."

"What kind of a computer problem?" Lars let out a yawn and a cough.

"An email or really, an instant message problem. It all needs to go away."

"Email doesn't really ever go away. It is always out there somewhere. Instant messages can only be retrieved from the hard drive and that's only most of the time. Depends on what's run over it."

Lars coughed and cleared his throat.

Brendan's stomach twisted. "Look, this is important. I believe the communications were primarily or really completely IM's."

"Well in that case, the problem is only with the two computers that went back and forth. It's the email that can always be retrieved."

Brendan tapped his fingers on his desk. "Are you positive?"

"As far as I know."

Brendan had to destroy Kate's hard drive. "My client would be compromised and some people might misunderstand the intent of these sensitive communications."

"Let me understand this. I haven't had any coffee yet," Lars grumbled. "Your client shared some IM's with someone he wasn't supposed to and now he's worried?"

"Something like that," Brendan responded.

"Look, as far as I know, without the hard drive, that stuff can't be retrieved. The only way, I guess, is if one of the two users was at another computer and accessed their accounts, but that's a stretch. I'll look into it and get back to you if I find anything else."

Brendan hung up the phone and tried to relax. Lars delved into the other side of the computer industry; he was a hacker. Brendan had been "creative" and saved him jail time. The guy was a genius, the original computer nerd on steroids. He crawled into people's homes and lives, mostly companies, learned all of their dirty little secrets and then sold them to the highest bidder. Through the court process, the fed's learned of Lars' abilities and became a client as part of his plea agreement, which kept him out of jail and "working." All from the security of his beautiful home, this now, at Brendan's recommendation, was under his mother's name. His dead mother.

Brendan didn't leave his office for lunch. He paced. At 1:30 Mel put through a return call from Lars. "Brendan, I've consulted with some acquaintances. But first of all, is our conversation still protected even though you called me?"

"Yes, of course." *It better be.*

"It looks like your client is safe, so long as he can secure both computers."

"What do you mean it looks like?"

"Well, one guy says that if it goes through the system, there's a track or a footprint somewhere. But hell if I know how to get to it. It's not like email. Email is forever. Now if one person discussed this information to a third party in an email, well..."

"Okay, thanks for your help. I appreciate it."

"You mean your client appreciates it, right?"

The attorney sunk in his chair. A piece he had no control over. Anything in print from Kate regarding their relationship would be disaster to his reputation and with his wife, however, would not prove murder. Information could just be out there floating around waiting to incriminate him.

Thursday morning brought two new assignments dropped on Mel's desk. The days were already full; they did not need more work. The dutiful, black clad assistant put off taking the paperwork to Brendan as long as she could. "Brendan, these contracts came in a little while ago. I have already started on one." She placed the files on his desk.

Brendan looked up from the pile of papers. Tie loose, shirt ruffled, he looked weary, with dark creases spreading across his face. Mel thought he had aged in just this past week.

"You have got to be KIDDING! Mel, I cannot take care of everything around here! I am out straight!"

The sound of his elevated voice became a staple this week. Though the workload was heavy, they'd been buried before. Other times, Brendan would rise to the challenge and even seem to enjoy it. Now, he just seemed overwhelmed. She tried not to take his rants personally. She turned to exit and his softer voice stopped her.

"Mel, I'm sorry. I know you are working hard, too. I'll take care of it. I'll work Saturday and take this new stuff home this weekend to get it started."

Mel returned to her desk, relieved that her weekend was not ruined.

The next morning, Friday, Mel came into his office, walked along side of his desk and told him that something was up. "I didn't realize, but Hessman hasn't been in much all week. The rumor is that he's sick; it may be serious."

"Well, what a shock," said Brendan. He had not left his desk long enough this week to notice anyone else. "He's only a hundred years old. What does Shelly say?"

"Officially nothing, he's unavailable, is all. But she's been crankier than usual. Everyone's been hiding from her. What would she do without him?" Mel smirked.

She collected the signatures she needed from Brendan and returned to her desk. Within a short time, she returned. "I just got buzzed by Shelly. She said there's a meeting for all partners in the conference room at 2. Something's definitely up!"

With only three other senior partners, Angus' exit would mean a shake-up in the status quo. He heard rumors that the other aging senior partners wanted to "open up" the firm and let the four junior partners buy into full partnership. They would be, in essence, selling some of their shares and cashing out some of their equity. Angus, who maintained the ultimate veto authority, thanks to well-written partnership contracts, would never agree to it. It would mean changing the dictatorship to a democracy. He and Shelly would no longer be the "first couple." Brendan felt exhilarated at the prospect. The buy-in would be a hefty amount, however, it meant procuring an equal vote and share of the profits. The future partner floated potential numbers through his mind. He worked fast through the morning and enjoyed a martini lunch.

At quarter to two, Brendan loitered outside the conference room, black suit jacket on and smoothing his navy print tie. Jared showed up soon after moving suavely in a new charcoal suit and maroon tie.

"What's the word, Jared?"

"Don't know," he said throwing his hands in the air. "I am not the sort to listen to rumors. How are you feeling? All better?" Jared patted down the front of his tie and smoothed back his jet-black hair.

"Just fine…back to normal." Brendan stood tall and straight trying to make up the difference in Jared's two-inch height advantage.

"Great, great. I was sorry to hear you were ill. If you ever want any help with that account…"

"Thanks so much, but it's pretty well worked out. Just the ironing to do now." Brendan planted his feet and his head high.

The two junior partners, as well as the seniors, trickled in and took their "assigned" seats in the conference room. Brendan looked at the vacant chair at the end of the table. The absence of Angus presented enormous opportunities for change. He anticipated the good news.

At two o'clock sharp, Shelly stepped into the conference room. She held nothing in her hands. She did not sit. She stood next to Angus' chair. "Angus has asked me to inform you that for personal reasons he will be unavailable to perform his usual daily duties and has asked the other senior partners to fill in these gaps." The senior men nodded, affirming previous arrangements. "It is unavoidable. We all hope this is brief. That is all. Any other questions or problems can be directed to me." That would assure none.

"Brendan, Angus would like to see you and Ronald in his office."

The room cleared out and Brendan shared a quick glance with Jared. Brendan followed the gray haired man down the short walk to Angus' office. Ronald Turner was the second most senior partner and as close a friend as Angus appeared to have. When they entered, Angus was sitting at his desk perched in front of two large windows, listening to the telephone he held to his ear. He jotted down some notes and grunted affirmatively several times. He looked fatigued and closer to two hundred years old. Brendan contained his optimism and sat in a brown leather chair facing the large, mahogany desk. And waited.

"Brendan, Ronald…" He nodded his head. "This will have to be shared with the rest of the staff, but for now, Brendan, I wanted to ask you for your help with some personal business."

Brendan nodded affirmatively. Ronald sat quiet.

"Everything that can be done…" Angus removed his glasses and rubbed his eyes. He pointed to a picture on the end of his desk. "Do you see this lovely thing? This is my granddaughter." The picture showed a pigtailed, smiling toddler decked out in pink, sitting on a much younger Angus' lap. "She's missing." The old gentleman removed a handkerchief from the pocket of his charcoal Brooks Brothers suit pocket and dried his eyes. "Brendan, you are the only one with any real experience with police. I would like to ask you to speak with the authorities and help me make sure that we or they are not overlooking anything."

"Well, of course, Angus. It would be my pleasure, but I am not really sure what I can do."

"Just be an extra set of eyes. I'm afraid I'm going to miss something. I am the only father she's ever known. We are so close."

"I will do anything I can. Was she abducted? Is there a chance she's with an estranged parent or relative?" Brendan realized how little he knew about Angus' family. He was so private, details were never shared.

"No, no. I'm sorry. Katherine's now twenty-four. I call her Katie," the old man said.

Brendan's hell broke loose.

"She's had emotional problems…lacked direction. I got her a job at Jean-Paul's last year; you know the men's store down the street? The owner and I are old friends…." Angus forged on about how Katie was the only grandchild he had, his daughter's only child. Her father had been killed in a drunk driving accident when she was two. She had never been the same.

Brendan's face lost all expression. His body went numb.

Twelve

Kyle's mind drifted off throughout the school committee meeting. The budget committee reported that there was no money and that the sky was falling. It was never a good year, even when it was a good year and the sky had fallen many times. Parents demanded new books, teachers and buildings. It was up to the school board to balance all these issues and figure out what was best for the students as well as the town.

Only one light outside was burning. Maggie lifted her head from the couch, saw Kyle, then went back to sleep. The kitchen was dark and the whole house seemed to be in slumber mode. As always Jason's and Jeffrey's belongings were left all over the kitchen island for easy access in the morning. Dinner dishes soaked in the sink.

Upstairs, she checked on her son. She eased the door open, Jeffrey's limbs hung over his bed, with most of the covers on the floor. His back lifted in a gentle movement while his arms embraced a big pillow. Kyle was well aware that her days and nights of such glimpses of security were numbered.

In silence, Kyle changed her clothes and tiptoed around the bedroom. She peeled off her tired, wrinkled black slacks and thin gray sweater. A calf length, pink nightshirt would help take away the November chill that filled the house. Jason snored, unconscious of the other human in the room.

Kyle headed back down to the kitchen, put water on for a cup of herbal tea, and loaded the dirty dishes into the dishwasher. Her eyes ached with fatigue. She sat in her favorite oversized chair and ottoman with the tea, and flipped on the television. Maggie joined her, curling up on the floor next to the chair. Maggie picked up her head and fixed a gaze at the useless cat. Pumpkin jumped onto Kyle's lap, crawled up her chest and rubbed her chin. After much petting, the feline settled into the ample space beside Kyle. By the time the news came on with a lead story about a missing young woman from Boston, the three were adrift in a deep slumber.

Opening her eyes only to small slivers, Kyle saw the television, alive with energy. Despite her attempts to go back to sleep in the chair, it was not going to happen. She got up, disturbing Pumpkin as little as possible. With the television turned off, Kyle found herself in her familiar, dark quiet. Her own personal mirror of time and she tried not to look. She leaned against the wood trim of the large window and looked out into the calm backyard. The pool appeared completely tucked in, sedate, with the green mess cover pulled over it. Leaves collected in the center from the winds. Through the bare branches, Kyle could see further into the woods. Scanning the backyard, she saw no figures and no black boots. Only the occasional wind woke the stillness of the moonlight among the trees.

Kyle crawled into bed at 3:37 a.m. She had hoped for more sleep, however she was pleased to have logged more than the previous night. Jason stirred, but did not wake when she pulled the covers up around her. Jason's 5 a.m. wake up was not far off.

When the alarm buzzed and it was still dark out, Kyle decided to get up and be useful. She started buckwheat pancakes for the men. Maggie was at attention by her side in the kitchen, Pumpkin stayed in Kyle's kitchen chair with her head curled into the pillow.

Jason adjusted his tie and surveyed the steaming pancakes. "Did you get any sleep?"

"Some."

"You need to relax," he said.

"I've got a lot on my mind with the school budget, and the holidays coming. I haven't even started to figure out Thanksgiving. It gets dark so early now, the days seem to go by faster."

Standing up, Jason inhaled a stack of pancakes with maple syrup. He kissed Kyle on the cheek and took off, armed with his usual weapons: cell phone, pager and palm pilot.

Minutes later, Jeffery devoured a feast of pancakes and was off to pick up Lindsay for school. Maggie and Kyle had the leftovers and then cleaned up.

Kyle decided that if they were going to indulge themselves with pancakes, they should go for a brisk walk. Maggie was enthusiastic until her nose hit the cold air. She took a moment to adjust. Kyle felt the chill only on her face, since she bundled herself up in lots of soft fleece, head to toe. She hit the road and headed up hill, just as an old blue pick-up truck drove past. Everyone was off to work early.

With the house locked up tight that evening and both of her men long asleep, Kyle sent the canine out the dog door for her last run. The news was about half way through when she heard the disturbance. At the window, through the shadows, she saw Maggie barking, yelping. Kyle banged on the window and yelled for her precious pup. Before she made it to the double glass doors, the dog flew in the entrance. The dog looked okay, except she pawed at one eye. Then the smell hit. SKUNK!

Now what? Her nose burned and Kyle gagged. Maggie whined and the smell was spreading. She began by shutting the dog door so the nasty visitors couldn't come in. Maggie never before had a tangle with much of anything. She flipped the floodlights, which cast some light on the situation. As far as she could see, 30 feet or so of the deck area the edge of the concrete decking leading to the pool, no black striped creatures. She dragged Maggie upstairs to inspect the damage.

Shut in the bathroom upstairs with the tub seemed like a good idea at first. But it was soon hard to breathe. She opened and shut the window. Being directly over the deck, it only let more odor in. She flipped on the exhaust fan and got to work. Rinsing the dog with shampoo did little. One eye of Maggie's was swollen and red. A direct hit. She needed to know what else to do. Tomato juice came to mind, but who kept that on hand.

Upon her exit from the bath, she glanced down both sides of the hallway, hoping the ruckus had stirred some assistance. Evidently not. She looked at her bedroom door with her husband sleeping on the other side and wondered if this met the threshold of an emergency. Instead, she chose the office and hopped on the internet. Soon she was back in the bath washing her smelly friend with a concoction of hydrogen peroxide and baking soda.

Upon coming home from the vet the next day, the smell in and around the house seemed worse. The stench seemed to permeate her skin and invaded her sinuses. Kyle bagged her clothes for the garbage, called cleaners for the house and hoped that a harsh New England winter would cleanse the backyard.

Pete watched Mrs. Sarah Reed drive away in her black Lexus. Then he checked his notepad. He waited in the woods for several minutes then put out his cigarette and entered the yard. The garage door was left open, so he went in. He found the door to enter the home locked. He would have to work on the windows. Garages often offered many valuable items, but required careful thought. Off-season items would not be missed for some time.

This was his first time at this house on Dove Lane. He poked and peered, but found most of the attractive pieces, like a chain saw, leaf blower, too large and heavy to risk moving. On the way out of the garage, a power cord sticking out from under a black tarp caught his eye. With one finger, he lifted a dusty brown material and uncovered an irresistible piece of merchandise: a black, Sony laptop.

It was in a ridiculous place. He wondered if it worked or was destined for the dump. It was bigger and more conspicuous than his usual fare. Pete decided it was worth the risk. Besides, if it were junk, it wouldn't be missed. And if it was functional, what a great find.

Before leaving the garage, he looked out back and surveyed again. With all quiet, he backtracked to the woods. A cold wind howled. After walking a short distance, he picked a spot close to the road and placed the computer on the ground. He piled leaves, rocks and sticks over it, then ran to the truck. A few minutes later, he jumped from his old truck and retrieved his treasure.

Back home, Pete opened up his pack and pulled out his most recent find, careful to leave the rest of the fruits of his labor at the bottom. He plugged in the laptop and turned it on. It flashed a login name of "Kate." Pete tried a few random passwords, but none were successful. He didn't really expect them to be. He closed it down and put it away. He liked the feel and size of the computer. He never kept anything before, but this tempted him.

In the morning, Pete made his trek to downtown Litchfield, with a stop to pick up a can of Fancy Feast. "So, Mac," he said to the proprietor. "Do you know anything about computers? Laptops?"

Mac's attention did not waver from the assorted pieces that "Jack" placed in front of him. Pete waited. He watched Pixie clean her beast paws after her snack. Mac took off his glasses and rested them next to him. "Nice stuff, Jack...how's $250?"

"Fine, whatever... So, you know anything about laptop computers?" Pete suspected the answer, but he also knew that Mac would know someone.

"Not much...but I know someone who 'collects' them, especially laptops."

"I want to use this one, not sell it. How do I get hold of him?" Pete asked.

"You don't. I do. Is this for you or..."

"I'd like to get it working."

"Oh. Well, in that case, there is someone who may be able to help you...should be in later this week. Call me and I will let you know."

"Thanks, Mac," Pete said as he rubbed the beast's head and left.

A few days later, "Jack" found himself sitting in the bar, outside Mac's office. He was not there long when a uniformed policeman entered. Pete eased his backpack under the seat with his foot. He sipped his soda and tried not to make eye contact.

Leeford, behind the bar, swayed over to greet the visitor. "Good afternoon, Officer Ceasar. The usual?" Leeford's wide smile stretched across his face. Jack watched with a close eye as the bartender mixed some type of concoction, poured it through a small funnel and into a soda bottle. The cop took the bottle, said something to Leeford and then departed. He did not look around; he did not ask any questions. Pete fought the impulse to ask about the cop. Communication was not the cornerstone of this business establishment.

Mac came out from behind his door, and summoned "Jack" into his office. He sat behind his desk and handed Pete a slip a paper. The company logo on the top was from a dry cleaners.

Pete looked up at Mac.

"No, not the cleaners, those are just pads I have around. The time and the place, that's your appointment with Ray. Consider it a bonus." Mac smiled as he stroked the cat-beast that fell over his lap.

"Great, thanks Mac. How will I find Ray?"

"Ray will find you, don't worry."

The next day, Pete confirmed the address and the name of the Book Store/Café that Mac noted. He entered into a small café full of coffee smells, cushy high-backed chairs and reading materials, not his normal venue. Pete focused his eyes down and tried to look as if he knew where he was going. He walked fast and chose an overstated, purple chair, with another chair open sharing a table. He stowed the heavy backpack next to his feet. The chair was soft, but Pete could not get comfortable.

Within five minutes, Ray sat herself down. "Okay, what's up? Make it quick. Time is money."

Pete took in Ray's look, and stared longer than he should. His mouth slid open.

"Hey, sweetie, are you sure that all you need is computer advice? Because that's all you'll get for free. And you are wasting your own time."

The long, dark haired woman, who looked to be in her twenties, wore tight black clothes and silver jewelry. Large hoops swung from her ears and sparkled in the light. Her green eyes had streaks of white fault lines running though them. She was slender, but her presence was huge. When she scraped the heel of her black cowboy boots across the floor, Pete saw that it was a spur that she cut into the wood planks. Pete had never seen anything like her before. She was like a horse wrangler from the old west who'd been transported into the computer age, then dropped into Litchfield. Annie Oakley meets Victoria's Secret and Microsoft.

"Sorry. I was…"

"What, expecting a man? Yeah, I get that a lot. Ray is short for Rachel." She winked.

"Yeah, I was. Sorry. Mac says you might be able to help me with this." Pete pulled out the laptop from his backpack.

"Let me guess, you're borrowing this from a friend and they forgot to give you the password… And they're away, right?" Ray laughed. "That's a common problem with laptops. I don't want to know anything else. You're a friend of Mac's… So, you just need this unlocked?" Ray said.

Pete nodded.

"Okay, give it here." Ray took the machine and plugged the cord into a nearby outlet.

"Do you think you can get it working?" Pete asked.

Ray didn't respond, but continued to smile. Pete peered over to get a look at Ray pulling out some things from her black sack. She started up a silver laptop and set it next to the black Sony. Then loaded a disk into Pete's.

As he waited, Pete noticed the same scratch marks made by

Ray's spur in other places near the chair. He looked around and saw the floor scarred with the same marks as far as he cold see. Ray's hands moved at lightning speed and grace, her fingers floated over both keyboards. Her black nail polish melted into the keys. Pete's computer flashed some lights. It stopped. Ray removed the disk and loaded it into her laptop. She watched scores of words zip over the screen. In about two minutes, she let out a yell. "Got ya!" Star symbols appeared across the line for the password on Pete's computer. Ray pressed enter and the machine accepted.

"Wow! How'd you do that?" Pete asked again.

"Piece a cake… Here's your password." Ray handed him a slip of paper. She began to pack up her things.

"No really, how'd you do that?" Pete asked.

Ray stopped her packing for a moment. "Think of it kind of as redial on a phone." She shrugged. "I just got the keyboard to tell me the last few things that were typed in. There's a few ways, but this usually does the trick." Then Ray smirked at Pete. "Okay, well you're all set. In this place, you can hook up to Internet for free."

Ray wrapped a gray wool scarf around her neck, zipped her worn leather jacket and left. Pete spent an hour or so looking over Kate's files and music collection of *Train, Three Doors Down* and *Coldplay.* He changed the name on two of the files to *Jack.*

The same password worked for the email, so Pete read a couple of new ones. Nothing interesting, just a couple asking her where she was.

Brendan drove his Jeep along the familiar route to Kate's apartment, with the aid of unneeded direction from Ronald, the other ancient partner and his new best friend. As they got closer, he fought the impulse to flee. Ronald, well into his sixties, had the personality of sheetrock. He said little and appeared depressed about everything. Going to meet the police at Kate's apartment did not help make Ronald any cheerier.

In his mind, Brendan reviewed with the actions of an innocent man. He rehearsed, he recited. Before he knew it, they pulled up in front of Kate's building and Ronald pronounced them "here." Brendan pulled on his new khaki colored trench coat. He ran his hand across his new crew cut, which his wife hated. The style was harsh, and the roots of his hair much darker than the sun-lightened version of his blond locks. Sarah said, "It makes you look like an entirely different person!"

When they reached the landing in front of Kate's door, Brendan appeared confused, looking at all the doors.

"Right here." Ronald said and unlocked the door. The key had been supplied by Angus, who was too upset to meet the police at his granddaughter's apartment. No one had heard from Kate for over two weeks, and a missing person's investigation had commenced. "I guess we're early," Ronald said. "Let's go in and wait."

Brendan resisted at first but realized it was the best thing for him. Both men mulled around the apartment in silence glancing at items. At the couch he recalled the vision of Kate's ice cold body. A chill ran over his skin. *An innocent man*, he told himself. He strolled toward the large windows and stood in a spot, looking out at the same street where they parked. He leaned and placed his hands where they rested before on one of his previous visits. His hot breath made a mark on the glass, then disappeared. His fingers made light contact with a bookcase, a glass table and a couple of other items in the apartment, out of Ronald's sight. He walked over to the couch and sat in the spot Kate last occupied, ignoring the turning of his stomach. Ronald pushed buttons on the answering machine. Brendan stopped the words of caution from coming out. The more red herrings the better. He leaned to one side and rubbed his forehead with one hand in an effort to control the headache, which was gaining strength.

"You okay?" Ronald asked.

Brendan nodded yes.

"I guess as okay as possible, considering we are helping Angus look for his missing granddaughter, the family's only heir."

Brendan faced the silver haired man. "Really, you mean be-sides his daughter, the granddaughter is the only one?"

"Yes," Ronald said. "Angus has outlived his two brothers and I think most cousins."

"So you mean she's the only heir to inherit an interest in the firm?"

"Oh sure, but that's just peanuts. Angus' brothers were load-ed and left half of it all to him…with some left out for their re-spective ex-wives, settlements and such, and I guess a little to children. Kind of the last guy standing. The brothers started up several international companies, venture capitol, and then sold them. They were ahead of everyone. They held onto stock from each transaction. At the beginning, of course it was worthless, but now, even with the market down, it's still worth millions. Be-fore the last brother died in the early nineties, he got into a big fight with Angus because he wanted to cash out most of the stock and buy real estate. Angus wanted to hold on to everything…you know Angus." He smiled at Brendan, looking green. "But since it was his stock, his brother cashed out seventy-five percent and bought up land and buildings all over the world. He put some into bonds and bank accounts in the Caymans. He died before he saw the fruition of his wisdom. The market started to fall not long after he died."

"With all that money involved, is there any chance this is a kidnapping?" Brendan asked.

"The thought crossed Angus' mind. The police, too. But, there hasn't been a call for ransom. Who knows? She has taken off before, but never this long. She's a flake. A nut. If she is just on another fun vacation, it's a sin what she's putting her family through." Ronald sat on the velvet moss-colored chair facing the multi-colored couch. Brendan now looked at the well-furnished apartment—with lots of windows, in a great location—with a new understanding. That's why she didn't have a roommate. She didn't need the money. Gramps paid all the bills.

"This unit is owned by Angus," Ronald said as if he had just read Brendan's mind. "He used to let the firm use it, but stopped a few years ago. He gave it to Kate so she'd have a nice, safe place to live."

Brendan popped up when the police arrived. The burly, over-sized Boston Detective, James Hayden, greeted them and intro-duced his obvious young trainee, named Scott Lordi. Officer Hayden came in and looked around.

"I don't suppose it occurred to either one of you legal geniuses to wait in the hall, huh?" said Detective Hayden.

Ronald and Brendan didn't respond. Ronald looked back at the officer confused.

"We have a girl missing; this could be a crime scene, folks. Has anyone other than you two have been in here?"

"The mom," Ronald blurted out. "I know at least she's been here. She came over to see if Kate was hurt or something. Here, she left her a note." Ronald pointed to a small kitchen table with two chairs and a single paper lying on top. Detective Hayden walked over to the table and read the note, taking care not to touch it, even with his gloved hands.

There was a knock on the door. Hayden didn't lift his head. "Get that," he barked at his assistant.

"That's the crime scene unit," Hayden reported. "Let's all step out into the hall and talk."

The men moved to the hall. Officer Lordi knocked on neigh-bor's doors while the other men talked.

"There doesn't seem to be any signs of disturbance, but we'll see what the lab guys come up with. Why don't we get together tomorrow and I'll go over anything we find here. I'll come to your office," Hayden said.

Brendan started down the hall before Ronald responded. His skin felt hot and his head ached filled with memories that haunted him. Even the smell of the place, the faint scent of her perfume lingered, to remind him. He used to feel like a big fish, now it seemed that his lake was turning into more of a pond.

Thirteen

Brendan tossed and thrashed around his bed, waking in a panic if he dozed off. After a few disturbed hours, he rose and stood at the windows, naked, staring up at the dark sky that held no comfort. He weighed through the mounds of mistakes he could have made. Did anyone see him leave, or see his Jeep? What if there was some sort of neighborhood watch that just recorded license plate numbers? And the damned potential computer records. He never used his phone to contact her as far as he could remember, thank god, but if she mentioned him in any emails to a friend, how would he explain that! Racing through every conversation, all of his movements caused gridlock in his brain. He would have to move Kate's body at some point, or could he? For the first time, he realized that putting the body in water was not a good call. It was a decision made under stress and some type of drug. What condition would the body be in? He envisioned a white swollen limb connected to the wire he connected it to. What would it be like to move? What if he left it there? He searched his brain for information on decomposition of bodies. He could recall little and he certainly couldn't ask anyone now.

The next morning, groggy with a Mount Fiji sized headache, Brendan came into the office to find a note on his desk informing him that Shelly cleared his schedule and he had a meeting with Angus, Ronald and Dt. Hayden at nine.

Brendan sat at the conference table with the men who were searching for Kate. He pulled his tie to loosen it a couple times, until he realized the anxious behavior. An innocent man, an innocent man…he recited to himself.

Sergeant Hayden's badge shined on his chest. Brendan put him to be about 50 and out of shape from sitting at a desk all day, maybe counting days to retirement. Time was now his ally. Trails got cold, evidence got dusty, and memories became distant images. For the first time he realized this was how the criminals he worked with must feel; stressed as the investigation unfolded, unable to take any action and everything beyond control. Of course, they were not sitting on the inside.

"First Mr. Hessman, let me say again that everything that can be done, is being done. Our first impression—there is a good chance foul play is connected to Katherine's disappearance, though she may have left her apartment initially on her own. Of course at this point, we have more questions than answers. This is what we have so far."

Brendan edged forward in his chair, wanting the words to hit his ears first. Angus noticed his eager lean and gave him a nod of appreciation.

"There was no sign of forced entry, no sign of a struggle inside the apartment. It appears she packed a bag of clothes. Her purse, make-up bag and laptop are presumably with her. All confirmed by her mother. Many of her recently filled medications are gone or empty. Most neighbors know nothing. They say they barely ever saw Kathleen. The only thing we have is the neighbor in the apartment directly across from hers, an elderly woman reports to have looked through her peephole to see a man in a black trench coat entering a couple of months ago. The woman is short, said she could not see well. Said this man and Katherine were talking in the hall, laughing a bit. So, we assume they knew each other. But, of course that was some time ago.

We spoke to many friends and we are interviewing an ex-boyfriend, Trevor. He says he hasn't seen her in a month and at that they have not been involved for several months. We hope to get additional information from friends we haven't been able to reach yet. We will be speaking with him again, of course. Besides the boyfriend, the only other item of mention was a friend reporting that she got the impression Katherine was seeing a married man. But, she could not say for sure. That *could* be the guy in the black raincoat. Trevor didn't look like a raincoat kind of guy."

The Sergeant paused and took a breath. He flipped pages in his notebook. "We served the warrants that you signed off on, Mr. Hessman, for her phone records and email." Brendan held his chin up and braced himself. "We have the phone records and we are going through them. The email will take a few more days, but unfortunately we will not be able to get any record of instant messages without the hard drive. And the problem is IM's are the main tool utilized these days by her age group." He rolled his eyes. "But we are always hopeful there will be some clues. There has been no new activity and since her laptop is gone, we feel that is significant. Her account has been flagged. We will be contacted immediately if there is any activity. We think if she was involved with someone, there would be a phone trail, so we don't think this will put us at too much of a disadvantage for the time being. And there are a couple more things…"

Brendan swallowed hard and hoped for the best.

"We recovered some trace evidence from around the apartment: hairs, fibers, etc. There is no way to know when they were left, but it may be helpful. But, there was one significant thing we found in the sink. A small vial in a bowl of soapy water. There are no fingerprints and we are analyzing what remains of the contents. The initial findings indicate it is the date rape drug, DHB, or liquid ecstasy. This concerns us, because if that container was full, the dosage would be dangerous."

Maybe make someone pass out for a couple days, or even longer. Brendan flinched. His stomach ached with the same pains he felt that day. What in the world had Kate planned for him!

"Mr. Hessman," he paused, "I need to inform you that we found something else…" The seasoned detective halted his words in search of a compassionate way to present this information.

He looked at Angus. "We found the wrappings of a pregnancy test in the kitchen trash. We did not recover the test itself. We think maybe it is with Kate. But, again, we don't know exactly what it means."

Angus sunk his head into his hands and signed an almost inaudible, "Oh my."

Brendan caught his mouth from hanging open and contained his shock.

The sergeant sat poised. "Any questions?"

"Have they double-checked the hospitals? Have they spoken to all of her friends?" His complexion was a gray paste, heavy rings circled under his eyes. Shelly brought in a pill and a glass of water. Brendan watched, with a little envy, as Angus swallowed the unknown medication.

"We have and will continue to check all those possibilities."

Detective Hayden left the attorneys and told them he would stay in touch.

Brendan fled to his office. He shut his door and made a phone call. "Lars, this is Brendan," he said speaking to an answering machine. "I need you to double check on those IM's. It's important you find out everything."

Brendan sat back in his chair. Hayden was much too competent for his taste. Not the donut eating, retirement obsessive hack that he had hoped. He reached into his desk drawer and swallowed a handful of antacid, then threw the empty bottle into the trash.

Brendan muddled through the week and collapsed at home on the weekend. Sarah hovered over him. She said he looked terrible, pale, even said he looked his age…for the first time! She told him he was working too hard and pestered him to take time off. His stomach turned each time he drove past the Mercer's home. On Monday morning, his stomach turned again answering his first call.

"Morning, its Detective Hayden."

Brendan's blood pressure jumped and he squeezed the phone.

"Ronald asked me to inform you of this new development. It's actually encouraging. We got a hit on Katherine's AOL account. It was at a café north of Boston, in Litchfield. We are working on it. This would lead us to believe she is alive. That's a step in the right direction. Frankly, between you and me, I was sure she was dead. But…maybe not. Someone checked her email. Besides that, we haven't found a body. I'll keep in touch."

Alive? Brendan felt that numb feeling come over his body. Who? How? The day moved at a snail's pace. He barked at Mel and left work early with a throbbing headache. He raced home. He reached the tarp in his garage and flipped it over. No laptop. Still in his suit and tie, he tore the garage apart. Halfway through he tossed his jacket and tie on the dusty floor. A concrete link, the only evidence he knew of that put the two of them together, and it was gone. Every piece of equipment, box or rake lay piled up in the center of the cement floor. Brendan yanked every piece off the shelves. He wondered if some sort of supernatural force was trying to undermine him. He cross-examined Sarah when she returned.

"Why were you storing an old laptop for someone in our garage?" as she stood looking at the disarray Brendan made tearing apart the garage. "Look at this mess! You know, Brendan, you have been moody and difficult. You're always tense and I just don't deserve this. What's wrong with you?"

He paused and realized that he needed to do some damage control. He took her by the hand and led her to two Adirondack chairs in their front yard. They sat and he looked in her eyes. "Look, Sarah, I have been under extreme pressure at work. They have saddled me with many accounts. I can just never seem to make the old man happy. My assistant is useless. It's not your fault. I'm sorry." His tired eyes and frantic demeanor helped him sell his words.

"Why don't you get another job? I don't want to live like this. What about Texas? I would love to move back."

For the first time, Brendan found the option appealing. "I can't consider it right now. Maybe, though in a couple months, it might make sense. Look, I'll clean this up. You go inside. I'll be in soon." He pushed her towards the door before she had a chance to get back to the question of the laptop.

Within a week, Detective Sergeant Hayden appeared in the doorway of Brendan's office wearing a stone, lifeless face. "Good morning, Mr. Reed, this is Officer Griffin from the Crime Lab. We're here for fingerprints and hair samples. May we come in?" Mel stood behind them poking her head around the officers, but still in Brendan's vision.

Brendan muttered a "come in" and offered the two chairs in front of his desk. He rubbed his sweaty palms up and down on his pant legs, hoping to keep the hand movements out of the Detective's line of vision. He repeated to himself his familiar mantra; an innocent man.

"I am not sure I understand, Detective. Why in the world would you need any of this from me? And there are certainly some privacy issues that—"

Hayden shook his hand, waving Brendan to stop. "Relax. The constitution is safe, counselor. We need your prints and hair to exclude from trace evidence found in the apartment, since you and Ronald were in before the lab guys. Remember? Shelly told me she was sure the entire firm would voluntarily supply anything we needed. Is there some reason you'd rather not?" Heavy creases in the detective's skin surrounded his dark eyes that fixed on Brendan. He sat, waiting for an answer.

Wasn't that nice of Shelly? Brendan wanted to go into an extended dissertation of unreasonable search and seizure, but instead uttered only, "No."

Officer Griffin, dressed in a different but equally authoritative uniform—a white shirt and black pants—clipped some hairs from the back of Brendan's head. The short hairs fell into a clear bag and were sealed. She pulled out one hair with a pair of tweezers to secure the root. Brendan winced at the brief pain. The hair dropped from the tweezers into another clear bag. The white labels on each bag served to document the gathered samples.

Next, the officer laid a fingerprint kit on Brendan's desk and asked for his hand. One at a time, the officer pressed each of his ten fingers into the moist ink. Starting with the edge of each finger, she transferred each print onto a form. As he wiped his fingers on the cleaning supplies provided, Shelly stopped in at the doorway. She observed, nodded and left. Mel watched the process, in horror, full of questions. Official channels informed everyone as to Kate's disappearance, but the police in the office collecting physical evidence came as quite a surprise. All staff had been questioned. Anyone with concerns was directed to Shelly. No one chose that option. Most people preferred bamboo stuck under their nails to arguing a request with Shelly.

"Well, thanks for your cooperation, Brendan." The detective departed with his evidence.

The attorney squirmed in his seat. He rose and shut his door. Behind his desk he paced and rubbed his palms at his sides. He reviewed his strategy from all sides, looking out his windows at the lightly falling snow. Fresh footsteps left a trail behind every pedestrian. Of course the following person mucked the prints of the last. He had just handed over physical evidence that could place him at the scene of the crime. Of course right now, there was no crime scene and, of course, no body.

Dt. Hayden called a couple of weeks before Christmas to "check in with Brendan". "Well, we traced the use of the internet access to a café in Litchfield, but the trail goes cold there. It really doesn't make sense. If Kate is checking her email, why doesn't she respond? At least to her friends? I am beginning to think her computer was stolen and someone wants us to believe she is alive."

Brendan grunted in the affirmative. No one was more curious than he as to who possessed of Kate's computer.

"And, if nothing turns soon, I am considering going public with the computer. You know…" The cop cleared his throat. His voice was harsh due to years of yelling in traffic detail and lots of black coffee. The pause, only seconds, seemed to be hours for Brendan to wait for him to finish his sentence. "You know, go public again with her picture and offer a reward for her laptop. Maybe someone has noticed a newly acquired laptop. What do you think?"

Courtroom training jumped to his aid, despite the adrenaline rush. "Well, it may help. It may not. It is likely that the person in possession of the laptop is involved with Kate's disappearance, or foul play. It might just get buried further. It is a risk. Do you really think it will flush out information?" Brendan sat back, pleased with his even tone and delivery. He discussed "the potential perpetrators" with great distance.

He spread his free hand across his desk like one would hold onto the helm of a ship. Fear and uncertainty crept in as the adrenaline leveled off. The computer was the only physical evidence. Emails to a third party could be lethal. But both were now beyond his control. Lars, the computer genius said that if nothing had shown up by now, they didn't have it. He said without one of the two hard drives in question, retrieving IM information was close to impossible.

Hayden said he would run it by his captain and let Brendan know what they decided to do about the laptop. He wished Brendan 'Happy Holidays.'

The law office took on a subdued tone with the holidays fast approaching. The dark cloud of Kate's disappearance lingered. Sparks of festivity, which would have lightened even this stale office, were muffled. Smiles were few. Angus and Shelly were seen only when necessary. Shelly now delegated tasks, which in the past would be guarded by the watchdog. Some T's went uncrossed.

Kate's picture circulated on television and the newspapers. A large reward was offered for her safe return or any information that led to her. As the mother reported Kate's laptop was missing.

The search for the missing black Sony laptop became public. The firm's name was mentioned on occasion. Sarah saw it one afternoon on television. She phoned Brendan at the office. "Brendan, what do you think happened to the poor girl?"

"I have no idea. Folks here say that she was a head case and prone to taking off. But, it is none of our business and I don't want to discuss it again."

"What about Texas? You need some time off and my parents are expecting us for the holidays. How long can you be gone?"

Brendan blew his stack. He felt safest at the office where information flowed through him. "I cannot afford to take any time away from the office. I HAVE TO WORK!"

Sarah seethed. "You don't have to work this much. Isn't there someone who can cover for you for a few days? You know, I think you want to stay there. Forget it. I'll go myself." She hung up.

It would work out well for her to be out of the house for a couple weeks. A welcome relief—one less front to watch. She could lunch and shop with her mother. Warm weather would only improve her temperament. He would send flowers to the in-laws with his regrets explaining that he was swamped with work. There are worse things than being a workaholic. Surely, they would understand.

Detective Hayden, as well as Angus kept him informed of the investigation. The mature man now looked old. His walk and movements were labored efforts. His once straight, square shoulders hung with weight. Angus directed various matters to other attorneys, but spoke only to Brendan, and sometimes Ronald, about his worries for his Katherine. Brendan listened. In his mind, he transcended from the man with the fatal flaw and commiserated with his mentor in his pain.

"Brendan, Shelly just called. Angus wants you in on the ten o'clock meeting with that retail company." Mel stood in the doorway.

The attorney lifted his head from the mass of papers in front of him. "Okay, Mel…can you move that nine AM meeting to…"

Brendan passed his finger down his calendar. "I don't know, Mel. Where are we going to move it?"

Mel, dressed in a tweed brown suit, walked over to his desk and leaned down. Brendan caught her scent.

"Boy, you smell good." A corner of his mouth turned up.

"This is the same perfume I always wear. You just haven't left your office in so long anything smells good to you."

Brendan smiled. He removed his glasses and loosened his tie.

"I can see if we can move the nine to eight. I am not sure they'll do it, but I can give them a call."

"Yeah, try that, and I'll meet you in here early."

"Early? Soon you're going to be asking for me to be in before the sun rises. We need a cot in here."

"A cot? Mel, this is a place of business."

Brendan let out a laugh and Mel knocked him in the arm with a light fist.

"Brendan, even with me getting help and delegating out much of the prep work, I'm not sure we can handle any more clients."

"We can't say no. We are getting the 'primo' clients. I've had other junior partners asking if I want any help. They are all looking to just get on these accounts, let alone quarterback them."

"You are certainly Angus' fair haired boy, lately. He has you in on everything. Any news on his granddaughter?"

"No." He directed his eyes back to his desk. "Do the best you can with the schedule. I'll get started on the new stuff tonight. I was going to stay late anyway."

"Tonight?" Mel razzed and left the office and started juggling appointments.

Brendan stretched back in his chair. Lately, he spent sporadic nights in Boston at a nearby hotel. Shelly suggested and cleared it on his expense account after finding out he had been sleeping more than a couple nights on his couch. He now kept a bag packed and a box of clean shirts in the office. The effort to drive home seemed worthless. He also enjoyed the freedom of those evenings to himself. He caught up with some of his law school friends. The pace over the last few months served to help Brendan distance himself from his involvement with Kate. Only nagging details forced him to again confront the hemorrhaging Pandora's Box.

Fourteen

Kyle and Annie strolled into the Four Seasons Hotel in Boston for the holiday party that Annie had been invited to. They shook off the dusting of snow, which clung to their coats. Lavish flower arrangements of white poinsettias and gold ornaments overflowed the main lobby. The host was a small company Annie worked for on occasion, but she made every party list. Go figure. Kyle watched Annie meet and greet everyone as they entered. She introduced Kyle to all of these people, most of whom were men she would never remember. She marveled at Annie's ability to recall names, children, wives and significant others in great detail. She joked and teased, knowing every line not to cross. She held secrets like a spy. Her flesh-colored party dress melted into her skin, with sparkles throughout. The feather-weight silk drifted as she walked. A single strand of pink hued pearls hung around her neck. Kyle sat in her black dress and sipped white wine. With Jason working all weekend filling in for someone at the last minute, this seemed like a good idea.

Kyle had accompanied Annie to other soirees at this hotel. The accommodations were always first rate. Kyle snacked on swordfish in mango sauce and drank her favorite white burgundy wine. Annie, the perfect companion, never left her side for long. When she returned from a brief chat, she whispered fun observations to Kyle. "The guy with the gray hair and red tie is CEO of a company that just got a big defense contract. That woman with the blonde hair looks like she just got bigger implants and her lips are going to explode."

Several male attendees inquired as to Annie's plans for the evening; more than one extended invitations for late night get-togethers. Tonight Kyle and Annie would dine; tomorrow they would shop along Newbury Street covered with a fresh coating of snow and white lights. It was the perfect December trip.

Kyle spent much of her evening speaking with the nearby waitress. Wanda worked there for years. She met many celebrities and liked most of them. She directed Kyle to the desserts, which were worth the calories. Even while Kyle spoke with her, she managed to top off every glass with wine or water. If anyone left their seat for a moment, upon their return they found their napkin folded or replaced by a new one.

Before midnight, the crowd thinned out. Kyle felt the effects of the many glasses of wine and champagne. Annie came to retrieve her for a trip to a nearby martini bar.

"No, honestly Annie, you go, I just want to go to bed. I'll go up to the room. You have fun." As usual, Annie could outlast most people and still look as fresh as a daisy. She accompanied Kyle to the room and made sure the door shut behind her. She told Kyle not to wait up. Some things never change.

Annie was in the shower when Kyle woke in the morning. Her bed was made.

While they gathered their things together to depart, Kyle's phone rang. "Hello?"

"Hi, it's me," Jason said. "You need to come to the hospital. Matt's wife, Kristen, is having complications. They're here."

A nurse recognized Kyle when she rushed into the Emergency Room. She led Kyle to where Matt paced in the hall in uniform. She hugged him and asked for an update.

"I think the baby will be okay. They have started her on a med to stop her contractions…Terbutylene; an asthma drug, which calms down the uterus and slows contractions, hopefully. She's only six and a half months. It's too early. Jason came around. He's been great. He told me that the doc covering obstetrics is good. Our regular doc isn't on. Do these doctors really need time off?" Matt smiled, as a trained paramedic, he knew much more about all this than Kyle. Like…this drug didn't always work.

Kyle went in for a short time to see Kristen. From the look of her pale skin, she was still experiencing some discomfort. Jason popped in and took Kyle into the hall to speak with her. Kyle took notice of his wrinkled clothing. He looked fatigued as he explained that this was all a waiting game. There was not much else they could do.

Kyle sat in an uncomfortable chair and waited. She got some stale coffee and paced the hall to stretch her legs.

Matt marched down the hall a few hours later with his eyes full. Kristen's water broke. They would monitor the baby, but had to deliver it over the next twenty-four hours, though they might try to delay more and add intravenous antibiotics. The baby had a good chance, but they were concerned with its lungs. He told Kyle to go home and get some sleep. He would call her if anything happened sooner than expected.

Baby Emily was born thirty hours later. She was the size of Matt's hand. Tubes twice her size fed necessary fluids. She survived the day. Later that week, after scrubbing and putting on hospital issue caps and gowns, they took turns slipping a finger into her tiny hands. She held on tight. Kyle got the opportunity to sit with the infant, by herself, when the other Birch children came to visit their mom and demanded her attention.

Kyle couldn't help but miss the second baby she never had. She held back the mournful tears, which pressed for an outlet. Everything happened for a reason, she knew. But, the reasons could never be good enough to make sense. What reason could there be to deprive Jeffrey of a sibling? Or from having another piece of a family long after she and Jason were gone.

Emily was just another example of the callousness levied by the disorder of the universe. Be it God, Buddha, or any other supreme force which was supposed to rule our existence, this vulnerable infant should still be in the security of her mother's womb, not exposed to this harsh world any sooner, to begin the struggle of survival.

Emily survived a long month in the hospital. She gained weight and the happy day came when the hospital released her. Kyle, her godmother, made the forty-minute drive to Birch's house often to hold and rock the tiny survivor craving more attention than the busy Mom could give. Emily's skin glowed from a flourishing internal spirit. Kyle told her stories about Matt, Jason, Jeffrey and, of course, about Annie.

As spring brought some warm rays of sun, Emily thrived. Kyle looked forward to her trip to Rome, but not to her separation from the new angel.

Kyle sat across from Annie, who was busy talking on her cell phone. "Sorry," she said as she finished. "I turned it off. So tell me, how's Emily?"

Annie flashed a warm smile. "She's great. She's still tiny, but she's healthy. She has a little rosebud mouth and a sweet smile…" Kyle stopped mid-thought, her eyes gone from Annie's face to another familiar face that entered the local restaurant.

Annie turned and looked at what stole Kyle's attention. She saw a tall, fit policeman in a dark blue uniform and thick, short dark hair. By this time, David noticed Kyle and made his way over to their table.

Annie stuck out her hand and introduced herself to the dark eyed man. "Hi, I'm Annie Watson. You must be Officer Linscott. Kyle has told me about you."

Kyle choked.

"All good, I hope?" David looked at Annie for a moment, but his eyes gravitated to Kyle at every opportunity.

"How's crime?" Kyle asked.

"Pretty quiet. The way we like it," David replied.

"Would you like to sit down?" Annie asked.

Kyle swallowed hard.

"No, thank you. I'm picking up take out for a few of us. I better run." He said goodbye with a big smile on his face.

"How did you know that was David?" Kyle asked.

"Because I'm a rocket scientist…" Annie was ever the smart ass. "How the hell do you think? You went off to never-never land. You two have a thing going on."

"What are you talking about? I would never…and you know if I did, I would tell you! But, Annie, don't say something like that. I wouldn't do that to Jason."

"Whoa." Annie held her hand up like a stop sign. "I didn't say you were sleeping with the guy; though…there are worse things. I mean that you two seem to be sharing a mutual appreciation. Relax. You're married, you're not dead. Crushes happen. You just happen to enjoy his company. And the uniform doesn't hurt either. He's adorable."

"Oh. I seem to be running into him everywhere I go. Last week, I ran into him at the Junior High. He is running the DARE Program. A couple nights ago, I slept, but when I woke…" Kyle's eyes fell and looked down at the table. "When I woke up, I realized that I had been dreaming of David. And it was one VIVID dream." Kyle covered the smirk on her face with her hand.

"Isn't it great that we dream in color? That's just your imagination having vacation. Enjoy the break."

"I guess."

"How is the eagle scout?"

"He's fine. Working a lot. We're looking forward to Italy."

They finished their tuna sandwiches and homemade coleslaw and set a time for next week.

Fifteen

Kyle wanted to take advantage of another beautiful spring day and work in the yard so she started errands early. Plenty of school committee work awaited her attention, but the day demanded some time outdoors. An eighty-degree day in mid May was a gift. After the long, dismal winter, she looked forward to the sun warming her face.

Unloading the car, Kyle froze as a noise in the back yard broke the springtime silence. But Maggie was not barking. There were no cars in the driveway. No one should be here. She heard something being pushed or moved. Her heart started to pick up its pace. Her muscles tensed. She looked to the far end of the yard and into the woods and saw nothing. Still with bags in hand, she walked around to the back of the house.

Someone sat in a lounge chair by the pool. She called out to the odd sight, but there was no response. Kyle approached, now not as frightened as annoyed. One of her white plush towels was stretched onto the chair and overflowed to the ground. It was not a pool towel.

Annie lay stretched out on the chaise lounge chair she'd dragged out of the poolhouse. Earphones and a CD player prevented her from hearing anything. She wore a tiny, bright pink bikini, which matched her sandals tossed nearby. A sheer pink fabric wrap hung over the bottom of the chair; the frayed edge twisted in the gentle breeze. Kyle couldn't believe that she still looked this good in a bathing suit with such a tight, flat stomach and small firm thighs. Her breasts were as full and perky as that of a twenty-year old. A martini glass half full of a familiar green potion sat on the ground with the sun pouring into it. Maggie, Annie's partner in crime, stirred and swung her tail as she got up.

"Hey…hey…" Kyle nudged the chair with her bags.

Annie came to life and smiled.

"What are you, Martini Barbie?"

"Hi. I tried calling. You didn't answer your cell. I brought lunch." Annie held up an open box of Pop Tarts. Strawberry frosted.

"Lunch?" Kyle shook her head. "Where's your car? How did you get here?" Kyle put the bags down on the ground.

Annie sat up. "Something's wrong with it. It's in the shop. I took a cab. It was such a nice day I figured you'd be working in the yard."

Kyle put away the groceries, changed into shorts, and pulled up another chair. She found that strawberry frosted Pop Tarts do, in fact, go well with Green Apple Martinis.

"I wish the pool was open. I like to see the water. You're not going to open it at all this year?" Annie refilled her drink from the pitcher beside the chair. She topped off Kyle's glass.

"If you want to take care of it, I'll open it. But we are just not going to be around enough. Jeffery barely uses it, anyway. I think you and I used it the most last year." Kyle's cheeks felt warm, a result of the combination of the sun and the refreshments.

"Well, maybe if I don't rent that place in Newport for the summer. I'll see."

"Okay. I'd have to give the pool guy a call. I just got an invoice for the work he did last week. He took the cover off, cleaned and added chemicals. I have to pay it before we leave. I could schedule him?" Kyle said.

"I'll let you know. I just put in for a project that would take me away for a big chunk of time. Let me see where I'm going to be."

The two friends chatted away the afternoon. They soaked up the warm sun, neither of them aware that the decomposed remnants of a corpse lingered just a couple of feet away.

Jeffery returned in the afternoon and drove Annie home. Though it was late, Kyle wanted to get something done in the yard. She took out her rake and headed for the back of the property. Starting at the fence, she would work her way in. After only two strokes of the rake at the leaves, her eye caught something just outside the fence. She dropped the rake and opened the gate. Maggie flew over and started eating something. Kyle hurried over and stopped her, pulling the thing from her mouth. In her hand, she held a large half-eaten dog biscuit.

Many things occurred to her. None good. She worried about what Maggie consumed. It could be tainted. Her eyes strained to look through the woods. She called Lt. Linscott.

"I'm going to take a look through the woods. I'll be back in a minute." David then spoke into a microphone clipped to his shirt.

Kyle watched as he left the backyard and was gone from sight behind the thick pines and a few white birches that speckled the woods. The occasional glimpse of him became visible, but even knowing someone was back there, it was hard to make him out. Not a comforting thought. She took a seat on her chaise, sinking her chin into her hands. Jeffery returned home and was full of questions when he saw the cruiser in the driveway. The policeman emerged from the woods.

"I found some cigarette butts. One pile looks new. Jeffrey, do you smoke?" he asked studying the teenager's face.

"No, never," Jeffrey responded.

"Okay. Well…" David stopped talking as Jeffrey's cell phone rang on his hip. He answered walking away. David looked at Kyle. "There really isn't anything else to do other than keep an eye out. You don't think anyone was in the house?"

"No, I was home most of the day. Outside, right here." Kyle

pointed to two martini glasses and Pop Tart refuse.

David smiled.

"This is not a frequent occurrence. My friend stopped by and..." Kyle smiled and rubbed her forehead. "What's bothering me is that Maggie barked a bit today, over in that corner of the yard. I told her to lie down. I thought it was a chipmunk or something. I didn't see anything, but I really couldn't see you back there, either. You don't think someone was watching us, do you?" Kyle hated sounding like a scared female, but she was.

"Even if some kid has been around, he's not likely to do anything. Probably just needs a place to smoke without getting caught. I will stop by now and then and take a look through the woods. If anyone is around, they'll see a cruiser and get lost. Try not to worry. And hey, next time call when you're serving martinis!"

"You wouldn't drink them anyway. You guys are boy scouts."

"Boy scouts, huh? Is that what Matt says?"

David returned to his cruiser, glanced back at the pristine home and pulled down the long driveway.

Jason returned home around seven p.m. Given the changing seasons, it was still light out, but the sun dropped fast, causing long shadows. Kyle reached him earlier on his cell phone, so he knew about the dog biscuit. He gave Kyle a hug and told her "not to worry." He was sure it was nothing. But, he didn't mind that his family would be leaving for an extended period.

After putting away the two chairs and securing the door to the shed, Jason walked through the pool area. He noticed a small wire caught on the edge of the pool cover. Darker now, with shadows cast from the trees, it was impossible to see into the pool. He bent and gave it a tug. It was stuck to something, so he pulled harder. The wire came up from the water and under the cover. Jason held a long twisted wire. "What in the world?"

Some unrecognizable debris hung, tangled in the wire. With the night sky upon him, Jason was unaware that the mess contained hair and leaves. He tossed it in the outdoor trash barrel. Crazy winter.

Kyle sat at the kitchen island sipping her tea, still stewing over Jason's news. "I thought that we were all going together."

"I'll be busy anyway. Those first few days are all business. Most families are coming along five days later." Kyle wanted them all to travel together. But, as if that wasn't disappointing enough, Dr. Drone and his wife would fly out with the families. He didn't want to leave the hospital for that long, so he was sending an administrative assistant for the first part of the trip. Kyle was sure she'd be the lucky soul seated next to them. Well, she thought, it *is* still a trip to Rome. Jason would leave in four weeks.

She looked at the pile of papers he left for her to sign…from the hospital, regarding the trip. Releases, insurance, Kyle didn't read past the first two, but signed her name next to Jason's. She began a check list of what she had to do and when.

The phone rang. "Hi Kyle…guess what?"

Kyle focused her attention on the conversation. "Oh hi, Annie, no you guess what? I had company after you left. Lieutenant Linscott." Kyle informed Annie of the dog biscuit mystery.

"That's kind of creepy. I'm glad I won't be hanging out in your backyard this summer." It took Kyle a moment to register Annie's comment. Both parts. Her backyard was now creepy and Annie had summer plans.

"I'm sorry. What was your news?"

"I got that assignment I wanted. It's for three months. I leave next week."

"That's great." Annie contracted for assignments all the time. Kyle didn't understand why Annie was so pleased with working for the summer. She usually kept a low profile, on a sandy beach surrounded by tan companions and exotic alcoholic connections.

"The assignment is in Rome! Isn't that great?" Kyle's face and mind lit up. She would have a trusted and experienced tour guide. Perfect! Annie went on to explain that she'd be leaving before

Kyle, but that she would be free for some long stretches during Kyle's visit. Annie signed off by saying, "Ciao."

Annie's news perked Kyle up. She shuffled through the pile of papers and signed on the "Xs", not once stopping to read any of it. Jason emerged into the kitchen. "Jason, Annie just called. She's going to be in Rome the same time as we are. Isn't that great?"

"So, the wanderer will be with us for the entire trip?"

"You don't care, do you?"

"No, of course not. It will be great for you and Jeffrey. Annie's a trip all by herself!" Jason looked at the papers. "Oh hey, did the pool guy come? Because I found some junk…"

Kyle jumped in, head still down at the paper pile. "Yes, as a matter of fact I have to pay them before we leave. Thanks for reminding me. The pool's all set." Kyle ran over the list as Jason gobbled down some leftover dinner and flipped through the newspaper. She determined that Jeffrey needed a new piece of luggage. "Oh, and I meant to ask you something…what's with all the pine needles stuck in your windshield?"

"What?" Jason replied.

"I saw a bunch of pine needles on your car. We don't have any pines here, and there's not even one tree anywhere close to the hospital, I was just curious where they were from. You've probably got pine tar on your car, too."

"I have no idea. It doesn't matter. I'll get it washed," Jason said and left the room.

At bedtime, she checked each door and window to make sure the house was secure. With the alarm system on, she looked out on her backyard from behind the large glass patio door. With fresh leaves now bursting from the trees, the view into the woods was camouflaged. Kyle strained her eyes, scanning the sway of the trees. The desire to find something remained, tempered only by the desire to see nothing.

Two weeks later Kyle was pulling into her driveway as a shiny black pick-up truck pulled out. Kyle stopped at the bottom of the driveway. The truck pulled to the side of the road. David Linscot climbed out and smiled at Kyle.

"I was just doing a random check of your house…and some others. There was nothing going on. I think whoever was around has moved on. But, I'll continue to keep an eye out. Oh, and that attack dog of yours is useless. She let out one bark, recognized me, and then came to me, tail wagging. Boy, she makes friends quick."

Kyle smiled. "It would be great if you'd come by. In three weeks we leave for vacation. No one will be here most of the summer, but I would appreciate your poking around once in awhile."

"Where are you going?"

"To Rome with my husband and my son. He's working. Jeffrey and I are tourists. I've never been. I'm looking forward to it."

"Good for you. If you are going to be away that long, you should really sign up for our home check list. Someone comes by each day. It is a good idea. Just come and fill out the form."

"Okay, I will." Kyle entered her safe home and didn't even glance at the backyard. Maggie lifted her head, then went back to sleep.

Sixteen

Bonuses handed out last month reflected Brendan's increased workload. In another six months, he expected even more. A breeze blew in from the many windows that lined the back office wall. It was a beautiful June day with low humidity and a strong sun. The thought of taking off to the Cape for the weekend crossed his mind. He ran his hand over his still crew-cut hair. The breeze invigorated his skin. Brendan had built up quite a nest egg between the accumulating raise in pay and the bonus. Now he needed a way to celebrate. Keeping his new bank account to himself, Sarah had no idea how much his finances changed over the past year. She still drew upon accounts that were set up for her as a child by her grandfather. They kept their money separate, except Sarah sometimes needed Brendan to help with legal matters. Brendan therefore, had a clear understanding of what she was worth, without the additional family fortune.

He wondered, considering what a pain in the ass she had been lately, if maybe he should "cash out" on her. He could hide his money with ease and cry poverty. Even with the pre-nup agreement in place, he'd still get a handsome settlement from her and argue truthfully that he was the sole support of their common property. In Texas right now, he imagined her father was giving her some type of speech. He decided to be prepared. He would secure the obscurity of his accounts. More and more this appeared to be a starter marriage. He could see himself with someone much younger.

The next day Sarah called Brendan from the Lone Star state.

"Hi Sarah, how's it going down there? Is the weather good?" he pushed his voice upbeat.

She exchanged few pleasantries and got down to business. "Brendan, I didn't really want to have this conversation over the phone, but you're never home anyway," Sarah said in a weighty voice.

"Is something wrong?"

"You can't be serious. You know we have gone from fighting all the time, to just not talking at all. You seem happiest when I am away. I think we should consider a trial separation. I have contacted an attorney."

No doubt an old family friend referred by Daddy. "Sarah, I know things have not been good with me working so much, but you know I am just trying to get ahead, for both of us. You know, your father didn't become so successful by sitting on his ass!" He inherited, of course. "I think you at least owe us to come back here so we can try to work things out. It hasn't been *that* bad."

"For who? Come back for what? So when you do take a Saturday off I can stay home while you golf? Even when you're home, your mind is elsewhere. You just take me for granted. You don't want children and—"

"Sarah, YOU AGREED! You agreed that we wanted to enjoy our life and have freedom. You agreed. Don't bring that up now!" Brendan snapped.

"Well, maybe I have changed my mind. I've run into so many old friends and their children. Maybe I want children. You're always working anyway. Why do you care? It wouldn't change your life." Sarah choked back years of resentment. The pressure slowly seeped out of her and sniffles started. "You always do this. It is all my fault, right? You twist everything. I can't talk to you. You don't really want to be married. You just don't want to be divorced!" Sarah erupted.

"Look, this is getting out of hand. Why don't you come home so we can talk in person?"

"I have tried to talk to you. You never pay attention. Good-bye." Click.

Brendan slammed down the phone. He spun his chair to face the window and the tremendous view of downtown Boston and smiled. This would be easier than he thought. He tried, right?

A couple of weeks later, after a couple of attempts by Brendan to talk to Sarah over the phone, he received a registered package in his office. It was a separation agreement and notice of a filing of divorce by Sarah. He was not to contact her, but only her attorneys. She retained attorneys in both Texas and New Hampshire. All bases covered. The best way to fight was with a larger number of attorneys. Brendan remained unconcerned. The separation agreement was more than reasonable. He felt certain that in order to expedite this distasteful situation and keep the family name out of the Texas newspapers, Daddy would offer a large settlement. It was all good.

There remained only one issue in his world of which he was not in control. Even in her death, Kate still caused him aggravation. There was nothing he could do now to bring her back. If he had it to do over, he would handle things much differently. He would have kept his distance from the psychotic bitch. Nothing would be served by him getting blamed for her murder. And, this god damned pregnancy test loomed over his mind. Disposing of the body permanently, presented a gamble. If pregnant, his DNA would be present in the fetus. Even if she was pregnant, how did he know it was his? Maybe that was the point of drugging him. She wanted to get pregnant! He wished he read those last few IMs she had sent. He sat at his desk, mulling over his situation, pressing for a way out of all this. He vacillated between work he needed done for tomorrow and his larger looming problem.

Before he realized it, the sun was setting. Mel came in preparing to leave for the day. "Hey, you look terrible. You need to get out of this office a little. You can't keep up these hours and this pressure!"

Brendan brushed off her concern. If she only knew.

"I've got some news." Sergeant Hayden sat facing Angus and Brendan. He asked to meet with them for an update and Shelly cleared time on this busy day in this long, hectic week.

Brendan rested his elbows on the arms of the brown high back chair. Hayden sat next to him with Angus behind his desk. The frail man awaited news. The collar of his white, button down, tailored shirt stood loose around his neck. Brendan noticed for the first time that Angus' wrinkled, spotted hands trembled as they lay clasped upon his desk.

"It's a small piece, but I wanted to pass it on. A second round of interviews with Kate's friends yielded an answer to one question. One of her friends told us that the last time she was at Kate's apartment, she used a pregnancy test. She wasn't pregnant, and took the test to show her nervous boyfriend. She didn't mention it to us, because she didn't think it had anything to do with Kate. At least that is one piece of the puzzle solved." Hayden looked at Angus' long face. "I'm sorry, Mr. Hessman, there's no other information at this time."

"What about the emails? Did anything turn up on the phone records that you can follow up on?" Angus asked.

"Nothing. That's why we are going back over every detail. No credit card activity, no prescription refills, no new hits on the email. The lab guys went through her car, but found nothing suspicious. I even spent some time on surveillance of the old boyfriend and the young guy who works at the clothing store, who is reported to be infatuated with Kate. I can't find any connection to anyone regarding her disappearance. I think we are going to have to wait for a lead," Hayden reported.

"Please keep looking. It's the not knowing...the uncertainty." Angus made a slow gesture, lifting his hand.

From his seat, Brendan focused on the broken man. Ill feelings welled up within him. Regret. A heavy hand strangled his soul. "Angus, I..." He rubbed his forehead with a sweaty hand titling his head down. Tears formed in his eyes.

Quiet filled the room and both men waited to hear Brendan words.

He looked at Angus and then the detective and caught himself. "Angus, I am so sorry."

"I appreciate it, Brendan. You're a good man."

Hayden walked out of the office with Brendan and down the hall to the elevators. "Mr. Hessman looks rough. How old is he?"

Brendan shrugged his shoulders. He didn't know the relic's age.

"I am reluctant to lay out reality for him. He doesn't seem like he can tolerate much. And at this point, it doesn't look good. A kid like that who has lived on a trust fund all of her life doesn't just walk away from it all."

"Well, Sergeant, perhaps it would be better to run things by me first. I can keep him updated. It's just; well…I think he gets anxious each time you come in. This way, if it's not substantial I can go over it with him, gently, when I think it's a good time. You think about it." Brendan stopped at the elevator with Hayden.

"That makes sense. It really doesn't look good."

"I know," said Brendan. "I know."

As Mel left to fetch him one of his favorite tall cups of complicated coffee, Brendan stood, leaning against the wall, looking out over the busy city with a heavy sense of relief. No pregnancy. This was promising news, one less hurdle to deal with. He again sifted his brain with a fine filter, searching for a permanent solution. Angus would not let this drop until Kate's body was found.

On his desk, piles of folders and memos promised to fill the day and even some of the night. But work would wait. He craved a drink to celebrate the relief of the recent news. He called an old friend from law school.

Jason got home later than expected and was up late into the night packing for the trip to Rome. A car would pick him up in four hours. Kyle didn't mind helping since she hadn't been sleeping much anyway. She did some of her best work in the middle of the night.

Kyle kissed and hugged him goodbye. They would be together in six days. She turned off all the lights, then paused and lit up the kitchen, like, as her father said when she was a kid, a Christmas tree. It was four-thirty in the morning, and the sun started to come up, but there remained sleepy shadows. After setting the house alarm, she climbed the stairs to her bedroom. Pumpkin waited, curled up on a pillow. Thick, cotton sheets caressed her skin as she crawled into bed. A thin blanket provided plenty of warmth for the tepid June air. A morning breeze pushed over the bed. Kyle began her ritual of review, which zapped much of her sleep. Plans and arrangements marched across her mind as she tossed within the soft bedding. Each item was rejected, soon replaced with a tempting one. She saw David in his black pick-up truck. It's a good thing that no one, especially spouses, could see into our minds, she thought. She fell asleep as the birds stirred. Pumpkin stretched out next to her, prepared for the long haul.

Transporting Maggie and Pumpkin to Massachusetts to her mother's home, took Kyle away for the next couple of days. She stayed and tried to help the traumatized pets acclimate to their temporary home. Maggie jumped around with excitement. She loved sleepovers. Pumpkin hid under a couch. When Kyle checked her cell phone, she found she missed a call from Jason. He sounded tired on the voicemail, but had arrived safely. Another call from Jeffrey; the teenager promised to return from his camping trip in plenty of time to pack and board a plane. He wanted to spend every last minute with his friends, whom he was being "ripped away" from.

Kyle went to bed in her old room, which now contained a daybed full of exotic pillows and a computer desk. The walls had long ago been repainted with a rich slate green tone. Black and white framed photos hung on all the walls, her mother's hobby and love. Pumpkin slinked up onto the bed, took a full bath and settled next to Kyle. She sat and curled her paws underneath her.

When Kyle turned off the light and in the darkness floods of memories streamed in; boyfriends, dressing for dances, and of course, walking into her home with Matt and finding her father in a puddle of sticky, dark blood. Years of healing allowed her to feel at peace in the home and share a link with her dad. She remembered going peach picking with him. Juice ran down their chins when they chomped into the ripe fruits. They brought their bounty home and Kyle made peach pies with her mother.

That was a good day with her father. The bad days were hidden from Kyle for the most part. Her mother, always upbeat, would say they were going out for the day because Daddy had been working too hard and needed to rest. He would leave his bedroom little over a weekend like that. He emerged for food, still in his pajama bottoms and a white t-shirt, then drag himself to work on Monday. As Kyle grew older, Mom explained that her father embodied a sensitive heart and that things hit him harder than they might other people. He seemed kind, until the one day when she found him and he had done the cruelest thing of all.

Kyle took her time driving home. It was a beautiful day. She turned the radio up loud and glided in the SUV. She arrived at the dry cleaners just before it closed. Three days would go by fast. Jeffrey would be home tomorrow. Her checklist was all set. Soon their adventure would begin, but she had no idea what waited for her at home.

Seventeen

Kyle pulled up her long drive, past the long line of thick trees, humming one of her favorite old songs about a reptile rocking, a song that aged her for even knowing the words, let alone knowing the artist and the year. Her back ached and her shoulders were stiff from sitting so long. She felt a headache coming on, but the lengthy packing list would not be put off. Italy awaited! But her thoughts crashed back to the present...at the top of the driveway. Two police vehicles waited for her. No lights flashed, no excitement or urgency was evident on the faces of the men: David and a man she recognized from the newspaper as the chief. She heard no house alarm. What ever happened must be over. Kyle exited her vehicle and swung her heavy overnight bag across her shoulder. She smiled as the uniformed men approached.

"What's going on? Did you see someone in the yard? Or..." she winced, "did someone break into the house or something?"

"Hi Kyle, this is Chief Fuller. I'm not sure if you two have met," David said. The chief reached out and shook Kyle's hand. "May we come in? We wanted to talk to you."

Kyle shrugged a shoulder and ran her fingers through her hair. "Well of course. What is this about?"

"Let's go in and sit down." David relieved her of the overnight bag and followed her toward the door.

Kyle went inside her home, finding the air dry and sticky from being unopened for a couple days, and threw purse her on the kitchen counter. She glanced around the room, stretching her neck to confirm that nothing was out of place. Everything looked as she left it with some books and newspaper scattered on the countertops. The three took seats around the kitchen island.

"Where is Jeffrey? Do you know how to reach him?" David asked.

"He's camping with friends. David, you're kind of scaring me. Is Jeffrey all right? Is something wrong? I assumed you were here because of the visitor I had."

"I promise I will explain everything. Would you just give me a number to reach your son? Does he have a cell phone?" David asked.

Kyle didn't respond, instead folded her arms across her chest. Her mouth wouldn't open. The stubborn front was an attempt to hide the sick feeling growing in her gut, such turmoil she had felt only one time before, on finding her father. It was not what David said that scared her. It was what he did not.

"Is there a number where I can reach Jeffrey?" David asked again, focused on getting as much information from Kyle as he could.

Kyle recited Jeffrey's cell phone number. David wrote it on a pad of paper that he took out of his shirt pocket. He pushed the paper to the chief. Then, David continued speaking. "Kyle, I want you to know that I just spoke to Matt and he is on his way. I would really like to wait until he gets here. He won't be long."

David's face held no expression. Kyle felt like she was in a poker game, betting without knowing the stakes.

"David, why would you call Matt? What's wrong? Jeffrey's fine, right?"

David shook his head in the affirmative. He pictured Matt breaking the sound barrier to get here, wanting him to fly.

Kyle's eyes swung back and forth to David and the Chief, searching for clues. "Jason's fine. I just got a message from him. What is going on?"

David dropped his chin just an inch. His eyes looked down.

"David, what's wrong? Jason? I just got a message from him. Tell me." His eyes met Kyle's. Kyle pressed. "TELL ME!"

"Kyle, I really want to wait for Matt to get here. Please." He shifted around in his seat. He met her eyes again. There was no textbook that gave him direction on handling this; late nights knocking on doors devastating parents and families. There was never a good way. David viewed the eyes full of concern and discontent, but wanted to contain her feelings to only that for just a few minutes more. Soon, she would hear news that would combust her secure world. Extending her ignorance would postpone her pain for a while longer. Once this bomb was dropped, there would be no escape. He fought his desire to fold his arms around her and protect her from the crush to follow. How ridiculous.

Kyle's eyes pressed on.

David looked away and she found the eyes of the Chief, whose head was tipped down. The Chief looked into his hat, which he held in his hands.

"David...David, you have got to tell me what's going on. It cannot be that bad. I know Jeffrey and Jason are fine. Nothing else matters." Tears pooled in her eyes.

David reassessed his plan. Better to know than continue the torture, though he was unsure that her imagination would sink to this. "Kyle, I am not sure how to tell you this. I would rather wait… We got a call from a Dr. Mulhorn, from the hospital. He asked for our help in contacting some people."

This has something to do with Dr. Drone and their trip, mulled Kyle. That's a relief. She took a breath. But why go through David, and the Chief?

David paused and cleared his throat. "Some time this morning, there was a small plane accident, just outside of Rome. I am so sorry to tell you…it was confirmed that twenty-five staff from the hospital were killed. Jason was one of the victims." David paused again, waiting for the words to settle. "I am so sorry, Kyle."

David watched Kyle's face. He wanted to reach out and catch her. Her expression remained inquisitive, but her body began to grieve through an involuntary response. The water in her eyes flooded. Tears dripped over her cheekbones and fell onto the island.

"What are you saying? Jason left me a message on my voicemail. He had landed and was at the hotel. You've made a horrible mistake." Kyle spoke free of emotion and unaware of her crying. She felt only cold.

David let some time pass before he answered. "Kyle, I'm sorry. It's not a mistake."

The tears came faster. Puddles formed on the island below her cheeks. Kyle didn't move. "No, no, there must be some mistake. He landed. He wasn't in a plane!" She glared at David, demanding he change his words.

"We were told they were taking a small plane to a hospital outside Rome, for a day trip."

"Are you sure? Are they sure? You know Jason is very strong. He runs every day. Have they really checked him? He could still be alive. They need to check again. They need to check. Maybe he's just unconscious." Kyle stayed in denial until the truth choked her. Then, she saw her terrifying confirmation. David's eyes were watery.

She labored to breath, feeling like there was no air in her lungs. Her hands rushed to hold her chest. Everything appeared to be in slow motion and she felt dizzy. She was unaware that she was doubling over and falling out of her chair. David caught her and assisted her to an arm chair in the living room area. He knelt in front of her, holding onto her arms. The chief went outside to call Jeffrey. He would go over the same drill. *Your mother needs you. You need to come home, do not speed, and everything will be explained to you when you get here.*

Alone with Kyle, David allowed his head to lean forward and touch hers. His strong hands supported her arms as she shook, constricting to a fetal tuck. With the violent tremors, it seemed like she would break off into pieces. When she shook, her tears flew; some landed on the backs of his hands and stung.

Matt arrived, running into the house. His eyes burned at David, "I thought you were going to wait!" Matt said.

David's only response was to shake his head, no. Matt took David's place, and then, with certain authority, pulled Kyle up and led her to the couch. There, without looking up, she crushed her face into his uniform shirt and sobbed. Matt said nothing, but sat and held his pal as he had done once before. Soon, his shirt was wet through.

David stood outside of the house. The Chief left him to stand guard. They shooed away one reporter. The tragedy would be on the late edition news with all the gory, high rated details. It was sure to be a devastating impact to the hospital as well as the community.

David stopped an unfamiliar car at the bottom of the driveway, around nine o'clock that evening. When the window rolled down, it revealed the strained and fatigued face of Jeffrey. "Is my mom okay? My grandmother? What's going on?"

David composed himself and responded to the young man in a gentle, calm tone. "Just go inside. Matt is with your mother. They will explain everything."

Jeffrey pressed the gas pedal down and sped up to the house.

David called into the station after midnight and asked the officers on the night shift to keep an eye on the house and that Matt was inside. David instructed them that he would be back in the morning.

Kyle woke and gasped for air. She sat straight up in bed. The linen curtains flew in the humid night air, rushing in from the open windows. Moonlight beamed between the sweeping fabrics, flashing the room with choppy light. Her skin was wet with perspiration and her clothing damp. It was three a.m. A terrible dream disturbed her sleep. It was chaos. Rubbing did not help her irritated eyes.

Thoughts of losing Jason, Matt at the house and Jeffrey home, spun around her mind. Horrible, all of it. She was so accustomed to managing on her own, she often didn't realize when she missed him. Just a few more days and she would be in Italy with Jason, Jeffrey and Annie.

Kyle rose from her bed and peeled her clothing away from her skin. Pumpkin stirred, but did not get up from the large bed. A collared shirt? No wonder why she was hot. Why had she gone to bed in shorts and a shirt? She reached into her closet for a thin-strapped cotton nightgown hanging on a hook. After removing her damp clothing, including underwear, she let the fresh garment fall over her head. She opened the door, entering the hallway. Through the shadows, she noticed all of the doors to the other bedrooms closed, except for the one to the office/spare room, which was wide open as if inviting a visitor in. She didn't remember closing the other doors. She reached the open door. Someone was asleep on top of the comforter, in a white t-shirt. Jason was the only one who ever slept in this disorganized room. Pressure and throbbing began, built; she felt pain in her head and rubbed her forehead. She approached the bed, confused. No one else should be home.

When Kyle saw the familiar head, crashed into a pillow, tears returned to her swollen eyes and ran down her puffy face. Her head, too heavy and painful to hold up, fell to her hands for support. The short reddish brown hair could only belong to one person: Matt. And if Matt was here, that meant the horrible nightmare was no dream. It meant Jeffrey was home; her mother and her aunt were here. It meant that Jason was not and would never be coming home.

She leaned up against Jason's desk and felt the shirt hanging across the chair. Her fingers identified Matt's uniform shirt from the buttons and ridged seams. Her sniffling grew louder than she realized and Matt woke. He got up, now fully alert and put his arm around his pal. "It will be okay. You and Jeffrey will be okay."

"I woke up…I thought it was a dream. I thought this all

wasn't true." Kyle's tears slowed down. There wasn't much water left in her system.

She and Matt walked downstairs, not wanting to wake up the entire house that she now knew to be full. Kyle made tea. The two sat across from each other at the island. Kyle vowed to pull herself together, for Jeffrey's sake. Jason would want her to be strong, to handle it. She tried to get Matt to go home to his family. He refused.

Kyle snuggled up to her pal, her security blanket, on the couch in the family room. Maggie circled their feet and lay down next to them on the floor. She was still there, by their feet, when the sun came up.

The hot sun beat down on David's head. Summer rolled in a few days earlier than its official later June start. He leaned against his cruiser. The sight of the vehicle would do most of the job for him today. Only one reporter dared even stop and ask David questions. That reporter would not be returning. He radioed the second officer stationed at the home in town of another victim from town. A much loved pediatrician who was also on that ill-fated plane. He told the officer to watch for the vehicle. There was little activity.

Close to noon a black Lexus pulled up. David leaned down to the window, hands on his hips to see two middle-aged men in dark suits. The man in the passenger seat emerged from the automobile and came over to shake David's hand.

"Thanks so much for your assistance. I'm Dr. Mulhorn, from the hospital. I'm here to see Mrs. Mercer."

David looked back at the man's pale face with dark circles under his eyes, no doubt from a speedy transcontinental trip. In sharp contrast to his fatigued demeanor his suit and shirt looked clean and crisp. David acknowledged him and sent them up. This would be a tough day for Kyle.

Matt's car remained in the driveway. Feelings of envy crept upon David knowing Matt was inside, consoling Kyle. He pushed away his selfish feelings. She needed Matt right now.

In the middle of the day, Matt emerged from the house, his uniform all back in place, but wrinkled. David watched him walk down the long driveway to the cruiser. He approached David with his hand straight out.

"How is she, Matt?" David asked as he shook his hand.

"Rough…Dr. Mulhorn just gave her some type of sedative. I had to really push her to take it. Jeffrey just isn't talking. His girlfriend is supposed to be arriving soon. Hey, Dave, thanks so much for all your help and for knowing enough to call me. You guys really handled this as well as possible." David shook his head in acknowledgement. "I know you had no choice but to tell Kyle. She can be pretty stubborn. I guess I just wanted to postpone it."

"Well, I hope she's okay. I'm taking off. We will have a detail guy covering the house for the rest of today. If they have any problems, just tell them to give us a call."

"I'm heading home myself. My wife is almost as upset as Kyle. We just worked out some of the funeral arrangements. The hospital is getting remains identified and sent back here. They expect within a few days. I'll stop back tomorrow. Oh, and Dave, keep an eye on Kyle and the house whenever you can. I'd appreciate it."

"No problem," David said to his friend.

David watched Matt walk back to house and enter. He drove away in the cruiser, wondering when he would be able to see Kyle again.

Eighteen

Her face held traces of make-up. She applied some, but re-alizing the futility, and wiped most of it off with tissues, leaving uneven steaks across her face. The simple navy blue dress that Kyle's mom picked out seemed as suitable as anything else. Kyle took little notice of it when she put it on in the morning, before leaving for the funeral home. Now, with Jeffrey flanked on one side and Matt on the other, both in dark suits, and her mother next to Jeffrey in a brown tailored skirt and jacket, the dark colors melted together. They stood next to the black, closed casket with shiny gold bars on the sides that everyone stopped at and prayed. Jason was in there, or whatever was supposed to Jason. When Kyle was alone earlier with her hands on top of it, she held no desire to inspect the contents. The outer shell felt cold and hard. None of this was the man that she spent her life with. He was gone.

Her mother was first to greet the people in the long line. She listened to their tale of how they knew Jason, their sympathy of the loss and then she handed them off to Jeffrey and Kyle with a synopsis. She kept the line moving, which lessened the time Kyle had to speak with any one person. Responding like a ro-bot, Kyle thanked everyone for coming and held her chin up, no matter how heavy it felt. Jeffrey said little and, every chance he got, looked off to his girlfriend.

Patients, hospital employees, friends, friends of Jeffrey's, and an assortment of other people stood in line waiting their turn.

The dark clothing worn by all of the visitors contrasted with the bountiful flower arrangements, stuffed into each and every crevice of the hallway and room. Tall stalks shot out the corners, their bases covered by the smaller vases standing in front of them. The Funeral Director said he never saw anything like it. The amount and quality of the arrangements were unsurpassed. He told Kyle the staff kept a detailed account of each arrangement, a description, the sender and their message. Kyle noticed little of it. Her nose ran. She stuffed tissues into her small pocket. It never occurred to her to take her allergy medication before coming here. When she glanced at the line winding back through the entrance and out the door, Kyle struggled not to run from the room. If not for the medication Dr. Mulhorn insisted she take, at least through today, her impulses would not have been controllable. The medicine dulled the ache through her body and slowed tomorrow and the next day from begging to be considered. She focused only on getting through today and the service tomorrow for Jason's cremation.

Even familiar faces blended together after three hours. Kyle had trouble remembering names. She just shook the hand and thanked the person for coming. And shook the next hand and thanked that one for coming. Her mind stayed buried in a fog until she saw a face that called her out. Touching her mother's hand, and then Jeffrey's, was David Linscot. He looked ahead to her. He looked different. Out of uniform and dressed in "civilian" clothes, he looked even more handsome. His skin glowed with a slight tan. He wore a white shirt, tie and a deep tan sports coat with black slacks. He waited with his hands folded in front of him. His hair looked freshly cut.

"Hi Kyle, how are you holding up?" David's deep brown eyes starred down at her pale face. She managed a reaction, a short piece of a smile. She shook his hand. He bent and kissed her check. For just a second, his lips touched her skin. She watched and listened as he spoke to Matt, and then left the line. He looked back at her, standing there, as he walked away through the crowd of people. Her eyes met his and stayed with him, until Kyle's mom introduced someone else.

"Kyle, this is Brendan Reed. And you know Dr. Mulhorn." Kyle shook their hands.

"Thank you for coming Mr. Reed. I remember…" She had met him at some time, but at first couldn't focus enough to figure out where. She remembered his delicate features, light skin and blond hair. The all-American.

"Call me, Brendan, please."

"Kyle, Brendan will be in touch to meet with you," Dr. Mulhorn said.

Kyle shook her head yes, but had no idea why they needed to meet. Dr. Mulhorn spoke more and Matt responded. The monotone words held no interest to Kyle. She merged back into her fog.

Brendan studied Kyle's drained face. She wasn't registering any of Mulhorn's words. He imagined she was medicated. He remained, mingled amongst the number of people and watched as Kyle survived the line of mourners. Soft, dirge music filled the air. Brendan took in the depressing scene. The loss of the respected doctor was felt by so many people, as well as being a tremendous loss to the hospital. Jason would now be remembered as the trusted surgeon and devoted family man. A hard shell to crack, or too good to be true, Brendan pondered. What type of secrets might emerge after someone passed and they were not available to defend themselves? Perhaps an involvement with a young girl that ended tragically. His way out!

Brendan chatted with other members of the hospital board who were in attendance, but his attention never left Kyle. His meeting with her next week would prove interesting. He had a lot of ground to cover.

A woman with sandy hair pulled back into a neat twist shook Kyle's hand. Her eyes were red and some water trickled from them. She introduced herself to Kyle as Chelsea, a staff administrator who worked with Jason. She looked to be younger than Kyle.

"Matt," Kyle put her hand over her mouth as she whispered

into his ear. "I don't think that I can do this much longer. I feel like I'm going to be sick. I have to go to the bathroom."

Matt put his hand on her back. "Go ahead, take a break. People will understand. Where's Annie?"

"Helping some of Jason's old aunts to their cars." Since Jason's parents were both deceased his family was represented by a couple old aunts and his sisters, who also assisted the frail women to a car waiting for them.

Kyle slipped out through a door behind them as the "funeral planner" earlier instructed. She walked across to another reception area, which was not in use. Hearing the buzz of the people further and further away helped Kyle to breath.

As soon as she pushed the door to the ladies room open, she heard someone else in the bathroom, crying. Around the corner, she found Chelsea, who shot straight up from her hunched over position by the sink. The beautiful, striking woman dabbed her face with tissues.

"Again Mrs. Mercer, I'm so sorry…I'll leave you to some privacy." Kyle had been crying so much, she didn't find this unusual.

Alone in the bathroom, Kyle took some deep breaths as she sat in a soft chair in the powder area. She couldn't wait to get this night over with. If it weren't for Jeffrey, she would not return at all. Thank God for Annie, Matt and her mother. They took her by the hand and told her what to do. She didn't know the rules for getting through all this, but was doing the best she could. Exhaustion loomed over her like a flock of buzzards, waiting for her to drop. Over the last fourteen days, she'd slept little. Calls from Dr. Mulhorn updating her on the impending arrival of her husband's remains, when they would be released, arrangements for the wake and the cremation service, filled her nights. The events and their details swirled around her mind in a tornado of images. When she did sleep, she woke only to find the surrounding storm of emotion pulsated with relentless pressure, nagging her every waking moment.

When Kyle descended the stairs, ready to go to the final cremation service, her mother jumped from her seat, and led Kyle back upstairs. She wore the same dress from the night before. Her mother retrieved something suitable from the closet and Kyle changed her clothes in a robotic mode, as Annie stood guard.

"How are you feeling? Forget that. I know how you feel." Annie held her coffee out and Kyle took a sip. She puckered her mouth, unhappy with the taste.

"Yuck, Annie, that's mud." Handing the black coffee back.

"Sorry, I needed it extra heavy duty today. Do you want me to get you a cup? I'll fill it up half way with cream." Annie paused, ready to jump at the request.

"No, that's okay, my stomach is killing me." Kyle's voice trailed off with every word.

"You could use some food. When was the last time you ate anything?" Annie sat herself down on the king size bed and patted Pumpkin, who wandered over. Her simple charcoal suit creased and wrinkled as she moved on the mattress. Annie didn't seem to care that her usual pristine appearance was compromised. Her hair was pulled back into a tight bun. Her face was make-up free, showing the wear and tear of the frantic trip back from Rome. Her complexion was dull, its color not regained since Annie viewed the wreckage, witnessing the crash scene first hand; an image which she did not share with Kyle or Jeffrey, not yet, and maybe never.

"I tried, but I just can't eat. Just the smell of the food downstairs is making me sick." The clanking and movements of the caterers setting up in the kitchen and dining room echoed upstairs. Aromas filled the room. The short service would be followed by a reception at the house.

"Kyle, you'll feel better. It will take time." Annie looked down to her dark coffee. By the time they came back from the service she would need something stronger than coffee to get through another afternoon of seeing Kyle and Jeffrey with their hearts bleeding.

Kyle checked her hair in the mirror. Annie stood and zipped the back of her dress. The lightweight piece of clothing did not grab at her body in the usual places. It did not cling at all. She noticed that it seemed loose, but the connection between the clothing and her body escaped her.

The service was "beautiful", that's what everyone said. Kyle walked from the house and leaned next to a tree in the back yard. The noise was too much and the smell of the food made her nauseous. She left Jeffrey well attended by her mom and Lindsay. Matt and his wife Kristen were lost in the sea of attendees. Kyle couldn't bear to hug someone else and cry with them, or on them. She hoped to hide out here long enough for some of the people to leave.

The air was humid for June. Kyle pulled at her dress, feeling hot and constricted. She stepped out of her shoes and ran her toes, covered with pantyhose, across the grass. Uneven blades stuck up between her toes. The sensation was a gentle distraction that Kyle could focus on. Yellow caught her eye. Beyond the fence where she once found the dog biscuits, she saw a bundle. She walked over and found a bouquet of flowers on the ground, just outside of the gate. A small, store-bought arrangement, the clear plastic still wrapped around them. She opened the gate and picked them up. Her eyes jumped to the woods and searched for any signs of black boots. Nothing.

A tap on her shoulder made her jump back a foot, and sent her heart racing.

"You scared the hell out of me!" Kyle gasped for breath, reaching for the fence to steady herself.

"Sorry...I wasn't sure what you were doing out here. You okay? It's almost over. People are starting to leave. Your mother is taking care of everything. Who are the flowers from?" Matt asked looking at the flowers in Kyle's hand.

"I don't know. Let's head back in. I want to see Emily."

"You know, she's only a few months old, but she's developing quite the attitude. She knows what she wants and she lets YOU know what she wants. I think she's going to be a handful...lots of spunk!" said the proud father.

"Perfect" said her godmother. The two returned into the house with the bouquet dangling from Kyle's hand.

From his desk, Brendan stared out the window, tapping a pen to his lips. The bright sunshine reflected on the landscape and sent up glare from all directions. A single tree had survived the harsh elements. It offered bits of shade over a bench. Pedestrians took turns enjoying the protection. In a forest, such a tree would go unnoticed. But, like everything else, scarcity drove its stock up. Here, it was a treasure.

The attorney, clad in a new, light gray suit, deliberated the fate of Kate's body. He always intended to remove the carcass, and deliver it to a final, ingenuous, disposal site, never to be found. Jason's death however, changed everything.

A recent news account of a missing, pregnant woman's body found in California, discovered after it had been in ocean for some time, also needed to be factored in. He hypothesized, without knowing what additional damage might be done due to pool chemicals that the body having gone through a winter might fall apart in transport. Not to mention the risk of getting caught. Jason's death was a huge stroke of luck. Brendan searched for a final and complete way out and it seemed that Jason provided the well-needed break. This could be too good to be true so he tried not to leap to a decision, although of late, found himself feeling like a heavy weight was lifted from his shoulders.

The vision of the remains being pulled from the pool at the Mercer's home pierced his thoughts. It would happen sooner or later. The only connection to Brendan at that point would be the town. No one else in the firm lived in Hollis. One other associate lived in the first town over the Massachusetts line, five minutes away. Jason and the hospital were a link. But, over the years, many attorneys pitched in, including Angus himself. Brendan was the newest in a long line. This would all be twisted on its head with just the right spin. Jason had connections to the firm for years and this is how HE must have met Kate, possibly on more than one occasion at a social event. Angus mentioned some events in the past that Kate attended. The old and stressed man would not be able to recall detailed accounts, when confronted with the discovery of Kate. The body put there for safe keeping by someone who had control of when the pool would be opened. Jason had no way of knowing that he would not return. This could work.

Brendan's fear and concern did not contain itself to only proof of his crime. He also needed to survive the popular opinion of the firm, most important, Angus. The tie to Hollis must be perceived as an unfortunate coincidence and a minor detail within the larger horror. In his favor would be his lack of time employed by the firm before Kate went missing. All other employees shared a much longer tenure than him. Hell, several guys in the firm admitted to be being a regular shopper in the men's store where Kate worked. Brendan had never been asked. Had Kate ever identified herself to him, none of this would have happened.

He decided. This mess sorted itself out. Staying close to the sources of information would give all the insight he needed and the ability to steer things in the right direction. Kate's murder would be brought to closure with Jason's death. Kate's laptop, floating around who knows where, with its hard drive memory contained the only physical evidence linking him to even having met the missing girl. Brendan envisioned the computer laying in pieces, stripped of its memory, which would identify it, and being used by some lowlife to download porn off the internet. By now, he expected it would be unrecognizable. Doubtful, even if it contained pictures of Kate, that anyone would connect them to the pictures of the missing young woman circulating through the news, with less and less frequency. For most people, energy and interest gave way to resolution and acceptance of a bad outcome. Little hope lingered.

Brendan turned his attention back to his desk. Time to get moving. Everything would fall into place. He picked up his phone and dialed the number on the paper in front of him. He reached a machine, which was understandable. He left a message for Kyle to get back to him at her earliest convenience. They needed to meet.

Nineteen

Pete sat in the café and as he had on many afternoons, waiting for Ray. He often caught up with her and enjoyed every minute of it. He brought his laptop, sifted threw some internet sites and sipped on an expensive orange-infused beverage. Or orange soda as he called it when he bought it for a third of the price at the corner convenience store. He felt his cigarettes in his pocket and craved one. The only smoking here was done outside when he and Ray took breaks.

Pete liked to watch Ray make her "connections." She helped people with all kinds of requests regarding computers. She asked as few questions as possible. Sometimes "acquaintances" needed help getting into a laptop. Some people wanted tutoring or a program to assist them in getting information from someone else's computer. She handed out discs and instructions. They handed her back rolls of bills. She never went to anyone's place of work to "help." Well, almost never. If the roll of bills exceeded her restraint, she sometimes took the bait. This was dangerous. Businesses now had cameras and security systems, even if you didn't see them. But, of course, even if they saw a woman on a video screen, it would not be her. She went in 'costume' on those adventures. She told her new male friend about wearing a black sweatsuit three sizes too big and stuffing it with other clothes. She put her dark hair up into a short blonde wig and a hat. Gloves covered her hands and dark glasses to hide her face. And even if they saw her face, her eyes were blue, not the color she was born with, that color was too striking for anyone not to remember. Thanks to color contacts now, without a prescription, her eyes could be any color she wanted.

Just as Pete finished his second beverage, the spur-bearing cowgirl sat down.

"Hey, buddy, how's it going?" Ray's dark hair was pulled back into a ponytail. Pete always took a second to adjust to the striking green-eyed beauty.

"Hi. What's up?" Pete sat back in his seat. A plain gray t-shirt hung from his shoulders. His torso offered no additional bulk to fill out the garment. Blue jeans with heavy creases and in need of a wash, bunched around his hips. He seemed to eat all of the time, but remained thin regardless. "You seen Mac, lately?"

"Not since he sent you." A smirk came over Ray's face. "He has a number he can get my voicemail at if he needs me."

"What do I have to do to get that number? What if I need you?" Pete asked.

Ray smiled. She valued and needed her privacy. But, she was spending more and more time with Pete, or Jack as she knew him.

"We'll see. Aren't you a little young for me? How old are you?" Ray asked.

Pete gave a quick assessment to his age, Ray's age, and what he thought she'd believe. "I'm 21." He thought she'd buy three years older than he was and that put him into his twenties. He thought her to be at least 26. "How old are you?"

"Older than you… But you're legal at least. I don't know. We'll see."

"What are you doing tonight? Want to go to the new Bruce Willis movie?"

Pete waited for a response. Ray rolled her emerald eyes and a smile broke out from her poker face. Her previous boyfriend would be away for two to five years. He experienced anger management problems when he drank cases of beer. This guy did not fit her usual mold and type. He appeared to be more of a house of correction type of guy majoring in misdemeanors rather than the prison type.

"Okay, we'll give it a try."

Automobiles flipping, police chases, rounds of ammunition fired, and potential destruction of the human race was all averted by Bruce Willis in two hours. Ray and Pete walked to their cars outside the enormous Cineplex. The parking lot was about half of a square mile, so the walk to their vehicles took more than a few steps. The warm night air brushed their faces.

Pete saw him first and it wiped the smile from his face. Leaning up against Pete's dusty truck was a disenfranchised associate of Pete's older brother. Pete only knew him as Chaser. It was some type of twist on his long, last name and unrelenting grudges. Knowing what he was capable of, he turned to Ray and spoke under his breath. "Just keep walking, and get in your car."

Ray didn't respond.

When Pete stopped, she stopped with him. With one foot, she pulled the spur down on the back of her other, short boot. She chose her ankle boots with her black shorts. It was summer after all.

"Pete, my man...what's up?" Chaser reached out his hand. Pete stopped about four feet from him and did not return the gesture.

"What do you want?"

"Okay, be that way." The greasy, dark haired male dropped his hand. He reached both pale hands into his vest pockets and continued talking, leaning again on the driver's side door of the car. Pete did not take his eyes off of the leather vest. It was too hot for a vest. "Your brother, Mike, owes me some money...and it's growing daily. Now, I can't seem to find him. Do you know where he is?"

"He hasn't been around for days. You know I'm not his keeper. What he does is none of my business and I plan to keep it that way."

Chaser didn't move a muscle. One corner of his mouth turned

up into a wicked grin. Pete stood, watching his hands.

"Who's your little friend? She looks like she's out of your league, Pete." Ray squared her shoulders next to Pete with one step forward.

"Shut the fuck up," snapped Ray.

Even Pete turned to look at Ray. Chaser bent and laughed at the outburst. "Well you're a feisty little bitch, aren't you? Pete, you better keep her on a leash before she bites someone. The little ones are always the ones that bite."

Ray started to speak up again but Pete interrupted her. Pete knew this was going in the wrong direction. Idiots you stand up to. Insane people you don't provoke. Chaser did things on a regular basis that he didn't remember. On or off narcotics, glue or whatever, Chaser's brain would just short circuit. Mike told him one day, sober, he got mad, stuffed a guy's head into a port-o-potty, nearly killed the guy and truly didn't remember it later that night. To this day he doesn't know why the guy isn't around anymore.

"Look Chaser, if I see Mike, I'll pass on the message. We're going." Pete gave Ray a nudge toward her car and took a couple steps to his. Chaser met him.

Ray stayed back, but gripped the blade in her pocket.

"Okay for now…but I will get my money…if not from Mike, then from you." Chaser stood inches from Pete. Turning his face towards Ray, he said, "See ya, honey." He puckered, blew her a kiss and swirled his thick, wet tongue around his lips.

Only because he was walking away did Ray not respond.

Pete motioned for her to get in his truck. From inside, they watched the psychotic, pale grunger get into a beat up white van and drive away. "So Jack, why did he call you Pete?" Ray asked.

"My real name is Pete. Sorry…I meant to tell you…tonight." Pete could not believe how bad this part of the night was going. "I am sorry about all this. That guy is crazy. You really shouldn't talk to him that way. Or really ANY way! He's always packing knives or something. My brother can be kind of a low life at times.

He's screwed up. Takes drugs, anything actually… and he gets into all of these situations." Pete could not believe that he had to explain about his loser, scrum brother to Ray, already. She'd probably run the next time she saw him!

"Look, Pete, in case you haven't noticed, I am not exactly an angel myself. It was cool the way you tried to protect me. Cute…" She leaned over and kissed him. When she pulled away, Pete eased her back and pressed her to him with his hands across her back. His tongue pursued hers. He didn't stop until Ray pushed hard.

"I've gotta get a breath here, big guy. I take it, it's been awhile."

Pete sat back and worried that he came on too strong. His right arm was still across her back and he couldn't resist touching her shiny black hair that fell from her ponytail. It felt like silk to his rough hands.

"Do you want to come over to my apartment to hang out?" Ray smiled. It had been a long time for her too.

"Sure," said Pete.

"You can follow me. Oh and one more thing…so you know, I can take care of myself. Chaser is a prick and I don't take any shit from anyone. If he ever meets up with me again, it's him that better be careful. I'm full of surprises. Got it?"

"Got it," Pete said.

A couple weeks later, Pete climbed the flights of stairs to the now familiar third floor apartment. Only a bare light bulb hanging from a black wire lit the way. Dust and dirt crunched beneath his feet with each step onto the worn wood stairs. Ruts formed a dip in the center from the thousands of shoes that worked their way up and down. They were so deformed; they were difficult to walk on without the added challenge of balancing a pizza and backpack. He reached the top, took a deep breath and wiped the sweat from his face with his forearm. He knocked on the door. A female voice yelled an impatient 'come in'.

"What took you so long? I'm starved!" Ray pulled the pizza box from Pete's hands. She halted, smiled and gave him a light kiss on the cheek, thanking him for his efforts. She usually had to fetch her own pizza pie. Pete placed his weighted backpack in the corner. He took off his shoes and placed them together under a row of hooks that held an assortment of Ray's clothing; a black, cracked leather coat, which she called "finally broken in", a hooded gray zip front sweatshirt, and long shirts that she used as jackets. Most of the hooks were overstuffed with too many items hanging on each.

Ray's apartment was one large room. A kitchen area contained a sink, a half size stove and an undersized refrigerator. Four cabinets offered the only storage. Ray's culinary talents consisted of frozen pizza and French fries. She subsisted on milk, cereal and take out. The cabinets held only microwave popcorn and soda.

A black futon functioned as Ray's sofa and bed. The cover was worn and tattered. A pile of pillows and blankets sat in a pile at one end of the upright sofa and hung over onto the floor. Two bean bag chairs and a trunk used as a table were the only other furniture, besides some shelving and boxes that held Ray's disorganized stuff. Bi-fold doors hid the sole closet. The only other door led to a minuscule bathroom. The white porcelain toilet and sink almost touched each other. Sunflowers colored the clear shower curtain that covered the compact shower stall. If he wasn't careful, Pete bumped his elbows in the small room. Standing, his feet took up most of the open floor. But, as he told Ray, it was better than his apartment.

Between bites of pizza, Ray checked her voicemail and then turned off her cell phone. She declared herself "off" for the Friday night. She would be reporting to her only official source of income tomorrow night, bartender at a neighborhood bar, which made Mac's place look like Disneyland. The overweight owner loved her because all the dirty, old, drunk men sat and drank just to hang around her. After working there for three years, she decided that alcohol was foul and she did not drink any of it. Her ex-boyfriend reeked of beer when he yelled and smacked her. She chain smoked at the bar and blew smoke at the drunks so she didn't have to smell their sour breath. But, the money was good.

"So, did you bring your pajamas?" Ray smiled.

"Yeah…" Pete responded with his eyes avoiding long periods of contact and a smirk breaking out on his face. He sat next to Ray eating a slice of pizza.

"What do you want to watch?" Ray handed Pete the remote. He placed it down without changing the channel. He didn't notice what was on the new twenty-inch television. He wanted to watch Ray. He stayed late last night and couldn't wait to return. He devoured the newness of her tight body. He restrained himself from stretching her out over the futon, now. She invited him to stay over tonight by telling him to bring his 'pajamas.' Both of them spent the previous night naked. He did bring his toothbrush. He told his mother he was staying at a friend's home to watch videos. Consumed by the care of his dad, his mother might not have noticed anyway. "Nothing on TV…what do you want to do?" Ray said and looked at Pete.

The pizza box hit the floor. Pete pressed his chest on top of Ray. He balanced his weight onto his knees and his elbows on the sofa, so as to not crush Ray's small frame. His hands cupped her face as he kissed her lips and penetrated her mouth with his tongue. Ray, ever the shy, petite female, unbuttoned Pete's pants and thrust her hand into his jeans. Ray turned off the television and they opened up the bed together.

Pete lay still and spied Ray as she breathed. A streetlight gleamed in, angling a slice of light across the room. He was unsure of the time since he woke from his short, 'exercise induced coma', but knew only hours remained before the sun would come up and he would have to leave. He watched her chest rise and take in silent breaths. The blanket covered only to her waist, which left her breasts exposed. Though he felt like this was unfair, he could not resist staring. In the center of her small, firm breasts was a tattoo of a black horseshoe. It formed a U to keep the good luck in, Ray told him. Pete thought that it was the most beautiful tattoo he had ever seen.

Pete drifted off. He woke to her lying on top of him, kissing his neck. "Did I wake you up?" Ray asked.

"I'm up, all right." The remaining covers hit the floor.

Twenty

"No, honestly Mom, I will be fine. Take home Aunt Ann. I'll be fine. Jeffrey is here. Annie should be back soon. We will be fine." Kyle carried everyone's bags out to her car. Five weeks passed since Jason's funeral. At some point, Kyle had to be alone with herself. She promised her mother that she would call and even come to her mother's home if she needed. Kyle watched them drive away.

"Hey, Mom," Jeffrey stood next to his mother in the driveway. "You didn't tell Gramma that I was leaving today, too. Are you sure it's okay?"

"Look, honey, I told you to go with Lindsay and her family. A couple weeks away at the Cape will be great for you. You need to get along in whatever way works for you. You want to be with Lindsay and she is going to be at the Cape. It's okay. Annie will be calling. She is going to try to come back from Italy soon. And, Jeff, you are going to be leaving in less than a month for school. I need to adjust. I have so much business to take care of…Dad's insurance and other legal stuff. Nothing for you to worry about… go and try to have some fun. Okay?" Kyle hugged her son. They walked back into the house together.

As Kyle walked to the kitchen, she passed by Jason's office. She avoided the room as much as possible. The pile of mail and paper stacks towered on the desk. Then, she remembered something she did needed to ask Jeffrey about. She retrieved a thick envelope and found Jeffrey upstairs in his room, packing.

"Jeffrey, this is from Bates. We need to send in a deposit."

"Mom." The young man hung his head as he spoke. "I figured I would just go to B.C. and give it a try. That's what Dad would want." Kyle sat on his bed.

"Jeffrey, I'll get the checkbook; we are sending in a deposit to Bates. You want to be there. It's a fine school. Just work hard and make us proud. Okay?" She spoke of his father like he was in the room with them.

"You sure, Mom?" He picked up his head.

"I'm sure." Kyle said.

Jeffrey loaded up his car, took his cell phone and departed for Cape Cod on a sunny July day. Kyle yelled behind him, "Drive carefully!"

She chose not to tell him that even though Annie tried to get out of her contract in Italy, she could not. She found that since she had not started on time, she would be "stuck" in Italy working for this company for some time. She asked Kyle to come. If it had been any other country, she would have considered it. Though she did not welcome being home alone, tripping over ghosts and memories of Jason, she knew at some point, she had to.

The next morning, clouds blocked the sun from heating up the air. The somber sky looked more like a fall day than a summer one. The off-season weather provided a welcome break from the heat, which seemed to have a stronghold. Kyle leashed Maggie and headed down the driveway. She needed to exercise and eat today. Small as they were, those were her goals. Those five extra pounds, or even ten, had been a struggle for some time. After the stress of the last several weeks, most of her clothing grew loose. The walk today served to relieve some tension. Her stomach felt like a constant traffic jam. She would have loved to add sleep to the list of things to do, but that would be too much to ask for.

Maggie dragged her further than the usual route. Kyle did not protest. The only thing waiting at home was everything in it. Maggie's tail wagged and her head perched high. She was happy to be on the move. Kyle turned onto the road that led to the center of town. When she got close, she turned around to head home. Her legs felt tight and her knees ached. But, for the first time in a long time, her shoulders dropped and some tension dripped out of her muscles. She did not see, or hear the shiny black truck pull to a stop next to her.

"I see your attack dog is hard at work." Maggie's tail did not stop. She recognized David Linscott, in his uniform.

"Hi, David," Kyle said. She cringed. She probably looked liked something from a bad Frankenstein movie. She ran her hand through her hair. Then, a shock came over her. She cared about her appearance. Was that okay?

"It was lucky to run into you." Not that lucky, since he made a habit of driving by her house at least three times a day. "I have been wondering how you've been."

"I'm fine." She couldn't eat, couldn't sleep and she didn't want to go home. But, she was fine. She wanted to talk with him more, but did not know what to say.

"You look a bit tired. Do you want a ride?" David asked.

Yes, Kyle thought. But, she wasn't tired. She opened her mouth. Nothing came out. She could not figure out what to say.

"Why don't you get in, and I will take you home." David exited his truck. He helped Maggie into the back cab seat. Kyle climbed into the passenger seat. David shut the door. He looked over at her, with his hand on the gearshift. "Are you okay?"

Kyle shook her head up and down. "I am. I thought I was…"

"Do you want a cup of coffee?"

Kyle nodded her head yes. The truck turned around and headed to the center of town towards the coffee shop. David went in and returned with coffees.

"Thanks." Kyle took the warm cup. Silence lingered.

David observed her pale skin and her sunken eyes.

Maggie whined in the backseat. "I guess I should get back." He started the engine and pulled out of the parking lot.

"So how is your son?" David asked.

"I am worried about him. He really hasn't talked much. He just wants to be with his girlfriend. I understand. I'd love to just keep him home and not let him leave the house, but I know…I know I can't." Kyle focused on her cup as she spoke. "He just left today. He'll be away for a while, then be leaving for college."

"But, you still have family staying with you?"

"No, I sent my mom home. She's exhausted. She would stay. God knows she's been great. I couldn't have gotten through this without her. But, she's got health issues and needs rest." They pulled up the driveway to her home. Kyle jumped out and let Maggie hop down. "Well, thanks for the coffee and the ride." David was out of his truck and patting the canine.

"Kyle, are you going to be okay?" She shrugged her shoulders and gave an affirmative nod. The truth was that she just did not know.

"Do you mind if I stop by after work, just to check on you?" David asked.

"Oh, you don't have to do that. I'll be fine."

"I'll stop by. Just to check the house and everything. Okay?" He shook his head. He waited as she walked to the house.

She looked down at her coffee and turned to David. "You remembered how I take it."

"I have a thing about details."

Fatigue hit hard. Kyle drifted through the kitchen, sipping the coffee and holding it with two hands as if it was a lifeline. She strolled into the study and sat in the brown leather chair that she'd been avoiding. Her eyes met the top of the biggest pile. She lifted off the first envelope. Only a bill. No problem. This one would be easy. Finding the checkbook in the top drawer, she wrote out the check and deposited it into the return envelope. Kyle repeated this sequence several times. Her work began to stack up. Pillaging through the drawer for stamps, her hand hit a set of keys. Jason's keys. Her hands ran over each link. She squeezed them in her hand hoping to choke out the last bit of essence of Jason. Something he had with him everyday, but he did not take with him on his trip. She recalled their last few conversations. All were about tasks: the plans for Italy, and whether or not she should trade in her vehicle. She couldn't remember the last time she said she loved him. Or he told her. Kyle pushed the tears out of her eyes and focused back on the pile. This room contained mine fields. It was a struggle to move forward.

By the time Kyle finished her coffee, she found a note in her mother's handwriting to call Brendan Reed at this number. Her mom had given her this message a couple times, but Kyle just put it off. With a heavy sigh, she picked up the phone.

Mel's voice came onto the line. "Mr. Reed's office, this is Melanie speaking. May I help you?"

"Hello, my name is Kyle Mercer. I am returning Mr. Reed's call."

"May I ask what this is regarding?" Mel asked.

"I believe it is something to do with hospital business and…" Kyle swallowed hard. "My husband's death."

"I am so sorry, Mrs. Mercer. Please hold…it should just take a moment." Mel buzzed into Brendan.

"Mrs. Mercer, this is Brendan Reed. How are you?" Brendan sat with his hands folded, starring into the speaker phone.

"I'm fine, thank you. Please call me, Kyle."

"I certainly hope you are adjusting the best you can. Again, you have my deepest sympathies, as well as those of the entire firm. Dr. Mulhorn has asked me to handle all of the estate and insurance issues. There is a fair amount of business to discuss. Do you have an attorney you would like me to contact? Not that you need one, but if you are more comfortable…"

"No, we…I don't have an attorney. The woman who drafted our will moved away a few years ago and we have had no need."

"Well, I can go over everything with you. But, if at any time you would like another attorney to review anything, please just let me know."

"I'm sure you'll be fine, Brendan." Kyle's head began to throb.

This was a mountain that she just did not have the energy to climb. Brendan offered to come by the house on Saturday afternoon, tomorrow. Kyle agreed.

A few minutes after six PM on Friday evening, David pulled up the driveway. He knocked on the door, carrying a bag of Chinese take out. Maggie barked. Kyle looked out the front door. She forgot. She looked down at her robe and felt her hair. She never even combed it. She opened the door. "I'm sorry. I lost track of time." David came in. Kyle excused herself and went upstairs to put on some clothes. She pulled on underwear, a long sleeved navy t-shirt and gray cropped sweatpants. Not great, but they were all clean.

She thanked David for the food that she ate little of. She asked him if he had any children. He told her no. He had never been married, but his niece, Jenny, was his sweetheart.

"Kyle, I guess I should go. But, you really don't look good. When was the last time you slept?"

"I don't know. It's been hard. They gave me some medication…I guess I should consider that again, at least to get a night's sleep. The problem is that I'm not a great sleeper anyway…"

"Have you tried watching a baseball game? That usually puts me out." David put on the Red Sox on the television in the family room. "It will relax you." David stood as Kyle sat down.

"Kyle, would it be okay if I stayed for a while?"

She looked up with sad, deep eyes. "That would be nice."

He sat on the same couch as Kyle, facing the television, but some distance away. He updated her on the most recent trials and tribulations of the team. At least the curse was broken. Kyle shook her head. She even laughed at some of the grave disappointments the team experienced over the years. David described the Red Sox as an addiction. You know it is bad for you, you know how it will end, but you do it anyway. That's how it had been for years anyway. Red Sox fans now held their heads high.

The game progressed and the talk between them was sporadic. Maggie slept on the rug next to David's feet. The useless cat poked around and settled behind Kyle's head on the back of the couch. Kyle's head seemed harder and harder to hold up feeling as if she was drunk. Her body zapped of sharpness, by fatigue.

"Kyle," David pulled a pillow down between them. "Why don't you try and go to sleep."

"Okay, maybe for a few minutes."

The game ended with the Red Sox winning a tough game against the Yankees. David turned off the television with the remote, but did not want to move and risk waking Kyle, who slumbered next to him, with her hand resting against his leg. He wondered if she was sleeping better because she was not alone. Assuming that since she fell asleep early, she would not sleep long, he loosened the buttons on his uniform shirt at his neck, revealing more of a white t-shirt. His boots were pushed away from his feet. He leaned back and let his head fall onto the back of the couch.

It was light out when he heard someone walking through the kitchen. He found Kyle's arm stretched across his lap and her head pushed next to his leg. She remained fast asleep. Maggie, ever alert, picked her head up, but did not bark. She rose, stretched and started her tail wagging. David got to his feet, with little disturbance to Kyle, just in time to meet the man standing at the entrance to the family room, starring at him, with his hands on his hips.

"Can I talk to you outside? Now!" Matt Birch demanded.

David followed Matt out the door, stuffing his feet in his boots, tucking in and buttoning his shirt. He thought he saw smoke come out of Matt's ears.

Kyle, rolled out of a dream, and surfaced from her nocturnal peace. Her head felt clear. Her neck was stiff. She looked around, knowing she was not alone. Getting up, she saw Maggie standing by the door and voices coming from behind it. The voices were low and serious.

David stood and listened to Matt. "You have got to be kidding me? Do you have any idea what she has been through? This is not just some piece of ass, Dave!"

"Matt, nothing happened…nothing! She just fell asleep. She was alone."

"I think you had better leave her alone. Jason was my friend, too, not just Kyle's husband. I knew him for twenty years!" Matt's voice rose.

Kyle opened the door revealing Matt and David. "Good morning. Do you guys want to come in?" Kyle rubbed her eyes.

"Dave was just on his way out," Matt reported.

"I'd better be going. I hope you feel better…" David turned and walked to his truck. Matt and Kyle went into the house.

"Thanks for the food, David," Kyle called out. "Do you want some coffee?" she asked Matt, seating himself at the kitchen island.

"Sure. Kyle, we have to talk. First of all, where is Jeffrey? Is he here? Was he around for this?"

Kyle put the coffee carafe down and squared her shoulders to Matt. "What are you, the ethics police? Nothing happened… well I shouldn't say that. I slept, for many hours, which is a minor miracle. And no, Jeffrey is not here. He's away. My mom left yesterday."

"I know. She called me to come and check on you and Jeff. She was worried." His voice reeled with irritation.

"So, that's what you're doing here. Look Matt, I know you're worried about me, but hey, join the club! I have no idea how I should be handling this. If you could supply me with a rulebook, that would help. I have never been through anything like this. I feel like a zombie. I still don't understand."

Matt let out a deep breath. "I just want you to be careful. You're not in any type of condition to get involved with someone. You need to be careful. People will take advantage."

"I thought you trusted David."

"I thought I did, too. If you need to talk, call me. You used to tell me everything."

"Matt, you have four kids and a wife. You cannot be taking

care of me all of the time." The two old friends shared some silence. Kyle made coffee and poured two cups. Her eyes filled and she fought back a full crying attack. "I am doing my best. I feel like I am losing Jason and Jeffrey at the same time. I don't want Jeff to go away to college, but what can I do? Disrupt his life further?"

"I don't mean to upset you. I just think you need to be careful."

Kyle shook her head in agreement.

"The lawyer for the hospital is coming this afternoon after lunch, to finalize insurance and everything."

"Do you want me to stay?" Matt asked.

"No, I got some sleep. I should be okay. I figure all I will have to do is sign some papers. It should be relatively painless. The attorney should be able to take care of everything."

After a pot of coffee, Matt got Kyle to laugh.

"Promise me you won't be angry with David. He didn't do anything wrong."

Matt grumbled.

"Now, get out of here so I can take a shower."

Twenty-One

Brendan pulled up to the Mercer's home in his latest acquisi-
tion: a silver convertible Mercedes. A splurge, provided for by his
generous, confidential divorce settlement. The previous weekend
with the aid of movers, Sarah retrieved all of her personal items
from the house. The process was speedy and civilized, just like a
roommate moving out.

Dark glasses with a platinum rim covered his eyes. He waited
at the front door after ringing the bell. Kyle peered out the front
door, recognizing Brendan Reed from the wake. He appeared
dressed down in a pistachio colored polo and khakis, which fell
smooth against him. The sunglasses were held high upon his
chiseled face. In jeans, Kyle felt underdressed. Maggie barked
when the door opened, but stopped when Brendan knelt down
and rubbed her head. "Beautiful animal...I love dogs."

Inside, Brendan pulled out a chair and sat down at the island.
His view, unobstructed by the open patio doors, was a clear shot
at the pool. He did not look directly into the yard, which pulled
him like a magnet, but looked around the kitchen.

"You have a lovely home, Kyle."

Brendan removed two thick folders from a camel colored
briefcase and placed them on the table. "There is no easy way to
get into this business. I will be as expedient as I can. If I go too
fast, or you have any questions, please let me know." He opened
the first folder. "We received the copy of the Will you provided.
It has been filed with the courts and I don't believe there will be

any trouble. You are the sole beneficiary, as you know. Payments of insurance and settlement monies will be made to you."

Brendan paused and looked at Kyle's blank face. "There will be insurance payments from the hospital's life insurance, which is carried on all employees. There was also an additional policy taken out specifically for the trip. You and Jason both filled out paperwork prior to the trip. There will also be a settlement from the airline, which is actually a subsidy of an American Company. A hired firm is negotiating the settlement. There are individual losses, as well as the loss to the hospital. I do not have all of the details; however, it appears that both sides want this settled quickly." Brendan moved several papers in front of Kyle. "I will need you to sign these. They say that you understand everything that I have explained to you and that you are the only beneficiary."

He put a pen down and motioned in front of the X's on lines."

Kyle signed those papers, and more. Brendan continued to speak about losses and settlements. She tried to pay attention. It was not that she didn't care about the money, she did. She needed it. Jason always handled most of the finances. He often tried to engage her, but her response was that she only cared that there was enough money in Jeffrey's college fund account, and that they could pay all of their bills.

"Kyle, I'm not sure if it is my place to tell you this, but I feel you should be made aware. I do not think you have calculated the amount of money we are working with. One policy had an accidental death clause...the settlement from the airline...Kyle; we are talking about millions of dollars, even after losing some to taxes. I just want to warn you that you and your son will be at risk of being taken advantage of. You could become targets for unscrupulous people. I would like to recommend we put his into a trust of some kind to protect both of you."

"This is the second time today. I guess I better pay attention. Brendan, I certainly do not need all of that. Can you set up a trust for Jeffrey and put most or all of the money in his name?"

"Yes. There are trusts that would protect you and your son. I can make sure that gets done."

Kyle watched Brendan's long hands work with the papers. He handled the documents like bank teller handled money, with grace and ease. "Kyle, may I have a glass of water? All that talking has dried out my throat." They shared a smile and Kyle fetched two glasses of ice water.

"I hope this was not too difficult. I can't imagine how you must feel." Brendan said.

Kyle looked down at the wedding ring on Brendan's finger. "Enjoy your wife. Things can change in a moment. What is her name?"

"Well…" Brendan rubbed his fingers over the gold band. "Her name is Sarah. I guess I should be taking this off soon. My wife and I have decided to divorce. I haven't told anyone in the firm yet. I am just not ready. I guess I work too much…take things for granted. I thought I was building a future for both of us. I won't make the same mistakes again."

"I'm sorry. That has got to be a great loss, also."

"Listen to me. You have enough to deal with without me going on." He pulled together the papers and folders. He returned them to his stylish briefcase. He handed Kyle a card. "That has my work, my cell and my home number on the back. Please call me if I can help with anything. I will have to meet with you again, as these policies get processed. I'll be in touch."

Brendan shook Kyle's hand and left. She saw the flashy car leave the driveway. Brendan's card was in her hand. She read the raised lettering, which listed Brendan's full name, the firm, the address in Boston, several phone numbers. The first half of the email address caught her attention: B.E.REED@...

Even late in the afternoon, a beautiful day lingered with crisp, dry air. Kyle sat out on the deck in an Adirondack chair and watched the sun start to set. Maggie sat by her side and Pumpkin nested on her lap, perched with a view of the pool still covered by leaves. The spring clean up was skipped in this unused area.

No furniture congregated on the concrete surrounding the water. It seemed to be a forgotten, desolate area. Kyle saw no reason to open the pool for herself, but wondered if it would at least not look so depressing. But, was it worth opening it for a month or so? Maggie would use it and the water would be refreshing. She picked up the cordless phone and dialed. No surprise, she got an answering machine late on a Saturday afternoon.

"Hi Bill, this is Kyle Mercer. We've had a change in plans. I was wondering what you thought of opening the pool now. I know it would not be for long, but I hate the way it looks. I know you're busy…if you could do it soon, give me a call. Otherwise, I'll just wait until next year. Thanks."

Within a minute of putting the phone down, it rang. A familiar man's voice spoke. "Hey, what are you doing for dinner?"

"Oh, I have big plans," Kyle said.

"Well, Emily would love to see you."

"Okay, tell her I'll be over soon, but only to see the kids. Not you." Kyle locked up the house, put Maggie in the SUV and was on her way. Maggie looked back at the house at the cat sitting in the window.

Brendan sipped twenty-five year old Glen Levet scotch. The single malt aged liquor rolled over his tongue with gentle sparks. He leaned against the back of the round upholstered sofa with one arm stretched out across the top. The seating area fit four adults in tight. Other heavy fabric chairs were pulled up to the half moon wooden table that uniquely fit the area. Nicole snuggled up next to him. Nicole was a beautiful brunette with whom Brendan connected since Law School. He reached out to Nicki, as he liked to call her, after it became clear that he would be available again. His marital status mattered little to her. She only honored promises she made. Brendan stopped enjoying time with her before his wedding, deciding that at some point he had to "grow up." He got together with her only a handful of times after his nuptials to celebrate a special occasion. As far as he was concerned, every man needed a Nicki—no problems, no strings, just recreation.

Tonight, he indulged her. She enjoyed going out with her "crew", as she called them, but Brendan did not agree to public appearances since his wedding. In return, she wore something she knew he'd like; a black slip dress with gray lace trim and black sandals with so few straps they looked as if they would fall, dangling from her foot. The thin dress twisted and covered little of her tall, lanky frame and full C-cup implants. Brendan watched as the lovely fellow attorney held court.

Nicki's spark remained contagious. The group erupted in laughs, often drowning out the piano being played in the corner of the room. Nicki continued her usual habit of regular trips to the ladies room. She gave new meaning to the phrase "powdering your nose." The table the group shared lay covered with glasses of all different shapes and sizes. They consumed fine vodkas, scotches and wines, leaving them well inebriated when they left in the first few hours of Sunday morning. Brendan returned with Nicki to her Back Bay condominium, spending the morning hours recreating between fine Egyptian sheets.

On his drive home, a little after noon, Brendan pondered how soon he could purchase a condo in the city. The home in the suburbs held promises of peace, quiet and a long commute into Boston. None were offerings he found appealing now. But, he resigned to staying in the bedroom community until after Kate's discovery and subsequent business concluded. The links of him to Kate and Hollis were enough for the authorities to look at him twice. The recent divorce already served as a "change", a small flag, which would draw attention. Moving out of town would be a smoke signal. Still, the process of discovering, identifying and investigating Kate's death would take at least months to even start, as he expected the Mercer's pool not to be open until next spring, or possibly, later. Impatient at the prospect of this time restriction, he decided it wouldn't hurt to search the Boston area real estate market.

Brendan sat in the Monday morning meeting with all the other attorneys in their sharp suits. Shelly, cloaked in her summer wool that hung on her bones, sat to the right of Angus, handing him papers to prompt him along. He coughed and gagged, stopping the meeting on two occasions. In the past, Angus relished the Monday morning sessions. He surveyed the week and "steered the ship" as he liked to say. The senior would assess each partner's projected agendas for the week, then reorganize or hand out new assignments according to his judgment and whim. Angus officially remained as the leader of the meeting. However now, Ronald and Shelly controlled the flow, agenda and decisions. Any new business that they were unprepared for was held back for further review. "Angus will get back to you," Shelly would respond. It appeared to everyone that Angus Hessman's days were numbered as top dog.

"Angus isn't looking well." Jared, the other junior partner, said to Brendan as they exited the morning meeting. "He never recovered since his granddaughter disappeared. Have you heard anything new?"

"Not a thing," said Brendan.

"What do you think happened to her? Do you think she just took off? I heard she was a mess."

"I have no idea." Brendan saw Mel coming down the hall, looking to him with an urgent glare. Regardless of what mess she wanted him for; it was welcome. "Excuse me, we've been out straight." Brendan left Jared standing in the hall.

"What is it, Mel?"

"The firm for the hospital has called twice. They really want your input before they proceed. There is a problem with the settlement being offered by the airline. They're concerned it could drag on, and the hospital has already incurred significant debt. This guy," Mel handed him a paper and a name, "wants to speak with you as soon as possible. He seemed stressed." Brendan shook his head.

"Fucking amateurs," he said to Mel in a hushed voice. "Get

him on the phone. I'll be in my office." He pushed the slip of paper back to her.

A few minutes later, sitting in his soft chair, Mel buzzed him and told him that she had Mr. Richard Deasero on the line.

"Richard, this is Brendan. What's going on?"

Richard spoke with chosen words, in a steady flow. He explained that the settlement, which they had hoped would be agreed to, was in jeopardy of falling through. The figures put on the table did not come close to their expectations. Richard wanted Brendan's opinion as to letting this drag out and what type of financial agreement would be acceptable, possibly less money, but saving the families from a lengthy process.

"Look, Richard, you guys have not been meeting with the families as much as I have. Our clients have been put through hell and are still there. Considering the maintenance records, or should I say the *lack* of maintenance, I would think these guys would be eager to get a confidentiality agreement in place. No one will set foot on these planes if this gets out. These families have been turned upside down and their pain is not going away. Go tell them that I am eager to take this to the court of public opinion. These surviving victims deserve fair compensation. They did nothing to deserve this. I don't want this to take forever, but if it does, we will be looking for twice the amount in damages. I know these usually take a long time to settle, but I would think that they would want this one sealed up. Haven't you guys had a case like this before?"

"Not quite this big," Richard responded.

The hospital Board really chose a crack firm, Brendan thought. "Just remember this, Richard, these people did nothing to deserve this. Lives have been devastated!"

The call ended. Brendan reflected in his chair, looking out the windows. His thoughts filled with regret that Kyle would have to handle the discovery of a body on her property, alone. At least she would be financially set and would not have to worry about money. She was now a rich woman.

Twenty-Two

Ray and Pete lounged across the open futon on the Monday morning. Pete scratched at his stubble and Ray stretched out her arms in a series of yawns. The look of two young people not caught up in the rat race. Cigarette butts overflowed from the two ashtrays on the side table. Empty bottles of soda and take-out containers spilled from the trash barrel. Sunlight pressed at the closed shades. The windows were open as they were all night; the occasional wind rattled the aluminum shades. Pete accompanied Ray more and more on her daily outings. So much so, that his finances became depleted. He told Ray he had to "do some stuff" this coming week to make some money.

"Pete, you know I "freelance" for extra cash. I know Mac, among his other talents, is a fence. So…"

"Yeah…" The young thief's eyes looked away. "I steal only little things from houses. Things that won't get noticed so easy. I want a real job though. I had a job at a gas station, but the guy was an asshole. I'm going to look around again."

"Have you asked Mac? He knows lots of people."

"That may be an idea… Mac has offered me some shit…well, it's not really regular work. Maybe I should ask anyway."

"I'll keep my ears open. I meet a lot of people. Ray picked up the laptop between them and set it on her lap. They surfed cool tattoo sites in between playing video games. "So where did you get the laptop? This is pretty nice."

"At the dump."

Ray looked at him with one eyebrow up.

"Well, it was going to the dump. Really. The thing was in a garage under a pile of shit…like trash."

"Works just fine. Tell me the truth, is that really how you found the laptop? With trash?"

"Yeah, Ray, honest. Under a bunch of trash."

"That doesn't make sense. This has got to retail for some bucks… can only be a year old at most because of the software. Why would someone want to toss it?"

"Who knows, Ray, some people in this area have so much money they throw good stuff out. I heard someone say a guy put in a fountain for 80 grand! Hey, I've got to head home for a while. Do you want me to come back over tonight?"

"Yeah, I should be back around six. I have to stop by the café for a while. Hey, leave the laptop here. I'm going to investigate. Oh, and here…" Ray handed him a key that she retrieved from a drawer. "In case I am not here. You can let yourself in. But only when I am expecting you. Understand?"

"Sure." Pete kissed Ray, pocketed the key with a smile on his face and left.

Ray began her excavation of the computer.

Bright sunlight greeted Kyle when she woke in her bed around nine a.m. She'd slept, piecemeal, for almost five hours. Not bad. It was a step in the right direction. Pumpkin stretched out next to her and cooed, as Kyle rubbed the cat's head. The feline, not yet ready to get up, hopped off the bed and found her cat bed. She curled up under the warmth streaming in from the window, eager to start her daily ritual.

The morning dragged along. Wanting to get something accomplished, her eyes found Jason's luggage stacked in a corner. The pieces sat waiting, patient that she would get to them sometime. Letting out a deep breath, she hoisted the bags onto her bed and unzipped them. The familiar scent of Jason's cologne lingered among clothing. Each garment conjured up memories. She pulled a gray matte suit up to her chin, and placed her hand on the back right shoulder, just where it would be when they danced last at a friend's wedding. If she knew that was to be her last dance with him, she would have hugged him just a bit tighter. She wanted the time back…the nights she did not wait up; the days that got so full they only spoke by phone…she wanted all the minutes, all of the seconds, back.

She made herself move along, forcing herself into a robot state, not looking directly at the clothing or registering any reaction. Focusing on the hangers, Kyle removed and placed rows of hangers on her husband's side of the closet. The next problem flashed through her mind; what was she going to do with all of these things? Probably donate them. One thing at a time, she told herself.

The last piece of luggage was a small bag. Kyle unpacked a shaving kit, underwear, folders and other small items, putting them back where Jason kept them. Finished, she ran her hand through a deep zip pocket inside the bag, and pulled out something in a smooth wrapper. She realized she held a long strip of condoms, like you would see hanging behind the cashier at a convenience store. The accessory bag fell to the floor as she sat on the bed. The condom packages lay across the back of her hand. She struggled to find an explanation that would decipher all the images pounding her thoughts. None held water. WHY?

When the phone rang, Kyle fell into her fantasy for a moment and thought it might be Jason. He often called in the middle of the day, when he was finished in surgery to let her know how his day was going, but now she realized, usually not inquiring about hers. Due to his schedule, the phone, sad to say, was their primary means of communication. The majority of their time was spent apart. Her hand stalled over the ringing telephone, before she picked it up. Of course, it was not Jason.

"Kyle, its Annie. How are you?"

Kyle held the cordless phone in one hand and her discovery

in the other. "I'm fine. How are you doing over there?" Kyle remained fixated.

"Well, I am not running off with any Italian men…yet. It would be more fun if you were here. How's Jeffrey?"

"Okay. He's with Lindsay. They will be moving to school next week. They are both trying out for the soccer team, so they're moving into the dorms early. They'll be busy. Boy, you have timing, Annie."

"What is it? Are you having a bad day?"

"You wouldn't believe what I just found."

"What?" Annie waited for her friend's response, but heard only silence. "Kyle, what is it?"

Kyle cleared her throat. "I was cleaning out Jason's luggage and…I just don't know what to think."

"What did you find?"

"Condoms."

"What?" Annie's voice halted.

"Exactly."

"Well, you don't know he was using them. There could be a very good explanation."

"Nice try. We haven't used them since college." The tears she had fought off rolled down her cheeks. She pushed them off her face. She stood and threw the latex products against the wall. "Damn it. I can't believe this. When did my marriage fall apart? And all this time, I thought he worked around the clock. I always felt bad for him. He'd walk into the house and get paged. How many trips did he take for training? For conferences? So I was a failure as a wife!"

"Don't go there. You have no idea how or why they were there. What if he brought them for Jeffrey? Or what if they are Jeffrey's? Has Jeff ever borrowed Jason's luggage? Or what if they were for someone else?"

"They could be the tooth fairy's," Kyle snapped.

"Even if it is what you think, and that's a big if, that doesn't mean Jason didn't love you and Jeffrey. You know that no one was more important to Jason than you." Annie spoke from experience on both sides of the affair sea-saw. "It doesn't mean anything. Besides, there's nothing you can do about it now. You have to let it go."

"I just can't believe this." Kyle said over and over. She spoke to Annie for almost an hour, before realizing the cost of this would be more than a plane ticket. Before she ended the call, Annie told Kyle that her cousins would be staying at her house in Hollis while their house was under construction, and that Kyle did not have to check on it any more. She said she would be home in a little over a month, so long as everything went well, and "hang in there."

Kyle fled from the bedroom, the room of love and intimacy, marching through the house. Items from around the home flew into the air. The first one to hit the floor was a crystal vase from their wedding. Next, she picked up Jason's favorite framed watercolor and smashed it on the floor. After that, anything nearby Jason loved, found its way into pieces. She even reached into the china cabinet and pulled out his favorite red wine glasses, expensive thin glass. They met the same fate. Maggie ran and hid as curse words and tears flowed from her master. Kyle called the dog, who came with her tail down, swooped up her purse and ran out of the house, slamming the door. She drove.

When she passed the 'Welcome to Maine' sign, she realized how far she traveled on Route 95 North to a section that held more trees than cars. She pulled off an exit and into a fast food restaurant. She let Maggie out to relieve herself. "I'm sorry puppy. You shouldn't have to listen to all this." As a consolation, she purchased a Happy Meal and gave it to the dog, fries and all.

Down the road, she made out a motel. It was a chain of Inns, which more resembled a strip mall than a residence. It was nothing special, in a nowhere town.

After some discussion with the manager, he allowed Kyle to rent a room on the first floor with Maggie. He required a large deposit, but said they did rent to customers with animals, on a case-by-case basis. In a lobby gift shop, Kyle purchased a toothbrush and paste. She and Maggie lay on the bed, secluded from the world, watching traffic pass from a large window.

Around 4 p.m. her phone vibrated from the bottom of her purse. It vibrated again five minutes later, and then every few minutes after that. The purse rested on a small table too far away from Kyle to notice. The sun set in no particular rush. Night fell and the stars came out. She watched the traffic pass with their lights now on. She alternated trying to sleep and taking Maggie out for relief.

Twenty-Three

Pete came over to Ray's apartment during the day and left in the evening. He needed to be home early in the morning to help Mom drive his dad to a doctor's appointment. Diabetes, high blood pressure, and other ailments were choking his body. His health grew more and more fragile.

Pete's early departure gave Ray free time to continue a question that was sticking in her craw. The laptop. She smelled something foul and wanted to find the source. It could be something simple: someone got mad and trashed a spouse's computer, or a disgruntled employee dumped company equipment. But, there had to be a reason why someone would discard a late model computer in good condition.

Not long after she got the computer in question up and running, there was a knock at the door. She looked up. "Pete, did you forget your key?" she shouted. The only response was another soft knock. Annoyed, she popped up and walked to the door.

"Well…" Ray pulled the door open to reveal a smiling Chaser leaning up against the frame, wearing the same worn black leather vest and a black t-shirt underneath.

"I saw Pete come and leave. So, he already has a key. You move fast, Ray." He planted his foot inside the doorway.

"Get the fuck out of here! I warned you when you came to the bar to stay away from me." Ray slammed the door on his foot. With barely an effort, he shoved the door open, crashing her small body to the floor. He stepped in, shut the door and in a moment lay over her. His coarse skinned hand stung her cheek with a hard slap.

"You disrespected me. You need to learn," Chaser said, close enough to Ray's face that she smelled his corpse breath. His weight pressed her back into the floor. She was pinned.

In survivor mode, she plotted. Dealing with drunken crazy people had to be the same as dealing with just plain crazy people, or close anyway.

"Okay, you want to do this. Let's get on the bed. This floor's too hard." She was not screaming and acted calm. Chaser leaned back and allowed her to get up. She did not move away from him, remaining within his range. Gripping the top of her sky blue t-shirt with two hands, she tore it down the middle, revealing her bare breasts and her horseshoe. She unbuttoned her jeans and zipped them half way down. A hint of a smile came to her face.

Chaser glued to her actions, watched with his mouth open. She motioned for him to sit on the futon as she slinked over to the light switch and turned off a bright light in the kitchen area. A lamp in a corner created shadows around the apartment. On her way past her shirts and coats hanging on the wall, she ran her hand across them, but distracted the Neanderthal by rubbing her nipple between two fingers, pulling on them and moaning. She reached her hands behind her back, swaying her hips in a slow dance, still with a smirk on her face. "Take off your shirt," she murmured.

She stood over him as he pulled up his grimy, sweat-soaked black tank t-shirt over his head. Aromas of body odor filled the air. When his face was covered for a split second with his own shirt, Ray lunged.

The knife delivered a deep wound into his abdomen. She twisted the blade back and forth and up and down to further the damage. Then without a word, she pulled the blade out. Chaser let out a wail and reached his hands to cover his bleeding stomach. Black blood spilled out between his hands. Ray stabbed him again on the side of the throat right above his collarbone, even though she had a clear shot to the center. It could not look too perfect. This was self-defense after all.

The dark haired intruder looked up at her and tried to speak. He made only gurgling sounds before he slumped over and hit the floor. The body fluid continued to pump, covering his torso and spreading beyond, forming a pool around him. Ray stood, motionless, assessing her work. Her best guess was that it would take at least fifteen minutes to bleed out. Most people think it's quick, but in reality it's not. Most lose their nerve and run too quickly for help. She learned long ago to be thorough. Then, she turned her attention to herself. She ran the long blade down the middle of her chest. Red dripped down from the cut onto her cream skin. She dropped the knife on the floor next to him, into the seeping blood, making sure the handle was well covered. The bigger the mess, the better. She bent down and, with one finger, lifted his head to look into his eyes and said, "I told you to stay the fuck away from me."

Her hands tossed her hair, infusing some blood into her dark locks, sticking some on her face, also pulling strands out and letting them fall to the floor. In a motion like she had fallen, she bent over, sticking her hands into the body fluid on the floor, covering herself. More blood, hers and his, was smeared on her body to complete the look. Taking a quick glance around the shadows of the room, she double-checked the scene. She pushed the door open with both of her bloody hands and fell onto the hallway still naked from the waist up. She screamed at the door across the hall, with the light escaping under it.

Within ten minutes, police and ambulances arrived. Ray, shaking, sat in her neighbor's apartment, an older married couple, Betty and Mike. The two were more shaken than Ray. They spoke to the police, leaving her with little opportunity. The couple reported that they asked their landlord on many occasions to increase the security of the building and that they witnessed the steady decline of their neighborhood. The lighting in the building was bad. The locks were old and undependable. Any idiot could walk in. Rachel had lived there for under a year, the poor thing.

A large, square bodied, female detective with a buzz cut arrived and asked to speak with Ray alone. Perfect, Ray thought. She pulled up a chair alongside the young woman covered with a borrowed blanket wrapped around her. Ray's black hair covered her face as she sat hunched over, sobbing.

"Hi Rachel, my name is Officer Reynolds. Can we talk for a minute? I need to ask you what happened."

Ray nodded.

The victim lifted her head, inch by inch, revealing her face to the policewoman. The now dried blood became streaked with the tears that ran over her cheeks. The sight of her battle-ridden face stunned the officer for a moment. With a gentle hand, she pushed some of the soaked hair away from Ray's face, so she could make eye contact.

"I opened the door and he was just on top of me. He said he was going to…" Ray stopped and choked back tears.

"It's okay. Tell me what he said. Exactly if you can."

"He said he was going to fuck me up, then kill me."

"What happened next?" The officer asked. Ray sniffled and took deep breaths.

"He told me to strip. He pressed on my throat and I felt dizzy. Then he cut me." She flashed open her blanket and presenting her chest, a work of art. "When he went to take off his shirt, he put the knife down. So I grabbed it. I told him to get out, that I was going to call the police. He laughed. When he went to get up, I just jumped. I think the knife got him then but I don't even really know how it all happened. He went to grab me again and I think I got him in the shoulder. I don't know. It was dark. I was so scared. I was dizzy. Then I got to the door."

"You're doing great, Rachel. Now tell me, do you know this guy?"

"Not really…I've seen him where I bartend. I think he has been following me around, at least I saw him once. I told him to stay away. I was afraid of him. He's creepy. I thought he'd get the message. I think someone called him Chase or something."

"Well, Rachel, you're a very lucky, brave woman. We know this guy. He has a record a mile long. We'll need to have you sign a statement. I would like to take you to the hospital to get checked out. Is there anyone I can call for you?"

"No. I don't have any family. Will you stay with me?"

"Yes, Rachel. I will stay with you. I'll be right back." The officer walked into the hall and spoke with a male officer. Ray put her head down, letting the blanket shelter her wounded body but listening to the voices.

The female officer spoke first. "She said she opened the door and that animal was all over her. He had a knife. Said he was going to fuck her up and kill her. Her clothing is ripped. She's been cut at least once. She got the knife and thinks she got him twice. It sounds like he was stalking her. She's lucky. He must have over a hundred pounds on her. Does that jive with the scene?"

The other officer responded. "Well, it's a mess in there. But it is contained to one place. No other disturbances around the apartment. There are at least two stab wounds. This is no great loss to the community."

"I'm going to get her to the hospital. Maybe you can talk to the landlord and tell him he had better do a better job with security. This guy had no trouble getting in."

"Will do. I guess this guy liked knives."

"Why?"

"Besides the one on top of him, we can see one sticking out from under his pant leg. I guess he brought a back-up."

On her way out, Ray saw her landlord in his pajamas talking to the police.

At the hospital, doctors examined her and ordered tests. Besides some cuts and scrapes, all superficial, they diagnosed a slight concussion. Her head ached and her body felt weak with exhaustion. When she got a moment alone in between nurses and doctors poking her, she called Pete on her cell phone and left him a voice mail. She said she would be tied up for a day or two and would call him when she was free. Under no circumstances was he to come over until she talked to him. She was crashing with a friend for a couple days.

Twenty-Four

Kyle exited the fast food restaurant and juggled a bag of breakfast. When she opened the door, Maggie flew out of the vehicle.
Kyle caught her leash and led her over to a picnic table in an outdoor eating area. The dog's nose worked overtime, following the
strong scent coming from the bag. Kyle sat, removed a breakfast
sandwich and dropped it on the ground. It met the grass only
for a moment before the ecstatic pooch devoured breakfast.

Staring off into space, Kyle sipped the hot brew. Her hand
covered her mouth during her many yawns. She now understood why some people turned to drugs. Sometimes you just
can't get away from yourself. She worked hard during the night
to push the inventory of her life away and bury it. Identified as
Jason Mercer's other half for twenty-one years, Kyle was half of
a happy couple who had everything. At least, Kyle thought they
did. She now felt regret at often finding her stable, predictable
life, boring. It seemed as if someone stole her identity and left
her to start over. Crawling back into that cave of naïve security
now was only a dream. Jeffrey would be around less and less.
The loss and gap left by Jeffrey's moving away loomed large during the last year. But, with no husband to turn her attention to,
her nest wouldn't just be empty, it would be demolished. Indulg-
ing herself by trying to keep Jeffrey home, would rob him of the
growth he needed to make. At eighteen, he should not be burdened with the responsibility of his mother's happiness or san-
ity. She needed to let her son get on with his life. And somehow,

she would have to get along with one herself. Annie was stuck in Italy. Matt was around, but busy and overextended. It struck her that she was in Maine and no one knew where she was. But then, it didn't matter. Dinner did not need to be made. Laundry would sit. No one needed her. She hoped someday she would embrace her new situation as independence instead of the isolation that gutted her chest. But who knows. Life was full of surprises. Things would have to get better.

The bright sun did not hold enough strength to warm the cooler fall air that crept in over night. August struggled to retain summer temperatures with September nipping on its heels. Kyle drove at the speed limit, sometimes falling below it. There was no rush. Her cell phone vibrated in her bag on the passenger's seat of the car. It went unnoticed.

Maggie lay across the back seat, air from the windows blowing over her brown coat, her stomach full with a special treat.

The drive seemed longer on the way home. It took over two hours to find her way back south to Hollis. In the center of town, she noticed the dry cleaners and realized she may have stacks of clothing ready. She could not recall when she was in last.

Inside, the clerk said her usual hello and gave a big smile. The fifty something woman and her husband opened the cleaners over twenty-five years ago and resisted many offers to be bought out. They made their home in town and cultivated many friends and customers. Millie knew everyone and everybody. She said you could learn everything about people, by their clothing and how it came in.

"Hi Millie, how are you today?"

"Oh fine, dear. How are you doing?" Her eyes grew wide waiting for Kyle's response. Kyle had not seen her since the services for Jason.

"I'm doing okay. Jeffrey's off to school soon." She drove her voice up to make every effort to appear 'on the mend' and to divert the subject from of herself.

"Wonderful," said Millie. "Hey, what's all the commotion

on your street? I tried to get through this morning, but finally gave up."

"Oh, I don't know. I was away. I'm sure it's nothing." The town grapevine worked fast and it started here. She was sure Millie would be privy to all details and have the full scoop on any disruption well before she did. If someone lost a cat, it was front page news. Kyle didn't have the energy to be concerned about anyone else's life.

Kyle gripped the hangers, said goodbye and headed home.

When she reached Bowen Street, she made out a couple of cars in the distance. She began to get concerned that something had happened to her neighbors, as the lights of a police cruiser became visible. It sat in front of their house.

At a reduced speed, she drove the SUV closer to her home and the flashing lights. Her foot hit the brake and she stopped in the middle of the road at the end of a trail of cars. At the end of HER driveway, a policeman stood outside a cruiser. An assortment of vehicles transformed the passage into a parking lot. Sticking out was a huge black truck with white lettering that read 'Major Crime Unit' The trail of cars and the remaining police on the road caused an overflow. Most of the vehicles were not "official." Several were private automobiles and trucks with bulb red lights on their roofs, still flashing.

Kyle did not see the patrolman waving her on. Her eyes remained fixed on her residence erupting with activity. None of this could be good and she was already at her limit. Something was wrong...Jeffery?

The young officer in uniform left his post and walked to her car, still stalled in the middle of the road. He knocked on her window. "Hi Ma'am, can you move along, please?"

Kyle took a second to respond. She lifted her hand and pointed to the house. "Can you tell me what's going on?"

"No ma'am, I can't. Would you move along, please?"

Kyle contemplated following his direction. Denial worked for some people and she really didn't want to take responsibly for this mess. She dropped her head down and held it with her hands and tried to breath. Kyle made out the back of an ambulance, but no one moving about with any urgency.

"That's my house," she said back to the officer.

"You live there? What's your name?"

"Kyle Mercer."

"Would you pull over please?" He motioned for Kyle to move her vehicle to the side of the road. He spoke into a microphone clipped to his collar. "Hey, Dave, I've got a woman out here that says she lives here. Kyle Mercer." The patrolman looked in the window and spoke. "Lieutenant Linscot is on his way out. Please wait here."

Kyle wrapped her hands around her elbows. Maggie now stood up in the back seat, tail wagging. It took a minute or two, but David strode down to the end of the driveway and focused on her SUV. Butterflies in her stomach congealed to full-fledged anxiety as she watched his fast, deliberate strides towards her. His badge hung sideways off of his gun belt, lopsided by the weight of the weapon. He could otherwise pass as a civilian, wearing a white-collared shirt and dark blue pants. Color flushed his cheeks, putting apples on his strong cheekbones. He spoke into a cell phone.

Deciding to confront her fear, Kyle pulled her keys from the ignition and stepped out of the car, pulling Maggie out, too. The pooch relieved herself at the same time, wagging her tail at the sight of David approaching. The two started walking towards the officer, a friend.

"I'm glad to see you're okay," David said when he met Kyle in the middle of the road. No expression seeped from his face.

"What's going on?"

"It's complicated. Matt is on the line. He wants to speak to you." He held out the phone to Kyle, who did not accept.

"Are you always the bearer of bad news?" Her voiced trembled. "First tell me that Jeffrey is all right. Anything else I don't care about. Remember, we've been through this before."

"Jeffrey is fine." Her eyes did not leave David's face as she took the phone and put it to her ear.

"Matt…" Kyle bit on her bottom lip.

"I'm on my way over. Where have you been? Why didn't you answer your cell?"

Kyle didn't answer. She didn't know where she'd been or why it mattered.

"Look, I don't know exactly how to put this…you have a crime scene in your backyard. David will explain. I'm on my way. Okay?"

"Okay." Kyle closed the phone and handed back to David. "You have got to tell me what's going on? This is still my house!"

"Let's go inside."

With Maggie in tow, the two walked up the driveway toward the house. The sounds of voices and radios became clearer the closer they got. Kyle fumbled with her keys at the front door and dropped them. Without a word, David retrieved them and opened the door. David motioned to her to wait behind him. He walked into the house first. He stopped when he heard the crunch of glass under his feet.

"Oh, I kind of left a mess. It's nothing," Kyle said.

David shot her a look and continued in to the kitchen. He looked around at the broken glass on the floor and picture frames underneath it.

Kyle looked up at David. "I had a bad day." Kyle glanced at a window and for the first time got a glimpse at the activity in the backyard. "It looks like I am having another!"

David moved to intercede her viewing, positioning himself between her and the windows. "Why don't we sit down?" He pulled a chair out at the island that would keep her back to the yard. Kyle took the seat.

David sat across from her. "I need to ask you some questions. Did you contact a guy named Bill recently to open your pool?"

"Yes. I was tired of looking at it this way. Did Bill get hurt?"

"No. Who else knew you were going to open it?"

"No one, I guess. Did someone get hurt?"

"Jeffrey? Did your son know that you were opening the pool?"

"No. He hasn't been around; he's leaving for college soon."

"Who else knew about your trip to Italy and the timeframe you expected to be gone?"

"Everyone, I guess. Certainly anyone in this small town." Kyle forced herself to focus on the questions, but what she really wanted were answers. "I forwarded the mail. I talked to Bill... everyone at the hospital. They made the arrangements. David, tell me what's wrong!"

"Human remains were found in your pool. Apparently, they have been there for some time."

Kyle felt her jaw fall. She reached both hands to her face and covered her open mouth. Her eyes filled. She fought back a tidal wave of emotion. "David, who is it?"

"That's what we are trying to figure out. We're hoping you can help us."

"Help you? Why would I have any idea?"

"We have to start somewhere."

The side door opened and Matt flew in. Without a word, he wrapped Kyle in a hug. He looked at David. "Dave..." Matt nodded his head to David. "Can I talk to you outside?"

"Sure."

"Kyle, I'll be right back."

The two officers exited through the garage. They turned the corner to the backyard and perused the busy property. They talked with hands on their hips.

"So what have you got since last night?" Matt asked.

"Not much. Major crime unit has taken over. The Attorney General has been on the phone with the Chief...everything done by the numbers. The Chief was happy to hand the scene over to them. This is a new one." David rubbed his forehead. "We've been trying to get fire and rescue out of here." Matt looked around at the "local volunteers" that comprised the majority of the Fire Department. "The guys are tripping over each other. Lab guys are here. They have been looking for as much trace evidence as possible. But, as you can see, any trace material has probably been compromised. The body has been there for awhile. There's only bones left. We think it might be a female, judging from long hair and some chips of paint on the fingernails. But, that's just a guess."

Matt shook his head, just as he did last night when he first arrived.

"Matt, you know that I have to question Kyle and Jeffrey. And, we're going to have to search the house."

"Dave," Matt spoke with one hand pointing. "You know that neither one of them had anything to do with this. I have known them their entire lives. Why aren't you looking for the Peeping Tom she's seen on the property?"

David let a few seconds pass before he responded. He knew Matt was upset. "You know someone is going to question them. Do you want it to be me or someone else?"

Matt dug his foot into the ground. He turned and walked back into the house. David followed.

The three sat at the island, Matt with his arm around Kyle. David removed a spiral pad and pen from his side pocket. He flipped some pages until he found an empty one.

"Kyle, I need to ask you and Jeffrey some questions. It will help us find out what happened. Can you reach Jeffrey?"

"I already left him a voicemail to call in as soon as possible. You can ask me whatever questions you want. I have no idea who would put a body in our pool."

"I have to inform you that you have the right to an attorney."

"I have what? Are you saying I am a suspect?" Kyle turned and looked to Matt.

"No one really believes you or Jeffrey had anything to do with this. I think it's clear that you are a victim in this. But, David has got to do things by the numbers. He has got to rule you and Jeffrey out," Matt said.

"Jeffrey? I won't have you questioning my son like some criminal. That child would not harm a fly. He has been through enough. Maybe I should consult an attorney."

"That is your right, but…why don't I give you and Matt a chance to talk." David closed his pad and went out the door.

Kyle covered her face with her hands. She hit her head with a fist a couple of times.

"Hey, knock it off." Matt pulled her fist.

"I am trying to wake myself up from this nightmare."

"Here's the deal. They want to question you and Jeffrey. You live here and there's a body, or what's left of one, in your backyard. They will want to search the house subpoena banking records, etc. This is all standard. Once they find nothing, they will move on. Also, when they get an ID on the body, it will help steer the investigation. You guys are the only lead they have. Do you understand?"

Kyle swallowed hard. "What do you think happened?"

"I just don't know. This is bizarre. Most people—especially women—are killed by people they know. It's odd that someone thought that your pool was a safe hiding place. It's probably a romance gone bad. A jealous boyfriend. An affair. They'll figure it out."

Kyle focused on the one word which haunted her for a couple days now; affair. She again felt the condoms in her hand. The word latex called out to her. Two days ago she would have sworn her husband had been faithful since she was eighteen. Were there more things she didn't know? Or worse, what if Jeffrey had something to do with this girl? Impossible. But, there was a body in her pool. It didn't just fall in. Right now, she didn't know what to do.

"Matt, should I speak to an attorney? I have never been involved in anything like this before."

"Lawyers." Matt made a face. All they ever did was muck up

their work. "I guess that wouldn't hurt. It's just that if you had nothing to do with this, why do you care what they look at or ask you?"

"Well, what happens if they can't solve this? I think I should at least consult an attorney. I just don't think I can handle all of this."

"Look, if you feel better talking to a lawyer, you should. Do you know any? Matt asked.

"Just one."

Twenty-Five

Ray shut the car door and swung the strap of her black bag over her shoulder. She walked through the front door of her apartment building that was propped open by a piece of wood. Power tools and sawdust littered the floor. She stepped over the mess and started up the worn wood stairs. A man in dusty carpenter pants and a tool belt passed her coming down. "Good morning," he said.

Her key would not fit the lock on her door, so she went back downstairs to the landlord's apartment, leaving her belongings in the hallway. She found him speaking with the man in carpenter pants on the first floor landing. The older man's eyes widened when he saw Ray.

"Are you feeling better?" the white haired man asked.

"Hey Joe, much better. My key doesn't…" Ray stopped as Joe reached into his pocket and retrieved a key ring with two shiny new keys hanging from it.

"Here. This is for you. I changed all the locks. One is for the front door, one is for your apartment. I put in some new lights with motion detectors inside and outside. And, I hope you don't mind…we cleaned up your apartment. I am very sorry what happened to you."

"Don't worry about it, Joe. I'm okay. Thanks for the new locks."

The new key worked on the first try. Ray perked at the sight of her apartment. Every inch looked as if it had been scrubbed or painted. A large sisal rug covered most of the wood floor. In the place of her old futon was a larger new one with a multi-colored cover. A silver standing lamp stood at one side. "Cool!"

Ray turned the new deadbolt on the door and secured herself inside. She looked out the new peephole and saw the empty hallway. Making her way around the apartment, she noticed a note on the fridge. It was from her neighbors across the hall. They hoped she got well soon and had made her some meals. Inside, she found several Tupperware containers. She checked two. One held lasagna, another beef stew.

So far, killing Chaser turned out to be a smart move. She called Pete but got his voicemail. "Hey Pete, its Ray…come over tonight, or call me. I'm back in my apartment." She tossed her bag and stretched out on the new futon.

Ray woke to the buzzer. She jumped and answered it. "Who is it?"

"It's me," Pete replied.

She buzzed him in and swung open the door. She waited it the hallway. Pete's steps echoed and came closer. Ray greeted him with a big smile. She stretched her arms over her head.

"What time is it, I must have fallen asleep."

"It's after six. So where have you been? I heard what happened. Are you okay? I couldn't find you."

They entered the apartment and Ray turned the deadbolt behind them. "Cool, huh? Joe felt bad for me, so they did all this." The pair sat down on the new furniture.

"Tell me what happened. You said you couldn't tell me over the phone."

"How's your brother?"

"He's *very* happy. He said he owes you one."

"He showed up here all Mr. Tough guy and stuff. You know, I didn't tell you I'd seen him around. I think he was following me. He showed up at the bar one night and I had Jimmy throw him out. I think that's what really pissed him off." Ray rubbed her eyes. "He pushed his way in, took out a knife…I got him to put it down and I got it. I got him before he got me. I considered it a public service."

"Ray, you could've been the one that wound up dead. You couldn't get away?"

"I didn't want to. I told you I could take care of myself."

"Why didn't you tell me he had been hassling you?" Pete asked.

"Because there was nothing you could do. I handled it. Hey, I've got to take a shower. Hang out." Ray kissed him and hopped up from the futon. Once she was in the bathroom, Pete sat back and clicked on the television. His attention strayed from the tube as he looked around the clean apartment imagining what took place. The rumor was that there was blood everywhere the pig had bled out. He was glad Ray was alright. He wondered how she learned to handle a knife and what else she was capable of.

Ray emerged from the shower wrapped in a familiar, white robe. "Hey, do you want some food? My neighbors felt bad for me. They made all this stuff."

They feasted on microwaved lasagna, then collapsed onto the futon. Ray lost her robe. The black laptop sat idle on the floor in the corner of room buried beneath stacks of magazines.

The next day Ray returned from her most recent espionage trip, exhausted. It took longer than expected because the guy who hired her was a wreck. Sent from a mutual acquaintance, a guy who she thought to be in his forties, hired her to break into his wife's computer. Convinced she was having an affair, he wanted proof. Ray followed him to a home and parked past it, not wanting to draw attention to the house, and met the guy in the garage. As soon as they entered the house, the guy started pacing. They were married for ten years, blah, blah, blah. Ray didn't care to hear his life story. The perils of working with others. She suggested they call the "investigation" off, but that only got him more upset. He led her to the home office of his wife and she got to work. Ray hit many blocks. Some, she herself would use if she needed to hide something on a computer. But that's why Ray did not do any business on her account. Email never went away. It was always out there somewhere. The man rocked back and forth, fearing his wife would come home and find them. At one point, he yelled at Ray to hurry up. She stopped working.

"Get a grip!" she told him or she was out of there. Finally, Ray broke into the hard drive and opened up all sorts of information. The few emails she saw were all directed to what appeared to be another female. The guy confirmed it to be a close family friend. There was talk of money, and when and how she was going to ditch her husband. They were milking the business she shared with him. She planned to leave him debt ridden and take off with this 'friend.' The guy went berserk. Ray let him rant for five minutes and then brought him back to task.

"Do you want to confront her or do you want to beat her at her own game?"

The man was all ears.

"Look, tell your wife you have some great news. You were offered a buy-out from a large company. They are going to audit the business to see if it looks as good as they think. If it's healthy, you guys will make a killing. This way, your wife will have to put back all of the assets if she wants a clean and easy payday. When everything is back in place, freeze the accounts and hand over copies of this stuff, as well as her computer…as evidence of fraud. You may be able take her for everything. You can even choose to clean out the business yourself."

The man watched as Ray showed him how to get back into her email and computer system. She even set up a program to forward all email to his account. He paid Ray more than her agreed fee. A tip. She just saved him a fortune.

Now, back at her apartment, she leaned over the sink and removed the brown contact lens. Her unique green eyes, red from the disturbance, were just too much of a flag. She flopped onto the futon and turned on the television. The remote slipped out of her hand. She bent down to pick it up and saw the laptop under a pile of magazines. "Oh yeah…" she said out loud.

Her fingers and brain worked slower than usual due to the long day. She found her way in and sifted through. Besides the stuff that Pete took over, the primary user of the machine appeared to be someone named Kate.

The late television shows were finishing for the night when Ray and Pete decided to get some sleep.

"I'm telling you Ray, from what I saw in the paper, they think I did it."

"So, what are you going to do? Go to the police and tell them you've been stealing and hanging around, but you didn't kill anyone? Forget about it. It doesn't matter."

"Guess so. But someone did kill that person and dump them, whoever it is."

"And the police will figure it out. They're not that stupid, all the time. That's a small town. They have nothing else to do. There's nothing putting you there, right?"

"No. I never took anything from the house. I got rid of everything from Hollis, except…the laptop. That's the only thing I ever kept."

Ray looked over at the black computer sitting on top of the rug. "Yeah, we should dump it. I'll take care of it."

"I feel bad for the woman who lives there. She's the one whose husband just died in a plane crash. He was a doctor."

"She has plenty of money. She'll be fine." Ray pulled her t-shirt over her head removing the only piece of clothing she had on. Revealing her tight, petite physique, she announced, "I'm ready for bed." This brought a smile to Pete's face. He pulled off his shirt and unzipped his jeans, ready for fun with Ray.

"Hey, it doesn't look like you'll even have a scar where Chaser cut you!"

Ray ran her fingers down the center of her breastbone. There remained only a pink mark. "Nah…no scar. It wasn't deep enough."

Mel entered the conference room and scanned the room. She picked out Brendan in his new black suit, blue shirt and tie and passed him a note. Shelly shot daggers from her eyes at both of them. Jared continued speaking. Brendan motioned to Mel to leave. He held the note in his hand, rubbing it between his fingers. It was a short note, but it could mean so many things. *Kyle Mercer, urgent.*

The meeting dripped along. Brendan sat, not removing his hands from the note. He couldn't wait any longer. As they took up the last topic on the agenda, Brendan rose and excused himself from the room. Angus, pale as ever, nodded with approval. Shelly scowled.

He walked to his office at the same pace he did every day. He stopped at Mel's desk. "What is this regarding?"

"Oh, I thought you'd remember…the widow of that surgeon from your town. Her number is on the note. Do you want me to call?"

"What's this about?"

"I don't know. She sounded upset and said it was an emergency."

"Fine…I'll call her now." He entered his office, closing the door behind him. The attorney paced before sitting at his desk. He loosened his silk tie and pushed the buttons on his large desk phone. He picked up the receiver as it rang, instead of leaving the speaker on that he usually spoke into.

Kyle answered. "Hello?"

"Hello, Mrs. Mercer, this is Brendan Reed returning your call. What can I do for you? My assistant said it was some sort of emergency."

"I didn't know who else to call. This horrible thing has happened at my house. I think I need your help." Kyle paused. "The police are here. They found the remains of a body in my pool."

Brendan pressed the phone to his forehead. He did not expect to be pulled into this mess this early on and from this end. Not directly. An innocent man…what would he have said to her if he had no idea who the corpse was? Think!

"Mrs. Mercer, I'm not a criminal attorney any longer. But, if you need some assistance, I will see what I can do."

"Oh thank you. Would you come here? Now?"

With only a slight hesitation, Brendan responded, "I'm on my way."

Twenty-Six

David stepped closer to the crime scene. The pool smelled like swamp water. With the cover removed, the pool exposed dark green water. Crime lab technicians dressed in plastic yellow suits gathered in the pool with masks to scour the bottom for even the smallest item of evidence that could be retrieved and bagged. Underwater pictures were taken of the scene by two techs. When all other tasks were completed, it was time to move the bones. The team worked at a snail's pace loading them onto a tarp with handles. Graceful manners were lost. As much respect as possible was given to the deceased, but the task was awkward. The workers lifted it from the pool, jostling the load from side to side. For the first time, David got a closer look. It was rough.

The lead scene investigator knelt next to the collection and through his mask, spoke into a handheld recorder. He motioned for his assistant to take pictures. He bagged what looked to be a clot of long blond hair, maybe, and leaves covered by a slimy film like clear jelly. He watched as the pieces were slid into bags. He recognized some fingernails and what was left of a zipper. Most likely she knew her killer, but did her killer live here?

Matt approached. "Some lawyer is on his way. I don't know who he is, but Kyle is petrified. I can't say I blame her. She's in shock. I'm sure that he'll just tell her to cooperate."

"Did you talk to Kyle about staying someplace else until this is over?

"No, but I'll take her to my house. She can't stay here." Matt re-entered the house to find Kyle sitting in the living room with her cat. "How are you holding up?"

Kyle smirked. "Besides losing my husband and finding bones in my pool, I'd say I was fine."

"Sarcasm's a good sign. You need to pack up a few things and come stay with me. It's going to take a few days for them to work the scene."

"Matt, I don't want to stay here either, but I can't stay with you. You and the kids are allergic to the cat and dog and besides, you don't have room. I'm not sure what I'm going to do. I can't go to a motel with them."

"Just come and stay with us. We'll be fine."

"Matt, I am not going to make you all miserable."

"Well, you can't stay here. Let me make a call." He pulled out his cell phone and walked away. He stood in the window, talking and watching the activity in the backyard.

A few minutes passed and he was back. He informed her that he arranged for her to stay at a nearby "extended stay" motel. He remembered another cop staying there with his family while his home was repaired after a fire. They kept their dog with them. "That'll work. Don't you think?"

"Fine...I'll get some things together." She started to walk away and stopped. "What do you pack to flee your own home?" She swept up the remaining glass on the floor, then holding on tight to Pumpkin, went upstairs.

Packing for Pumpkin was easy and hard: food, a carrier and litter. But, something easy to use as a litter box would not be simple. With little ability to focus, the task seemed monumental. "Something that will hold litter," she said out loud.

In her closet, she found a clear, plastic storage container full of sweaters. Kyle dumped the contents onto the floor. It wouldn't be pretty, but it would work.

She pulled her toothbrush from the stand, which still contained two. She could not resist looking out the window into the backyard. It was her first observation. She saw David and other people hunched over something. Suddenly all stood back for a photographer, clearing the view. The sun hit the area, highlighting the site. Kyle gagged. A tarp was stretched over the lawn with a collection of large and small bones. Gloved and masked technicians fished through mounds of leaves. Kyle jumped back. Her eyes filled. This thing had been in her pool for months. She dropped to the toilet and vomited. Only coffee came up. She had to leave.

In an overnight bag, she threw a toothbrush, underwear, a t-shirt, socks and jeans. Nothing seemed very important. Before leaving the room, she took off her wedding ring and put it in the jewelry box.

She entered the kitchen, juggling her bag and the kitty supplies. Matt rose and took them out of her hands. Brendan Reed stood looking back at her.

"Hi, Mr. Reed...thanks for coming," Kyle said.

Brendan nodded. His stomach felt like a wrench tightening each time he moved. He wanted to get out of here as soon as possible. After some awkward moments and a deep swallow, he spoke. "Matt, would you give us a few minutes alone?"

Matt's eyes opened wide. "Kyle, do you want me to leave?"

"Maybe that would be best."

It took a moment for the words to register. Matt was shocked. He knew her better than she knew herself. He just loved lawyers. Finally, he threw his hands up and went outside.

Brendan suggested they speak in another room to get away from the obvious commotion in the backyard. Kyle led him to the living room with a view of police cruisers and emergency vehicles.

Brendan removed his black suit jacket and put it over the side of the chair. "Matt is an old friend?" He said this as more of a question than a statement.

"Yes."

"Well, I'd advise you to remember that he is a policeman, first and foremost. Speaking with me is protected under attorney/client privilege. Anything you say to Matt, is not." Brendan paused for effect. "You can trust me. Why don't you tell me what you know."

"I don't know anything. I came home and found police all over my yard." Her eyes filled and she pushed the water away. "I had no idea what was going on."

"If you don't know anything about this, then you have no reason not to answer anything the police ask. There must be something else." Brendan fished and hoped. Everyone had some type of dirty laundry.

"I just don't know how to handle this. It's such a nightmare. Kyle fought to push the images in her backyard from her mind. "How did it get here? What could have happened?" Kyle said this, but knew Brendan had no answer he could give.

"Try and remain calm. This will all get figured out in time." Brendan put his hand on her shoulder.

"I guess what I need to know is what I should tell them." Brendan was all ears. Kyle looked up, straight into his eyes. "I think my husband was having an affair before he died. What if…"

"Are you concerned about your husband's actions or your son's?"

"Jeffrey couldn't hurt a fly. He doesn't even know anything about this yet. I need to talk to him."

"What makes you think your husband was having an affair?" This news could only help muck up the water as far as Brendan was concerned. Jackpot.

"I found condoms in his luggage. We didn't use them. When I think back on it, he was never home. He came in at all hours. I only reached him through his cell or his pager when he was out. He could have been anywhere. The wife is always the last to know, right? I feel like a fool."

"He was a surgeon, wasn't he?" Brendan did not want to jump onto the bandwagon too soon.

"I never questioned his fidelity until I found the condoms. Now they've found a body, I think I should be questioning everything!"

"I understand. Why don't you wait and see what the police find out. Once they identify the remains that should give them a direction. For now, I don't think they need to know anything about your suspicions. So you are aware, they do have enough probable cause to get search warrants for your home and records. You were planning on leaving for a few days?"

Kyle explained where she'd be. "I don't know if I ever want to come back here."

"You've already told the police you have no idea who this could be, correct?"

"Yes. But, they said they want to question Jeffrey. Is that okay?"

"Yes, but I'll let them know a meeting will be arranged through me. I want to speak with Jeffrey first. To prepare him… all right?"

"Yes. I still have your card."

"I'll take good care of you and your son," Brendan said.

Kyle gave him her cell phone number and promised to make sure it was on. Brendan rose to leave. "I will let you know if, at some point, you need to retain a criminal attorney, but I don't see the need at this point. You have been through enough. I will be happy to do everything I can, at no cost. But, please be sure to tell me everything. Otherwise, I won't be able to give you the best advice. Call me, day or night. I will be in touch. I'll speak to the police on my way out. Why don't you leave as soon as you can?" Brendan placed his hands on her shoulders. In her stocking feet, Kyle was more than a couple inches shorter than him. She angled her neck up to look him in the eye.

"Everything will be all right." He gave her a reassuring look. "You really didn't need any more stress." Brendan ran his hand across one side of her head, pressing on her hair.

Kyle felt a great sense of relief that someone other than her would be dealing with the nightmare.

Brendan exited the house and looked upon the recovery scene. He glanced only a moment towards the pool and the tarp. Yellow suits and uniformed officers speckled the lawn. He couldn't resist a peek, but he saw only edges of what looked like bones. An officer approached.

Brendan composed himself. "Do you know who is in charge?"

"The Chief or Dave...just a minute." He left and returned with one of the few people not in uniform.

Brendan saw David's badge on his belt. He put his hand out to him. "Hello, I'm Brendan Reed. And you are?"

"Lieutenant Linscot, Hollis P.D."

"I will be representing Mrs. Mercer and her son. If you have any questions, please contact me." He handed David a card.

"We'll be getting warrants."

"Of course. Just keep me informed...of everything, please." He kept his back to the activity in the yard. Brendan let out a deep breath, when he reached the sanctity of his car. Being pulled to the inside of this would gain him the best view possible. Let the games begin.

Matt helped Kyle carry things to her car. On her way out, her eyes caught David with his notepad, writing, being a police officer.

She followed Matt to a motel that looked more like a condominium development with much of it concealed by thick pine trees. Matt accompanied her into the office and up to her unit. He opened the door and looked around. The two of them carried her things inside. Pumpkin cried from the carrier.

"I've got to go. I have been out of my office for most of two days, now. Let me see your cell phone." He checked it to be sure it was on. "Make sure you keep it charged. I'll call you later. Have you spoken to Jeff, yet?"

"No, but I will do nothing else until I find him."

Maggie hopped onto one of the beds, tail wagging. Loose, Pumpkin ran under a bed.

Matt came to her and gave her a big hug. "Everything will be okay. I promise." He kissed her forehead. "Lock the door behind me."

Kyle did as he asked. After setting up a litter box in the bath-room, she sat on a bed and dialed every phone number she had for Jeffrey. She got an answer at Lindsay's parents' house. Lindsay's mother informed her that the kids were out on the boat for the day, but she expected them back within an hour or so. She would have Jeffrey call as soon as he got in. Was everything okay? Kyle said, 'fine', not knowing how best to describe the morbid day.

Jeffrey called as the sun was setting. Kyle instructed him to drive back—now—and where to meet her. There had been an accident at the house. She said she'd explain more when he re-turned. He should be there in a couple of hours.

Pumpkin hissed when Kyle retrieved her from under the bed and shut her back in the carrier. She leashed Maggie and exited the room. Whether she liked it or not, she needed to give Maggie a walk and find food for the both of them. The lights were on in the parking lot, which held few vehicles. Right away, she noticed a familiar truck facing her. She walked up to it.

"Am I under surveillance?" Kyle was only half joking, but she did smile.

David looked back at her. "I just wanted to keep an eye out. I don't understand what's going on at your house."

"Neither do I."

"Where are you going?"

"Walking the dog and then grabbing something to eat. I'm not very hungry, but I've got to feed her."

"Why don't you let me drive you?" He jumped out of the truck.

Kyle protested, waving a hand back and forth.

"I promise I won't ask you any questions Mr. Reed would object to."

"Don't you ever go home?"

David shrugged and took the dog's leash. The walk was short and then David drove the three to a small restaurant with outdoor picnic tables. Kyle insisted on paying for her food. Quite happy with this sleepover thing, Maggie gobbled down her dinner, a steak tip sandwich, then finished the majority of Kyle's chicken kabobs.

"Oh, I've got to get back. Jeffrey will be there. I don't even know where to begin." David didn't respond. He rubbed his red eyes.

Kyle took notice of the circles under the red eyes. "You look beat."

"It's been a long couple days. I've got to tell you I was worried when we couldn't reach you."

Jeffrey was leaning up against her SUV when they returned to the motel.

"I'll see you later," David said, let them out and drove off.

Maggie dashed to Jeffrey. Kyle greeted her son and they entered their temporary home. They took seats at the small pine table with round chairs, which took up most of the area in the kitchenette. Maggie attached herself to Jeffrey's leg. Pumpkin, now free, sat on Kyle's lap. Kyle began the slow explanation of the discovery of a body, or really remains, in their swimming pool. She told her son everything she knew, which did not take long.

"Jeffrey, the police want to ask you some questions. It's all routine."

"Ask me? What can I tell them? I have no idea what happened."

"They asked me. I want you to think about anything that you may have heard, or something odd that someone asked you. Did anyone make any comments about us being away? Or ask how long we'd be gone? Can you think of anyone who's missing?" Seeing Jeffrey confirmed Kyle's first impression. Jeffrey knew nothing about this. She was upset with herself for even needing to be reassured.

"Don't worry about it. Mr. Reed, the attorney I told you about, will be with us. They'll ask questions. You'll just tell them the truth. Then you'll be off to school and this will all get taken care of."

Her son sat looking at her like a deer in the headlights. He squirmed in the chair and then pulled out his cell phone. "I'm calling Lindsay."

"Do you have to?" Kyle asked, then shook her head. "Forget it. Of course you can tell her." Even though this was not the kind of news Kyle wanted to share, she realized it would not be kept a secret. Jeffrey walked outside to make his call.

Kyle picked up a paper cup and filled it with cold water. The cool liquid hit her parched throat. She rubbed her forehead. This long day needed to be over soon. She picked up the remote and turned on the television. The eleven o'clock news was underway. The weather was predicted to be cooler this week. Kyle kicked off her shoes and pulled her legs underneath her. The news anchor began to speak about a breaking story. "Today in Hollis, New Hampshire, remains of a body were discovered. Reports are not clear, however it is believed that the unidentified female was murdered on the property and discovered by a worker at the home." A picture of Kyle's home flashed onto the screen. "The home belongs to the Mercer family. Dr. Mercer was killed in a plane crash while traveling in Italy this past June. His family did not accompany him on the trip." Kyle snapped off the TV. She leaped up for her cell phone. "Matt, it's me. Did you see the news?"

"I'm sorry. I should have warned you. Leave the TV and radio off. It will wear off in a couple days." Matt stayed on the phone with her for a few minutes. She told him that Jeffrey was back and that she'd be calling Brendan in the morning.

"They can ask him some questions and then I'm getting him out of here. This is a nightmare." Kyle got off the phone when Jeffrey returned. He walked in with the same dazed look that he went out with.

"Lindsay said there was a story on the news about all this. Mom, are people going to think that we had something to do with this?"

"No, honey, I just spoke to Matt. He said this will all blow over. You'll be at school and no one there will know anything about this. It will be okay." She stood face to face with him. "We're just having a bad few days. I'm so sorry."

"Mom, this is more than a couple bad days." Smiles broke out on both of their faces.

The two retired onto the beds. Maggie stretched out next to Jeffrey. Kyle on the other with the still-miffed Pumpkin next to her. The family together.

After a brief catnap, Kyle woke, uncomfortable on the old mattress. She rose and pulled back the heavy lined curtain and looked out at the night sky. Moonlight filled the room and illuminated Jeffrey sleeping, his face filled with peace. Kyle wanted him away from this mess.

Jason having an affair was still a fresh wound. But kill someone? It just wasn't in him. Of course, two months ago she would have sworn her husband was faithful. The one in a million perfect, devoted husband. What else could she have been wrong about?

In the morning, Jeffrey was awake when Kyle returned from walking Maggie. She told him to take a shower and they would go have breakfast. She called Brendan Reed on his cell phone. She told him what Jeffrey told her, nothing. Brendan said he would arrange a short meeting with the police for later today, at their motel.

Brendan contacted Lt. David Linscott and set up a meeting at four that afternoon. He would be at the Inn by three to speak with Jeffrey. He sat back in his soft leather chair, with his hands folded behind his head. He faced out the large windows of his office, but saw none of the view. His thoughts jumped over many calculations. He hoped the police search would yield some type of questions regarding Jason. Many times he witnessed police investigations turning up 'issues.' Brendan informed many of his clients: If they look hard enough, they'll find something. It might not be what they expected, but it may still be a problem. After hearing Kyle's concerns, he was hopeful that Jason's past may not be as squeaky clean as he first thought. The next few weeks of the investigation were crucial. He needed more questions to arise rather than answers. The attorney's plotting and planning was never more important. He couldn't place facts, but he could put the facts in place. He imagined how his clients felt when he told them there was nothing more he could do; they would just have to face the music. Confess and own up to the wrongdoing. Unacceptable. He refused to trash his entire life over one moment of bad judgment. Positioning and bracing himself for Kate's identification consumed his focus.

David Linscot hung up the phone and ended his conversation with the attorney. David would bet his badge that neither Kyle nor Jeffrey had anything to do with this murder. The formality of the dealing with an attorney was overkill. They really didn't need to be represented and protected from him. He felt certain the attorney had some other agenda. Probably the almighty dollar. There was talk that Kyle had inherited large sums of money.

David tapped his desk with his pen, reading the computer screen. He imputed the rough description they had to work with into the National Crime Information Computer (NCIC). His call to the crime scene investigator yielded at least something to work with: maybe female with what may be long light, or blonde, hair. The chemicals in the pool altered the color. The body obviously was in the pool for quite some time. But, he told David he would just have to wait a while for a full report.

The limited information yielded several hits. David expected as much with such vague information. He decided to first narrow the search to New England, as bodies are generally found not that far from where they were last seen. That brought the number lower. Narrowing the time frame down to missing persons less than two years cut the matches further. He ended up with two still-open cases. The first, a young female from the northern most part of the state had been reported missing and was a suspected runaway. She was only seventeen, but she was a dirty blonde. The report was filed after she did not return at Christmas. They suspected she took off to Canada with an older man;

there had been no leads since. The second was a young female from Boston. No apparent leads. David contacted the appropriate Police departments via email and let them know what was found and that they would be requesting DNA. He would scan the list again and again. He needed to identify this woman before he could figure out who killed her. Since the case now rested in the hands of the Attorney General, it was not required for David to continue his work. The State of New Hampshire enjoyed such a low homicide rate that the state's lead prosecutor handled all. It would receive the office's full attention as well as their complete bureaucracy and politics. David wanted answers.

The pool was closed in late September and opened now in August. Almost a year. The body could have been put in at any time. This morning at the station, David met with Bill, the owner of the pool maintenance company, and his assistant, Kevin. This was Kevin's first season of pool care. He found the work, out in the heat, overwhelming. On the day that Bill sent him to the Mercer's home in June to pull back the cover and add chemicals, it was a hot and humid. Instead of going to the Mercer's home, he chose to go to a friend's air conditioned home to rest. He figured no one would know if he actually did the work or not. Bill believed the pool was opened and re-stocked with chemicals by his assistant. Kevin expressed a great deal of remorse, having not completed his work. David felt they were telling the truth. He informed them State Police would also be questioning them.

This information cleared up a few things for David. It did not make sense that the pool was opened and someone did not notice a body or something wrong, in June. To be put in after June, did not fit with what the forensics leaned towards as a time frame. It appeared anyway that the body was deposited much earlier.

The struggle with the news media was underway. David and the Chief fielded calls all morning: all reporters looking for a scoop. One reporter got under David's skin. "I understand that an intruder had been seen on the property several times. Did the police have a description? Care to comment?"

"No. And where are you getting your information?" David asked.

"Girl's gotta protect her sources," was all she'd say. The investigator spent most of his day in front of his computer and on the phone. David left the station well before his 4 p.m. appointment, stopping at Kyle's first. He walked past the young officer on duty and stood in the back yard. The yellow police tape circled much of the yard and encompassed all of the pool. He could see inside the house. State Police, armed with a warrant, were finishing their search. A judge granted a narrow search, limiting it to evidence of a crime and materials, which could lead to an identification of the victim. David chose not to participate. He did not want to be going through Kyle's personal items. She would later feel violated and he did not want to be personally involved.

He walked through the backyard and entered the woods. After twenty feet, he stopped and looked back. The trees and brush around the yard and house provided excellent coverage. Whoever put that body there would be safe from detection, except for anyone inside of the home. David strolled the area, able to look close at the ground now that it was not covered with police. Spreading his search deeper into the woods, he came across two separate piles of cigarette butts.

He returned to the house and entered. He flagged down the first investigator he found. "Hey, I found a couple piles of butts in the woods. You got a camera and a bag?" The forensic investigator looked up from his bent knee where he peered under some large pieces of furniture.

"You never know what can roll under furniture." The young, nimble man popped up and collected his black case. "We were going to take a look outside next."

"Okay, but, I just want to show you this. I was called here on two occasions about someone in the woods watching the house."

David led him to the two sites to be collected. He watched as the young officer clicked off several pictures and removed the trash with gloved hands, putting it into clear bags. "Thanks. Hey, have you found anything in the house?" David asked.

"Not really. We're going to take some phone and bank records with us, but so far, nothing saying 'regarding body in pool.'

David drove to the meeting with Kyle and her attorney.

He pulled up to the motel complex and spotted the SUV. Parked next to it, a sparkling convertible Mercedes. The lawyer. He knocked on the door. Kyle opened it and let him in. Seated already at the small table were Jeffrey and Brendan.

Twenty-Seven

Aided by years of training, Brendan forced himself to appear relaxed. Sitting in a room with a policeman asking questions about Kate's death was a strain, but with the questions directed at someone else, it was tolerable. It also gave him all the information he needed.

"Good afternoon, Lieutenant. Jeffrey and Kyle will answer any questions you have." Brendan sat back and listened. Hearing earlier about the reported stranger in the woods was a bonus. All previously reported and documented. This could be all the muck he needed.

David took out his notepad and went to work. The answers did not surprise him. No, they had no idea who the poor person was. No, they could not think of anything unusual, other than their backyard visitor. David asked questions and studied their reactions. "When was the last time the pool was open? Did anyone offer to watch your house while you were going to be away?" This was getting him nowhere, but making the high paid attorney richer so David cut his questions short. He told them he would be in touch with other questions as they came up.

"There's one more thing. We exercised a warrant today. Your home was searched," David said.

"You searched the house! Looking for what?" Kyle asked.

"Not us, State Police." David paused to be sure Kyle heard him. "The scope was limited. I will supply you with a list of anything taken."

"Kyle," Brendan spoke up. "That's to be expected. Lieutenant, you will supply me with a list as well, please." Brendan, ever the thoughtful attorney, wanted to stay abreast of the situation.

"Of course," said David. He rose from the chair. "Thank you for your cooperation."

Kyle walked outside with David. "Thanks. I don't think that was too bad for Jeffrey," she said. Her eyes were deep and big, almost as big as the circles beneath them.

"It's really not my place, but you really don't need to have a hired gun at this point. Ask Matt."

"Oh, Brendan isn't charging me, at least he hasn't mentioned it. I offered."

A lawyer who works for free! David's concern grew.

"How long is your son staying?"

"I'm sending him away in the morning. He's going back to the Cape and then off to school next week. I want him out of here."

"I understand. I'll be in touch." David stalled his walking away and turned back to Kyle. "You know how to reach me." He tapped the cell phone on his belt. "Mine's always on."

The comment brought a slight smile to her face. Brendan opened the door and spoke. "Everything all set, Kyle?"

David watched as she returned inside, with the charitable attorney.

Brendan made his exit a short time later. He asked Kyle to step outside with him. "How are you doing, really?" Brendan stood inches away, making it impossible for her to miss his Armani aftershave. He placed his hands around her upper arms. Cool air brushed passed them. "Are you getting any rest? You look exhausted."

She had not considered how she looked over the last few days. A mirror might be a scary place. "I haven't been sleeping much. But, that's not..." She did not want to go into any more of her problems. "But under the circumstances..."

"You poor thing. This summer has been quite an ordeal. I wish there was more I could do." He paused. "You know, with

Jeffrey leaving tomorrow…why don't we go grab a bite to eat Friday evening? It will be good for both of us."

"Oh, I don't know…I don't think I'd be very good company."

"I won't take no for an answer. I'll come by around seven." Brendan left before Kyle had a chance to respond.

He needed to get as close as possible. After Kate's body was identified, circumstances would change.

Through the dark, Kyle watched her son sleep with the dog curled up next to him on his bed. Familiar shadows blanketed the area. Bizarre that they had a spacious home and here they slept, in a cramped room. Pumpkin remained unsettled with no good spots to curl up in and hide. She scoured at Kyle and hissed on occasion. She wanted to go home. Kyle concurred in spirit, but wasn't sure what they'd be going back to. The night was longer than usual.

Kyle reached over from her sitting position on the full size, strange bed and picked up the cat. "It will be okay, baby." She petted the moody animal. Sitting up straighter, she stared at the moon, visible between the break in the drapes. She waited for sunrise. Tonight, she fell on the losing side of the battle in her brain. What was happening in her life? The chaos and violence must in some way be her fault. If not resulting from her actions, then from inaction. Had she coasted through her years in an apathy that led to this? And what did all this mean for her son? What twisted wreckage was now left as his parents' legacy? She could look back and see that maybe her marriage wasn't perfect, but this! She always prided herself on being independent, but was she really? Or had she simply fooled herself into believing she had it all? She stuffed her head in a pillow to muffle the sounds of her crying. Her body convulsed with pain, unleashed from weeks of oppression.

The daylight went fast. Jeffrey and Kyle shopped for clothing and other items Jeffrey needed. All things that were waiting for him in his room, but for now unavailable. "You go back to the Cape and try not to worry. This will all get straightened out," Kyle said as they strolled through the trendy teenage clothing store.

"Mom, are you sure you're going to be okay?"

"Positive!" Kyle cursed the wetness that continued to come to her eyes at the insistence that her son leave, but she wouldn't have it any other way. She packed him up and sent him away, first to the Cape, to a place where people weren't aware that his home was a crime scene. Well, at least besides Lindsay's parents. Then in a few days, she would meet him up at his new residence at college.

Brendan Reed pulled up in his shiny car at 7 p.m. All the way to the restaurant he chatted away, never mentioning the case. He took Kyle to what he described as his favorite Italian restaurant, Cucina Banca, which resided inside an old stone building in downtown Nashua. The interior was crisp and clean with simple white tablecloths and mahogany chairs. The Chianti served did not come from fat bottomed glass, but rather from sleek dark bottles. Finely crafted smells filled the air. The owner, a rotund Italian gentleman, came to the table and greeted Brendan.

Kyle ate small bits of food that she did not taste. She sipped from a single glass of wine and left it half full. Brendan was fine company and did not comment on her lack of enthusiasm. He seemed to barely notice. He elicited a small laugh from her after many failed stories.

"It's nice to see you smile," Brendan said. "How's your dinner?"

"Oh, it's fine." Kyle twirled some of the lobster pesto pasta on her fork.

"Is there anything I can do for you?" Brendan flashed his blue eyes.

"There's really nothing else you can do, unless you can tell me whose body that is and how it ended up in my pool."

Brendan gulped down wine. "I'm sure it will all get worked out in time."

After dinner, Kyle felt relief when the owner came back to chat. He drew Brendan's attention. Kyle watched his hands motion as he spoke. Starched cuffs of his deep blue shirt dressed his wrists and contrasted with his dark suit. It appeared to be fine clothing. The black one-piece dress that Kyle purchased today at a discount store and pulled the tags off of only a couple hours ago, paled in comparison. Kyle did not even wear jewelry. Her head bobbed from fatigue. Her eyes felt weighted.

Brendan took a good look at his dining companion and announced that it was time to go. Back at the Inn, he insisted on walking her to the door. She fumbled with her key into the old lock and opened the door. Unsure of proper etiquette for a dinner with your attorney representing you after your husband's death and subsequent body is found on your property, Kyle did not invite him in. He took her hand between his and wished her a good night's sleep.

Kyle watched the silver car depart the lot. Maggie begged to go out. She slipped her feet into her sneakers and headed to the door. A slight drizzle started and mixed in with the cool night air, chilling her skin. She considered going back for a jacket, but Maggie bolted ahead of her. She picked up the pace going down the stairs with the leash in her hand but without the dog attached. She kicked herself for not using it. The dog was well behaved, until lately.

Kyle trailed after her to the side of the building. Maggie's nose worked overtime. She was hot on the trail of an exotic animal, or so she thought. The canine flipped to her back and rolled on the patch of ground that held the delectable scent. From previous adventures, Kyle recognized the behavior to be a smelly one. God knows she also did not want to revisit the skunk fiasco!

"Maggie, GET UP!" Kyle yelled. The precipitation turned to rain as Kyle closed in on the dog. "Maggie, come. We're going in. You don't have to pee." The lab did not hear a thing. Her head pointed into the patch of woods surrounding the back of the parking lot where the lighting ended. She took off like a teen getting the freedom of a car for the first time.

Several yells from Kyle went unheeded. The dog flew down a small opening to the woods. Barely a path, the opening was not wide enough for Kyle to pass without being hit by branches sticking out. Her arms gathered scratches as she pushed her way in. The rain burst and came hard. Thick trees blocked some of the water, but the gushing rain grew loud. She heard Maggie running ahead with leaves crackling under her feet. She kept moving, shivering with every step. The wet leaves reflected bits of light, but with the cloud cover there was little moonlight.

Mud under her feet rose up around the sides of her sneakers. Disgusted, she paused in her tracks. She should just turn around and let the dog find her way back. But Kyle couldn't get the sight of the nearby highway out of her head.

Kyle turned her head around looking behind her. She heard something. Had Maggie gone full circle? She stood still and listened. The sounds were muffled by the heavy rain. Kyle wiped her face, dripping with water. Footsteps! She heard the deliberate movements of a person, not an animal. Shit. Who would be out here, at night, in the rain? Is this what Maggie was interested in?

Her heart pounded. Adrenaline kicked in. She pushed through the branches, closing her eyes at times, to move as fast as she could. She wanted to find the other end of this path and Maggie. Her feet sloshed in her mud filled sneakers. Bits of dirt sprayed her nylons and the hem of her dress. The weight slowed her down. She tried to calm herself by repeating that there was a simple explanation and she would feel silly later. However, unidentified human remains lingered in her thoughts. She gulped for air.

After what seemed like hours, but only minutes, a soaked and winded Kyle found the other end of the path. It ended at the back of a large cement block building with sparse lighting. The lot was empty, except for some out of commission trucks rotting away at the other end. She made out a tail moving at the end of one. She raced across the desolate pavement. Rain washed over her.

When she got close to Maggie, she resisted the urge to call out, not wanting to draw more attention. She gripped the dog's tail. Maggie spun around. Kyle leashed her collar and pulled her behind the truck, getting them both out of sight. She looked into the dog's eyes, and saved her words for later.

Squatting in an endless puddle, Kyle peered under the truck to the opening of the woods. She and Maggie were concealed by a set of large wheels. She waited.

Dark shoes and pants that came out at the edge of the woods did nothing to help make an identification. She stood and leaned, getting ready to take a better look when she heard her name being called. She thought she recognized the voice, but did look to confirm. Her head poked out to give her a look at a profile of David, peering in the opposite direction. She called back.

"David…" She took a deep breath and emerged from her hiding place.

He turned and rushed over. He too, was soaked, but at least he wore a jacket. His face dripped.

"Kyle, what are you doing?" David elevated his voice to be heard over the pounding noise.

"I was just letting the dog out."

"Tough night." David put his jacket over her shoulders. He took the leash and pointed in the direction for them to return to the motel. They walked around to the front of the cement block building to the main road. They were soon at the front entrance and inside Kyle's room.

She stood and shivered. Her teeth chattered while she spoke. "Maggie took off. I went after her… I heard someone. I panicked." She dropped her head. "I know it seems ridiculous."

"It's okay. I saw you go into the woods and I didn't want you out there alone." David held her shoulders. "Why don't you get into some dry clothes?"

Kyle entered the only other room, the bath. She pulled on the sweatpants and shirt that hung on the back of the door. She used them to sleep in each night. Hot water splashed on her hands and face helped stop the shivering. A towel removed some of the excess water from her hair. A wet rat looked better.

"So, you were spying on me again?"

"I thought I'd make sure you were okay."

"Do you want a cup of tea? I don't have anything else," Kyle offered.

"Tea sounds great." David removed his wet shoes. His jacket hung on a back of a chair. Water drops rolled off onto the floor. He used a towel Kyle offered to pat dry his clothes, but he was soaked through.

They sat on the couch in front of the two beds. "So how are you holding up? This must be hard."

Pumpkin decided to make an appearance, hopping up on the middle cushion of the couch, between them. She brushed up against David but feeling the wet leg of his jeans, she moved away.

"I'm about ready for this to all be over. Have you found out anything?" Kyle wrapped a blanket around her back.

"No, but I have some leads. You look exhausted."

"Do you think Jason killed this girl?" Her voice cracked and she cleared her throat. The words were like stones.

"I don't know. But, we'll figure it out. Have you remembered anything that may help?"

"No." She rubbed her eyes with her hand.

"Are you getting any rest?"

"Hey, you've got bags under your eyes too, now."

It was true. David put in long days and often slept in his truck outside the motel. "Let's see if there's a ballgame on."

Kyle switched on the TV with the remote. Surfing the few channels offered, she found a Red Sox game after a short search. "My son says they are going to win the wildcard again this year."

"That's the only way they can get into the playoffs, most of the time anyway." David gave her a brief description of the playoff draw and the woes of the burdened pitching staff. Kyle curled up in the blanket. It was not long before her eyes were heavy and she laid her head against the back of the couch. She dozed off. David rose and turned off the lights and the television. He returned to Kyle and sat down. He eased her head down onto a pillow in the center. This served the same purpose and beat the hell out of sleeping in a truck again.

In the early hours of the morning, Kyle woke to a wet sensation pressing to the side of her face. A look provided the answer. Her head was across David's lap and his pants were still damp. Her hands were around his waist. One of his arms fell next to her back. He was breathing heavy. If she moved, would she wake him? And then he would leave and she would be alone again. She decided to let him sleep and enjoy the small sense of security, wet and temporary as it may be.

Her hands were against him and she allowed herself to enjoy the feel of his body, to touch him. Her mind ran. What would he be like to kiss? How did his shoulders feel? Images of lovemaking with Jason flashed, before her imagining David in his place…she drifted off. Her face tucked in his waist.

Twenty-Eight

At 6 a.m. Maggie whined at the door. The noise stirred the sleeping lump inside a twisted blanket. Kyle uncoiled her arms and moved away. She looked at David, stretching and opening his eyes.

"Good morning," he said.

"Good morning." Kyle smiled and popped up from the couch. She stood. "I um…I fell asleep," she said avoiding eye contact.

David reached up, took her hand and said, "Its okay." For a moment, she considered sitting down and wrapping her hands back around him and having a dream.

"I've got to take the dog out…with a leash this time." Kyle moved away.

She exited the room, leaving David sitting on the couch. He got up to fix his clothes and use the bathroom. His jeans and shirt were still damp, pasted to him. His socks stuck to his feet. He was putting on his shoes when Kyle's cell phone rang.

She returned to the room with a happy pooch. Maggie ran to David. She enjoyed the big sleepover.

"Do you want to get some breakfast?" David's words were interrupted by the cell phone. "Oh, it rang while you were outside, too."

Kyle picked up the phone and stopped the noise. "Oh, hi Matt." She locked eyes with David. "Sure, I can do breakfast. Where are you? Okay, I'll see you soon." She closed the phone. "Matt's on his way."

David picked up his damp jacket and went to the door. "I'd better be going. Thanks for the tea." He ran his fingers over his dark crew-cut hair.

Kyle did not know exactly what to say. It had been forever since she said an awkward goodbye to a guy at 6:45 a.m. She felt like she was back in college shuffling Jason out of her room. Just what she needed, regression. She shrugged.

"To serve and protect," David said and smiled. He pointed to his cell phone on his hip. "Anytime…"

The door closed behind David. Kyle flopped down onto the couch. She pulled up the blanket over her, hugging it and remembering. She looked over at Maggie and said, "Good dog!"

She stayed on the couch until Matt knocked. The time elapsed so fast, she hoped Matt and David did not pass each other. That was a conversation she didn't need to have.

Matt and Kyle found an old diner on the main street. A shiny bubble of metal blossomed from the mouth of a brick building. The original neon sign remained on top, but no longer lit: *Harding Diner*. When they entered every patron turned in their direction. Kyle assumed it was Matt's uniform, but soon realized it was also the fact that everyone else in the place was on a first name basis, staff and customers. The apron-clad waitress came with coffee. Betsy, as her nametag read, wore black sensible shoes, thick, support pantyhose and her hair whipped up into a bun, frozen by several cans of Breck hairspray last week.

"What can I get for you folks?" She smiled at Matt. "Our hash is the best. Everyone raves about it."

Matt was about to say yes, but Kyle stared him down. He could eat healthy when he was with her. He never gained weight, but his cholesterol crept up.

"I'll have an egg white omelet and wheat toast," Kyle said.

"I'll have the same," Matt said.

Betsy wrote the order and stuck the pencil back into her hair as she walked away.

"Okay…ever hear the expression when in Rome? Egg whites

at a greasy spoon?" Matt pleaded.

"Save it. You have four small children. You don't have the luxury."

Matt knew to stop a losing argument with Kyle. "So, how are you doing? Getting any sleep?"

"As a matter of fact, I slept better last night. Any chance you brought encouraging news?" Kyle replied and gulped down strong coffee, her main source of sustenance lately.

"No, I haven't heard from Dave. I'm going to give him a call when I get through with court this morning. I'll let you know what he says."

"Great." Kyle choked a bit on her coffee and coughed. She wondered if David was out of his wet clothes yet, and pictured the process. "I spoke to my mom again yesterday. She's feeling a little better. I think I convinced her to stay home for now. She thinks she should be here with me. But, I told her you were taking care of everything and any day she'd read in the paper that the case was solved."

Matt eyes opened wide.

"Okay, I lied. I didn't want her to worry any more than necessary."

"Kyle, it will get figured out. As soon as they make an ID, the list will get smaller."

"Well, I'm tired of this living out of a motel with animals. I think I'm going back home."

"Are you sure? I wish you'd stay put until we find out who did what to who."

"The house is alarmed and I have Maggie. I think I'm safer at home. Besides, I rarely sleep. Being there will be gross, but I have to go back sometime."

"Let me first call Dave and see if they are done processing the scene."

"Even if they're not, I'd be safer there with police around, right?"

"Would you at least let me talk to Dave about this?"

"Knock yourself out."

"I mean before you go back," Matt said and studied her face. "Damn, you're stubborn."

"I can't stand this anymore! My life is happening to me. I have to at least try to take control of something."

The two finished their healthy breakfasts and Matt dropped Kyle back at the motel, leaving her with a big hug. Before going inside she studied the small path into the trees, which she followed on her adventure last night. In the daylight without the rain, it looked serene, just a small patch of trees dividing two parking lots. She'd really let her imagination get away from her.

She was not in the door yet when her phone rang. She dug the phone from her bag. "Hello?"

"Good morning, Kyle. It's Brendan. How are you?" All of the men in her life were checking in this morning. She spoke as she passed inside, without letting either the cat or the dog out.

"Hi, Brendan."

"I just wanted to see how you are. I trust you slept well. You looked exhausted last night."

"Oh, well, it was a crazy night. But, I did finally get some sleep. My dog took off into the woods just as it started to pour. It was a mess out there."

"You think it's wise for you to be off in the woods at night, alone? I mean, given all that's happened…"

"As it turned out, I couldn't have been safer. Lt. Linscot showed up."

Kyle continued to speak, but Brendan did not hear a word. He wanted the rich widow left alone in his sole care.

"Brendan, are you there?"

"Yes. The lieutenant should not be following you."

"It's not a problem. Really." Kyle said omitting any further details.

"He has no right." The call ended with Brendan promising to be in touch soon. He had the final papers for her to sign to set up the trust for her and her son. All to be processed soon, before

Angus did what lawyers do when they've been injured; sue.

Brendan flipped through some notes and found the number he wanted. The line rang.

"Lt. Linscot," David answered.

"Lieutenant, this is Brendan Reed, the attorney representing Mrs. Mercer."

"Yes, I remember who you are." David sat up in his chair. His free fingers tapped the desk. Visions of venomous reptiles flashed before him.

"I understand you have been following my client."

"Following? Not exactly…"

"She has cooperated fully. If you have any further questions, those should be taken up with me."

Well, David thought, she hasn't cooperated that fully. "Look Mr. Reed, Mrs. Mercer and I knew each other prior to all this."

Just enough rope for the attorney. "Are you telling me you have a personal relationship with someone you are investigating?"

"There is no conflict of interest here, Mr. Reed. Besides, you're not a criminal attorney, are you?"

"I will be contacting your chief and informing him that any further surveillance will be considered harassment and I will file a complaint. Are we clear?"

"Oh, I think I understand you, Mr. Reed."

Click. Brendan hung up. A few minutes later the Chief came by David's office. "Dave," he said, "I just got off the phone with Attorney Reed. Says you've been harassing a Mrs. Mercer. What's the story?" He took a seat in front of David's desk.

"You want the short version or the long one?" David said.

"Short."

"He's a leach and I don't trust him."

"Well, so long as it's not personal… Perhaps you better fill me in a little more."

"I can't put my finger on it, but he's up to something."

"Is there something going on between you and Mrs. Mercer?"

"Nothing that's a problem. I have been kind of keeping an eye on her. Until we figure out what happened at her home…"

"I know she's a friend of Matt's. Maybe you better back off, if she's complaining to her attorney. Just use your judgment and keep me posted." The chief left his office.

Kyle complained to Reed? She was the only one person who could have told him. David answered his ringing cell phone.

"Hey, Dave, it's Matt. How's it going?"

"Okay. How you doing?" David asked, sitting straight up in his chair.

"Okay. Hey, any news on the ID?"

"Nothing yet. I was hoping for a match, but so far nothing."

"Kyle wants to go home. Wait, let me rephrase, she is going back home today. Is crime scene done?"

"I think so. I can check into it. Do you think it's wise for her to go back?"

"This is not my call. She must have had a rough night."

"Oh," said David.

"Anyway, I guess she'll be back today. Do me a favor and keep and eye on the house. She has an alarm system and the dog, but who knows what's going on."

"Sure thing, Matt. I don't have to tell you that it's unlikely the perp is hanging around the scene."

"Yeah, I know. He's probably half way across the country by now."

Twenty-Nine

Days were numbered. Brendan pressed Mel trying to complete as much as possible. Kate's ID was imminent. When it happened it would be difficult to concentrate. His link to Kate and the Mercer's home would surface. He didn't need any small town cop working overtime on this case. He wanted it left to apathetic State Prosecutors who would look for all of the pieces to fit neatly. He returned his attention to work, paperwork that needed to be filed as soon as possible. Once Kate's body was identified the next logical step for Angus, an attorney, would be legal action.

Brendan jumped from his chair and began a search of his folders. It was here somewhere. The papers were ready. There had been no rush before. Items from his desk crashed to the floor. "Mel…MEL…MEL…." He called out.

His assistant entered the office. "What is it?"

"Where is the trust agreement set up for the Mercer estate?"

"It's been on your desk for at least a week. It's around here somewhere. Is there a problem?"

"Yes, there's a problem. I can't find it. This has to get processed!"

Mel let out a deep breath. *Where's the friggin' fire?* She helped search the piles of folders. She found Brendan to be in one of his moods. He vacillated so much she considered it cyclical, like PMS. The folder was found and Mel left the office as Brendan buried his nose in it without a thank-you.

Brendan called Kyle's cell phone. He reached her and told her that he would be by this evening to finalize some paperwork. She informed him she would be back in her home and no she could not be talked out of it.

After settling up her bill with the manager of the motel, Kyle packed up her things and tossed them in her SUV. Last in were the cat and dog. Pumpkin hissed at Maggie who got too close to the carrier in the back of the vehicle. "You two get along!" Kyle pulled away and drove home to a house that she didn't know anymore.

Half-way home, her phone rang. Stopped at a light, she just looked at it. Will this thing ever stop? She fantasized about throwing it out the window. Then, she realized it could be Jeffrey. "Hello?" The warm voice on the other end of the line brought a smile to her face.

"Ciao! How are you? What's new? Any more bodies? Or just the one still?"

Kyle laughed at the sound of her friend's voice with watery eyes. "Just the one. I think that's enough. When are you coming home, Annie?"

"I told them they have me for another month and that's it. Why don't you come here? Jeffrey's at school now."

Fleeing the country was tempting. Italy was not. Kyle pulled over into a shopping center parking lot. She caught Annie up on current events, or the lack of them; they still had not identified the victim.

"What's wrong with David? He seems nice, in an incredibly sexy, makes you want to tear his clothes off kind of way."

"He's working a case. And besides, I am in no position to start anything."

"So what was dinner like with the attorney?"

"Fine...he's very polite. But, it is odd being out with a man who is better dressed and prettier than me."

Annie let out a big laugh. "Well, it sounds like you have men all around you."

"I miss Jason, Annie. Then I get mad at myself. My life is such a mess."

"Of course you miss him. It hasn't been that long."

"That's just it, it feels like he was gone long before he died." Memories Kyle pushed from her head on a daily basis came front and center. Her favorite times, which happened less and less, were the rare occasions when Jason came home after a long stretch and turned off every device that could summon him. He left his phone and pager in the car and even turned off the phone in the house. He would just be there to enjoy them or help with a menial task that he normally would never get to. They all retired early in a peaceful house. But then of course, the more recent memories took hold...pine needles on his car from an unknown source, condoms, and now a corpse.

The animals got restless, reminding Kyle where she headed. They finished up and Annie promised to call her again soon.

No policeman sat at the end of the driveway...a good sign. She rolled up to the house and met no one. She let out a deep breath then unpacked the car, avoiding even a glance at the back yard. Maggie hopped around, tail wagging. Pumpkin made a beeline for her bed.

The big windows in the kitchen made it impossible not to look out to the back. Kyle gave in. She stood at the large doors to the patio and inspected her yard, the crime scene. The pool was drained and empty. Yellow tape circled the extended area. The first few leaves of autumn littered the lawn and the concrete decking around the pool. She hoped the foliage would bury the entire site.

After several passes during the day, she stopped at the doorway to Jason's office. It was difficult to avoid being just off the kitchen. She entered the room. She paced around the desk. A large pile of mail spilled over from the desk onto the floor. Bills? When was the last time she paid any? This appeared to be a task she could focus on without hitting too many landmines. Kyle sat on the edge of the chair behind the desk. The leather felt cold and stiff. She reached for the first envelope and got to work.

Her focus was disturbed in the late afternoon by the doorbell.

"Hi Brendan, come in. You're early."

He appeared casual, leaving his suit jacket in the car. His shirt was crisp white contrasted by a celery-colored silk tie with a black square design. Kyle made a slight attempt to smooth her t-shirt and rumpled hair. They took seats in the kitchen. Brendan wasted no time in opening up a leather folder and pulling out stacks of papers.

"I know I'm early, but these have to be completed. I spoke to the bank and set up the trust. I need you to sign these papers and we'll get everything processed. You will not have to do anything else. Monies resulting from Jason's death will be automatically deposited to this account. The life insurance has been settled and will be sent in. A settlement with the airline may take some time. The money is safest in the trust."

Kyle signed where Brendan pointed. She read none of it.

"Okay, that's all of them. I will get these processed tomorrow."

"What's the rush?" Kyle asked.

"No time like the present! But enough of business…how are you doing? Are you alright in the house?"

"Yes, I'll be fine. I'm actually going to leave again tomorrow to go visit with my son."

"That sounds like a great way to spend the weekend. I will check with you next week."

David Linscott slowed going by Kyle's house. He saw the flashy car in the driveway and continued on his way home.

Thirty

A fresh shaven and showered David Linscot walked into the Hollis Police Station. Sleeping in his own bed instead of his truck, or a wet couch, gained him better sleep. Kyle was on his mind. She did not seem to dislike his company, but she'd complained to her attorney, so he would just have to leave her alone. The shift duty officer sitting behind the safety glass buzzed him in. The flashing light on his desk phone lit up the shadowed office before he turned on the light. He sat on the edge of the desk. He picked up the phone and retrieved his voicemail.

He listened to the message, scribbling notes. When he got all it, he hung up and went straight to the chief's office. "Morning, Chief. We got a DNA match on the remains."

"Who is she?" David read the notes from pad.

"Kathleen Thompson of Boston, Massachusetts. Twenty-four years old. Missing person's filed in November of last year. Suspected foul play."

"Gee, you think?" the Chief smirked.

"The Attorney General is organizing an Interstate Task force. I am supposed to send in a full report to the AG's office, ASAP. They also requested that we send a representative to the first meeting. Next Tuesday, 9 a.m." David looked at the chief.

"I'm not meeting with those bureaucrats. They're all yours. Keep me posted."

Back at his desk, David gathered up all of his notes and began typing. He reviewed the reports from the first call-in from the pool guys to his interviews with Kyle, Jeffrey and the attorney. This information must be included but were mainly dead ends. He was eager to get hold of the coroner's report and information from the search warrant.

Impatient with the number of days until the Task Force met, David pulled up the missing person's information on Kathleen Thompson. He read through the file, but it told him little. No leads. He picked up the phone to call Kyle, but first heard Reed's voice in his head. The attorney would be the one he should call. Screw it. He could wait for the official report. It wouldn't matter to him who the poor victim was.

The following Tuesday, David headed to the state office buildings in downtown Concord, New Hampshire, which were visible from Route 93. David Linscott took the exit to 'State Offices' and headed for the Attorney General's office. He parked his truck thirty minutes early for the meeting. He hoped to get in early and secure a copy of the autopsy. He pulled on his jacket and fastened the polished brass buttons of his full dress uniform. His shiny black boots pounded the pavement up to the stone building with the granite foyer. The polished, gray 'state stone' covered the walls and floor.

David found his way to the correct office. A woman dressed in navy clothing showed him to an empty conference room. "You're early." She checked him off her list on a clipboard. "You can have a seat. It is requested that you fill out and wear the nametag." David followed orders and picked up the black Sharpie. The room offered little stimulation to make the wait pass any faster. A large, rectangular mahogany table centered the room surrounded by at least twenty chairs. A strip of paneled windows ran along one side with a great view of another building.

By 9 a.m. the chairs were half filled with nametag wearers. A Major from the state police investigation unit introduced himself. They traded some stories about their common friend, Matt Birch. As the room filled, David noticed a Massachusetts policeman.

"Good morning. David Linscot, Hollis," he said introducing himself to the out-of-stater.

"Jim Hayden, Boston. You guys found her, right?"

"Yes…I've been looking for some more details. What can you tell me?" Hayden told David as much as he knew: they looked hard at her ex-boyfriend, but got nothing. They had no leads, until now. The victim's grandfather was some old lawyer who's one cough away from a headstone. A lot of money involved.

"Hey, there's one thing though, the old guy assigned this other lawyer to work with us, as a contact. Guess he's got a criminal background. Anyway he's been representing the widow of the home where the victim was found. Guy's name is Reed."

"You're kidding me. Reed knows the victim?"

"Not really, at least as far as we can tell. But, I guess it's a pretty odd coincidence."

"That's some coincidence. He's been kind of a prick."

"Oh, you must be who he referred to. He said some of the Hollis P.D. was overzealous. Said you guys were bored and had nothing better to do than harass a new widow. Don't sweat it."

The Attorney General, Ron Dupruis, paraded into the room with several aides in tow. He introduced himself and a representative from the Commonwealth's Attorney General's office. Thick, white folders were handed out. Dupruis discussed the cooperation between the two neighboring states and the opportunity for more efficient criminal investigations in the future. He praised both states for their quality police work. David listened to the speech. Dupruis all but announced his candidacy for governor in next year's election.

After a few more introductions, Dupruis got to the case. "Here is what we have so far. The victim was a twenty-four year old female, reported missing last November. Stray fibers were recovered, nothing conclusive. No obvious trauma to the remains, so cause of death is still in question. They're doing more tests on the bones, but not sure if we are really going to get too much more. A vial containing traces of GXB was recovered at her apartment. At this point, we have to assume this was a recreational drug used by the victim, who has some history of drug use and emotional problems. Boston crime scene went through the apartment. No obvious signs of struggle. Some stray hairs and fingerprints...the mother's and other investigators, all attributed to persons entering the residence after the missing person's was filed."

"Mother of the victim reports that the young woman canceled lunch abruptly on a Thursday with her mother and grandfather in November. That was the last they heard from her. Mother also reports that the victim's weekend bag, make-up, medications and some clothing were missing." Dupruis paused and adjusted his tie, practicing for the cameras.

"Now, as for friends and neighbors. One friend relayed to investigators she got the impression from Miss Thompson that she was involved with a married man. Neighbors report nothing unusual, with the exception of an older woman who resides across the hall. She reports seeing a man wearing a black trench coat. She is short, so she could not see much through her peephole. With no signs of forced entry or any disturbances, it appears that the young woman left willingly."

"The only sign of any disturbance was to the victim's automobile. The vehicle sustained some superficial damage to the driver's side. No accident report was filed by the victim, however, that does lead us to a connection to our suspect."

The AG stopped for a sip of water. He picked up another pile of papers. In it, David's latest report would be included. "We put Jason Mercer, one of the owner's of the house where the victim was found, together with the victim on at least one occasion. We have an accident report filed by Jason Mercer on the evening of November 8. The insurance report states that Jason Mercer describes a collision with a vehicle without lights on the side of the road, belonging to Kathleen Thompson. He filed a report with his insurance company for minor damages. Again, we find it curious that no such accident report was filed by Miss Thompson. These incidents, along with the obvious discovery of the body on his property, lead us to present Jason Mercer as our primary and only suspect at this time."

"A search of phone and email records of both the suspect and the victim came up clear. We have seen in other cases involving extra marital affairs, the use of pre-paid cell phones as a method of communicating undetected and that the suspect disposed of the evidence. We presume that to be the case here. One thing which was revealed in looking at some bank statements of Mr. Mercer secured at the search of the home was the purchase of a diamond bracelet in the month of August last year. A check with the insurance carrier of the Mercer's home owners' insurance revealed no such piece scheduled for insurance, yet all other items owned by Mrs. Mercer appear to be fully insured. This is something that we will check on with Mrs. Mercer."

"I would remind all of you that we have heard from both governors on this, and that a speedy resolution and conclusion to this case is of the highest priority. We would like to bring closure to the victim's family as soon as possible. Now, does anyone have anything they wish to add?" With that Dupruis sat down and gazed over his disciples.

David listened as a couple of the officials sitting closest to the Dupruis reiterated the high profile nature of the case and the need for closure. That was code for the press is breathing down our backs and the pressure is on to solve this. The public felt safe when crimes were solved, especially the murder of a young, blonde woman from a prominent family in Boston. When the public felt safe, it re-elected public servants.

Investigators liked it when the pieces all fit together. But the pieces gnawed at David. Some of them fell together too easily, like someone cutting jig-saw puzzle pieces to size. There were leftover material and large gaps. It concerned David that there was no dissention.

David motioned with his hand and introduced himself. "With all due respect, Attorney Dupruis, it seems like we are at a loss to explain the circumstances around this murder. Do we have a

motive? Should we have narrowed our investigation so early on?"
That was as diplomatic as David could muster.

Dupruis grinned with only one side of his mouth. "Lieutenant Linscot, I can assure you that many manpower hours have gone into reviewing the evidence, carefully. We do not rush to judgment. One of the benefits of being somewhat removed from the immediate locale, is that our eyes see only the facts."

David felt his blood pressure go up. Someone relayed the information to Dupruis' office that the locals were not objective, a conflict of interest. He knew the source. "It just seems to be a bit too obvious," David replied.

This brought another smirk to Dupruis face. "Are you saying someone framed a dead guy, before he died, accidentally?" The smirks now spread to most of the lackeys in the room.

"Well, no... but doesn't it seem pretty stupid to store a victim on your own property?"

"Lieutenant, I fully agree with your assessment that this is a bizarre case." The AG removed his glasses and let them dangle from his hand. "For anyone to use a swimming pool as cold storage for a body is definitely a new one for this office. However, it is much harder to believe that anyone else would have put the body there, though I understand the house was to be vacant for some time. Mr. Mercer knew the victim and knew that no one would be at his home or staying at his home while he was away. Being a physician he, better than most, would understand what the condition of the body would be over time. No cause of death, less to dispose of. He could have cleaned out the pool later himself and deposited the bones elsewhere to cover up his own crime. People snap. This action gives him time. He was conveniently taking his family out of the country." He paused. "I've been involved with criminal investigations for many years now. More than I would like to admit...but one thing still holds true, if you hear a stampede, it's probably not zebras!" Gentle laughter scattered around the table. "Let's not make this horrible situation any more difficult on the families. I will be holding a press conference later today to discuss our findings to date. We have identified the victim and have a suspect. The investigation is ongoing, but we expect to conclude soon."

Route 3 maintained a steady flow of traffic heading south from Concord. David's return trip to Hollis was smooth, but the congestion in his head caused much frustration. Something just wasn't right with this case. And it seemed that the self righteous, charitable attorneys kept cropping up on both sides. As always, there was pressure to put it to bed. He appeared to be the only one who felt there were still several loose ends. Before he left, one of the aides to the AG, a well-dressed son of some senator, gave David a copy of the purchase information regarding the bracelet. He requested an answer from the widow as soon as possible.

It was to be the nail in the coffin.

Thirty-One

Detective Hayden, as ordered by his superior, drove directly from Concord, New Hampshire, to the law office of Angus Hessman. In an earlier conversation with Brendan Reed, he arranged a meeting, scheduled around his return from New Hampshire this Tuesday. He needed to update the family and prepare them for the news, which would be hitting the press at a 5 p.m. press conference.

Brendan waited in his office, pacing, sitting, and standing. He knew what was coming. He reacted with shock and amazement when Hayden phoned him last week and discussed the breaks in the case and the potential ID. At that time, Brendan considered it wise to divulge his 'distant' association with the Mercers made only at the request of Angus. The hospital connection was all that it was. Living in the same town, well… "It's a small world, isn't it?" he said to the detective.

Mel buzzed. "Detective Hayden has arrived and is waiting for you in Angus' office."

Brendan checked his appearance in a mirror, which sat in the corner of the office. He buttoned his jacket and smoothed it with his hands. "This is it," he muttered. "Get through this and you should be home free."

Brendan greeted Shelly and Angus inside the elder's private office. Shelly, ever pleasant, made no eye contact, her expression unchanged. Brendan assumed it saved her a great deal of energy. She could go from a wake to a circus without changing a facial expression.

Angus sat in a chair behind his desk. What white strands of hair he had left were combed over in perfect order. His tie was straight, and his suit jacket hung slightly open, but symmetrical in appearance. Shelly had spruced him up, staged him. He looked old and tired. Brendan could relate.

Shelly returned with Detective Hayden following. The two men sat chairs arranged in front of Angus' desk. Shelly strode to her place a few steps behind the desk.

"Thank you for coming, Detective. Brendan reported to me some things...Could you tell me what you know for sure?"

"Well, I am sorry to inform you the DNA match was made with the sample you provided to the remains of a woman found in New Hampshire."

Without moving Angus responded, "Are you positive it's Kate?" The red swollen eyes of the distraught grandpa teared.

"Yes, Sir. I'm sorry. The medical examiner has no question. An interstate task force has been formed. We have a suspect. The man whose property Miss Thompson was found. We believe your granddaughter was involved with Dr. Jason Mercer. Her body was stored on his property where he knew it would be undisturbed. It was only discovered after his death."

"I think I met Jason Mercer some time ago, at a reception of some kind, I can't believe he would be capable of such an atrocity," Angus said.

"He has no history of violence, so it does appear out of character, however, sometimes people...well...react badly under pressure. Kate may have been frustrated and threatened to go public with their relationship. Dr. Mercer's reputation would have been destroyed. We may never know for sure."

Brendan decided this is as good a time as any to speak. "In a horrible twist of fate, I have been working with the widow, Mrs. Mercer, regarding estate business for one of the families of the hospital…a lovely woman, who is as much of a victim in all of this." He did not need to look up to feel Shelly's eyes on him.

The words registered little with the old man. He raised his finger. "As soon as the investigation is concluded, I want a wrongful death suit for twenty million dollars filed on behalf of my family." Shelly patted him on the shoulder. Her eyes did not leave Brendan.

"I will put Jared on it right away." She had not missed a word.

"Shelly, would you get my daughter on the phone. Tell her that I am on my way over." He looked up at the men in front of him. "I don't know how I am going to tell my only daughter, that her only child is gone."

Brendan and Hayden rose from their chairs, expressed their sympathies again and exited the room. As they walked down the hall to the elevators, Brendan found it a perfect opportunity to pick Hayden's brain.

"Are you serving any additional warrants? Are there any other avenues you're looking at?"

"I'm not. Both AGs seem fairly satisfied with the case as it stands. It's an easy resolution. No one to put on trial…hard for a dead guy to plead not guilty." Hayden paused and looked Brendan in the eyes. "As I said earlier, your connection in this is quite a coincidence. I passed it on to the guys in charge. It is possible someone may want to ask you some questions."

The attorney responded, "Of course, I understand. This is quite disturbing to me, as well as a shock. A very dark day for all of us. Angus has been like a father to me. You know how to reach me." The men parted without shaking hands.

Back in the haven of his office, Brendan let out a deep breath, took off his jacket and fell into his chair. A great weight had been lifted from his shoulders. By the time anyone got over the shock and took time to think about his links, the case would be closed. Kate would be buried and this entire nightmare would be behind him. He could see the light at the end of a long tunnel.

It was Tuesday, but he felt the need to let out some steam. He picked up the phone. "Hey Nicki, its Brendan. You free this evening? Give me a call." Leaning back in his chair, he pondered the future. Angus and Shelly thank God, would be on their way out. The entire firm would be reorganized, this unpleasant chapter in his life reduced to a water cooler story about Angus' wild granddaughter. And Brendan would assist in the development of just the right details to stir gossip.

Mel's voice on the intercom jolted him back to the office. "Brendan, a Lieutenant Linscot from the Hollis Police Department is holding for you. Are you in?"

"Good afternoon, Lieutenant, what can I do for you?"

"I understand you have a conflict of interest in our mutual case."

"Yes," Brendan replied.

"I need to ask Mrs. Mercer a couple more questions. To whom should I direct that request?" Brendan squeezed the phone and thought for a moment. Mel walked into his office. With quick hand motions he shooed her away. She closed the door behind her.

"Why don't you relay them to me. Maybe I can help you."

David smiled. Reed still wants to be in the loop. Interesting. "No thank-you, Mr. Reed. At this time, I don't think that would be appropriate."

"In that case, I suggest you contact Mrs. Mercer yourself and ask her if she has retained another attorney."

"I will. Quite a coincidence…you seem to be all over this case. Are there going to be any more surprises?"

"Goodbye, Lieutenant." He hung up. Brendan's gut stirred. That call from Linscot was unnecessary. He was fishing. This case needed to be closed before the irritating investigator had too much time to think.

Something…something was all wrong. From the beginning, David felt the lawyer served private motives, but now the detective questioned the depth of greed. And he did not believe in coincidence. He picked up his phone and called Kyle at home. No answer. He dialed her cell phone.

"Hello." A flustered voice came on the line. "Sorry, I dropped my phone."

"Hi, Kyle, it's David. How are you?"

"I'm too many things to pick just one. Everything seems upside down."

"I need to meet with you. It shouldn't take long."

"That would be fine." Kyle found herself eager to see him, even if to discuss this case. "Just so you know, Brendan already told me about the young woman's identity. He called me a couple hours ago. This is all just getting more and more bizarre. He also mentioned there was some type of task force meeting today, but he didn't give me many details."

"I just need to go over a few things with you."

"Okay. Well, I am on my way back from visiting with my son."

"Did you have a nice time?"

"Great. I almost didn't come back. I should be back home within an hour."

"I'll meet you at your house in an hour. Drive carefully."

David hung up. The folder he received from the Task Force lay open on his desk. He studied each line of each report. There had to be something here. Or a hole large enough to fit a slippery lawyer.

Thirty-Two

The walk around the yard and the edge of the woods was un-eventful. David stood outside the yellow crime scene tape. The marker rattled in the gentle wind. One loose piece rippled like a flag, still secured on one end. Did David believe someone else would have the balls to dump a body on someone else's proper-ty? Stranger things had happened. The right person, who knew enough about the law, would understand what a successful diver-sion this would be. An investigation would be uphill from here. The water was enough to compromise any physical evidence. The property-line provided enough cover. It was only a matter of a window of opportunity. If that was the case, Jason's death was a simple stroke of luck. Instead of the respected surgeon fighting for his reputation, he was presumed guilty from the grave, even his widow having no choice but to accept the morbid details. Cer-tainly a roll of the dice, but better than being caught holding the bag-or the body.

Reed remained front and center in David's thoughts. The at-torney was all around this case, but was he in the middle of it?

David stood at the top of the driveway as Kyle's SUV rolled up. Her face warmed to a smile when she saw him. David's did the same. Not the response he was expecting since she complained about him to her attorney. He helped her in the house with some bags. They took seats in the kitchen. Just as they sat down, there was a quick knock at the door. It swung open.

"Who invited you?" Kyle said to her unexpected guest.

Matt smiled. "I love you, too." He moved to Kyle and gave her a kiss on the cheek. "David called me."

"Well, this can't be good."

"First, I have to ask you if you have retained another lawyer." Her mood had deflated when Matt walked in but crashed as the discussion moved so quickly to business. She had to accept that despite how David looked, with rugged shoulders, strong cheekbones, fair skin and dark hair, he was working. That's why David's presence became scarce over the last few weeks, his work focused him elsewhere. He was not interested in her, but her case.

"You said I didn't need to get another." Kyle looked at her old friend.

"No, I don't believe you need a criminal attorney."

Lawyers are lawyers, Kyle thought, and shrugged it off. "Okay, so what is it now?" She prepared for whatever bombshell was about to drop.

"During the course of the investigation, a few questions came up and they have some theories that they are following. And by *them* I mean the Attorney General's office. Let me start with the questions." David paused and took a breath. He hated dragging Kyle down into this garbage, again. "Did Jason own a black trench coat?"

"Yes."

"Do you still have it?"

"No, it was lost in the accident. He was wearing it."

David wrote on his pad. "Okay. Do you own or know about a diamond bracelet, which would have been purchased last August by your husband?"

Kyle's eyes opened wide. "No, what does that mean?" She looked at Matt. "Who was he buying...?" And then it hit her; you didn't buy diamond bracelets for casual acquaintances.

Matt struggled with his explanation. Kyle needed to have all the cards put on the table, but it was hard to spell this all out in plain English. There was no better time. "Whether we like it or not, this is evidence which would lead us to believe Jason was having an affair. If he didn't give you the jewelry he bought, then who has it? The young woman who was killed went missing a little over two months from the time of this purchase."

"She had this bracelet?" Kyle asked, pissed. She didn't own a diamond bracelet. She never asked and Jason never insisted.

"No!" David was quick to respond. "Much of this is simple circumstantial evidence. It speaks more to behavior than proof."

Kyle rested her forehead in her hands. The tears arrived, but she was able to force them back. The tears were getting old. This mess was her life and she had to handle it. She lifted her head. "I didn't tell anyone. Well, I told Annie. When I unpacked Jason's luggage, I found condoms. We didn't use them. I think Jason was having an affair. And now, I find out he's been buying jewelry! I guess I shouldn't be surprised anymore..." Her voice trailed off.

"You never told me any of this. You should have," Matt said.

"It's not exactly something I wanted to discuss. And you guys are policemen. I didn't want things to get any worse."

"I have been your friend longer than I've been a cop."

"It just wasn't the type of thing...and Brendan told me to be careful about anything I told you guys."

"Reed!" David reeled. "Let's talk about Reed. Is there any other advice he gave you? What kind of questions did he ask?"

"I don't know. He told me I should run everything by him first."

David gave Matt a long look. David marveled at the convenience of that practice. He finished the circle in his head. The grandfather and police also included Reed from the beginning.

"Kyle, you need to know about how the big guys are seeing this case." Matt took a deep breath. This was the big elephant in the room that no one really wanted to make real. But if someone was going to tell her all of this, together, it would be him. "They are following the theory that Jason was involved with this girl, she threatened to go public and he killed her in a crime of passion.

He stored the body until he could decide what to do with it. Of course when he was killed..." Matt stopped.

"Is that what you think?"

"No. Not the man I knew. But at this point, it's hard to find another explanation. Everything seems to be stacking up. I'm sorry, but I think at this point we are going to have to accept this."

"Well..." Kyle kept her head high. "At this point." She decided right then and there, that there would be no more tears from her puffy eyes. "At this point," she repeated Matt's own words, "it really doesn't matter. What's done is done. We will never know all the details. I just want this put behind me. But, I don't care what anyone says, Jason would never kill anyone. I can buy the affair, but not murder." When Kyle heard her own words, she felt a great sense of relief.

"There is one other thing. The grandfather of the victim is the senior partner of some large firm in Boston. They have expressed their intention for filing a wrongful death suit against the estate. It is possible that when some of this settles down, they'll change their mind."

"But, Jeffrey and I had nothing to do with this," Kyle responded.

David sensed Matt was struggling, so he stepped in. "Kyle, they can go after Jason's estate. It is not as easy, but it can be done. And the family is headed by a well known attorney so seeking financial compensation would not be a surprise."

"Can they go after Jeffrey's college fund?" Kyle asked.

"I don't think so, but you will need to get an attorney that handles these things," David said.

"Brendan did give me the name of someone."

David cut her off. "Matt knows a couple lawyers in New Hampshire. Why don't you meet with one of them? I don't think you should take any more advice from Reed. With his firm involved, it's too much of a conflict of interest. And one more thing."

"There's more! What could you have possibly left out?" Kyle replied feeling naked and drained.

"The Attorney General has scheduled a press conference. It should be on the news at anytime now. He is going to discuss the case and their only suspect." Kyle swallowed hard as David mentioned the press. "You may not want to answer your phone for the next couple days." He wanted to suggest going to stay with someone for a few days and hoped Matt would have some luck on that front.

When they were through, Matt walked David out to his car. "Thanks for calling me. I am going to stick around for a while… make sure she's okay. I am going to try to take her to my house, but I'm not sure she'll go for it."

"You know Matt, like I told you; I am not convinced her husband did this."

A smile came over Matt's face; he reached to place his hand on his comrade's shoulder. "I appreciate the thought, but we are going to have to stop denying what happened…we have to accept, and go on. That's the best thing we can do. I guess you really never know what people are capable of until they get pushed."

David's gut grumbled all the way home. Did anyone really look at this case, or did they just let it unfold in front of them? Evidence did have a way of falling in line, but there was also such a thing as a "dog and pony show." He could not help but think they should be looking in another direction.

It was an hour before Kyle got Matt to leave. She sat at the kitchen island just like she had many times before, by herself. For the first time since this nightmare began, her fear fell away. She was able to focus clearly on the situation at hand. Her thoughts fell together and one thing became clear. The man she had spent her entire adult life with was not capable of killing anyone. But what should she do? Jason would tell her to 'do her homework.' If she couldn't, maybe someone else could.

A short search yielded a phonebook. She flipped the yellow

pages to private investigators. She found a listing for a woman from Hollis. She thought that was an omen. She dialed the number.

"Hi, you reached the office of Ceece Deluca, Private Investigator. I am away in Arizona on vacation, but will be back soon and would like to speak with you. Please leave your information and I will get back to you." *Beep.*

Kyle turned off the phone. This just might be a good idea. She wanted to speak with someone who might be able help. She dialed. "Hello, this is Kyle Mercer. I was wondering if Brendan Reed was in."

"Just a moment, please," Mel said.

Brendan came on the line quickly. "Kyle, how are you?" He'd known she would need comfort after the news got broken to her, but was surprised to hear from her so soon.

"I need your help."

"Anything," Brendan said.

"I want to hire a private investigator," Kyle said.

Brendan heard the calm determination in her voice. It unnerved him. He sat up in his chair and went into damage control. "I know you must be disturbed by the news today, but I can assure you Kyle, everything that could be done, has been."

"Jason didn't do this. It doesn't make sense. I know what the police are saying, but I'm telling you, he didn't do this. I cannot just let them blame this on him without a fight."

Brendan's shoulders tensed. "Okay. Why don't you let me handle this? I know someone that I have used in a few cases who is very discreet. Let me put him onto this. I can't promise anything."

"I understand. I just feel like I need to do something more. There has got to be some other explanation."

"I'll be in touch," Brendan said as he hung up the phone. He would just give her some fictitious updates every so often, and tell her that he insisted on paying for it. He didn't need anyone else looking at anything.

"Hey, hurry up! I want to show you something," Pete yelled to Ray inside her tiny bathroom. Steam escaped from the cracked open door. He spread the morning newspaper over the table reading the front page article again. *Respected deceased surgeon only suspect in the murder of young woman.*

Ray emerged from the shower with a towel containing her volumes of dark hair and a loose thin robe covering the majority of her petite body. Pete lost his focus for a moment catching the edge of the horseshoe against her pale skin. "So where's the fire?" She looked down at the newspaper. "Since when are you so literate?"

"Remember I told you about that house…where they found the bones in the pool? I was afraid they were going to blame me. As it turns out, they think this girl, Kathleen, was killed by this surgeon. Freaky, huh?"

"You know that computer belonged to a woman named Kate. Some of the emails said Kathleen, but I didn't pay much attention. Think it's the same?" Ray asked, face down studying the article.

"That's weird, though. I know I didn't take anything from that house. How could her laptop be at another nearby house?" They looked at each other.

Ray spoke first. "Why are you so sure it did not come from the house where the body was?"

"Because I took nothing from there. I just hung around a few times."

"But, why would you watch a house and then not take anything?" Ray asked.

"I don't know. It doesn't matter."

Ray threw up her hands, giving up on the discussion. With her hair still wrapped, Ray retrieved the laptop and sat down on the couch. She pulled it in and powered it up. Pete took a seat beside her. Her fingers flew over the keyboard.

"Look, this may take a while. Why don't you let me work on it and I'll let you know what I find."

"Okay, I have to get to work anyway."

Ray stood to usher him out of the apartment. "How's the new job at Home Depot?"

"Great. Mac really came through for me. I get benefits and everything. I'm just a stocker now, but I can move up." He paused and looked at Ray. "I like it better. I like having a real job."

"Good for you." Ray cut him off before he started again on the straight and narrow routine. He wanted Ray to get a real job. Which meant to Ray answering to real assholes. No thank-you. "See you tonight?"

"Yeah, I should be out by seven. I'll be by then," he said and kissed her goodbye.

Ray set to work on the computer pulling up old email on the mainframe. Easy as pie. She began her search as far back as she could see, then scanned and moved to more current correspondence. Boring....boring....boring...blah, blah, blah. Kate finishes college. She gets a job at a men's clothing store, blah, blah. Bored with what she found so far, Ray began looking at files. It did not take long before she found a treasure trove of information. A file labeled with just, B. Inside were saved IM's. All were from 'BER' to 'KATwToys.' Each brief message discussed getting together, what they had done and what they planned on doing. Even with the small bits of information, Ray could sniff out the rat.

She hit pay dirt with the last couple messages saved from KAT to BER. They went from spirited to nasty. KAT was pregnant and wanted to get together with B to discuss THEIR options. KAT's demeanor in the messages got more desperate with each. Then nothing. But the best was what followed.

Ray ran through a collection of pictures. They began with a man sleeping on his back in a bed. Good looking in a G.Q. kind of way. Next, they showed the same man with the covers pulled back, revealing full frontal nudity. Ray lingered on it. Even in a small picture, the guy's package was impressive. The next few were of a young woman with blond hair with her head tucked next to the sleeping guy. It was a closer picture of their faces with her smiling. The remaining shots weren't so interesting; a white house viewed through some trees. On the side was pasted in information. It looked like a scanned/pasted business card: Hessman, Coughlin & Associates...Brendan E. Reed. It contained the business and email addresses.

The file itself was odd, as if someone was compiling information just in case they needed it handy. Ray sat back and ran through a sequence of events. Married guy gets involved with a twenty-something woman. She gets prego. All communication stops. She gets dead. He works in Boston. But this guy isn't a doctor. Even if BER had nothing to do with the murder, he still might not want all of this nasty stuff released to the press or police.

Ray dressed and was out the door in five minutes, laptop in tow. She got to her favorite fishing spot and decided to throw a line in.

Thirty-Three

"Look Jared, it was the right thing to do." Brendan sat in Jared's office having a conversation, which he knew was unavoidable. He squirmed in his seat. "You're telling me the money from the estate is in a trust and can't be touched?" Jared steamed.

"You know it's standard to protect assets, especially in the case of a widow coming into a large sum of money."

"Some of the money yes, but all? Why wasn't some left in the wife's name? She needs something." Jared held a stack of papers in his hand and waved them in the air. His face was red.

"She has full access through the trust. I thought this would be the safest way to protect them both against folks who might take advantage of the situation."

"Well, this is just perfect. Do you realize what you've done? What am I supposed to tell Angus?" Jared glared at Brendan as if this entire mess was his fault. "If we fight the trust and win, we leave the firm open for liability for setting up a faulty trust? We can't touch this!"

"Angus doesn't need the money anyway. He's just reacting. He'll cool down. The wife and son had nothing to do with his granddaughter's death. And by the way, Angus is the one who told me to take care of everything involving the hospital families."

"Angus wasn't going to keep anything; any monies would be donated to a shelter for woman and children in Boston. He's going to be pissed."

"He'll cool off," Brendan said and rose from his chair.

Jared raised his voice. He was not through. "I will still be look-ing at other angles. I'll have more questions." Jared pointed his finger at Brendan. He enjoyed putting the screws to the fair-haired boy of the moment surely to fall from grace at least a bit.

Brendan appeared unconcerned and walked down the hall to return to the sanctuary of his office. This Wednesday was already long and it was only 9 a.m. He passed Mel with little more than a grunt when she held out papers for him to look at. With all the talk in the office, she almost felt bad for him but his moodiness of late prevented it. His unlucky acquaintance with the murderer's family did not sit well. He slammed his door. Mel decided that if he really needed these documents, he'd ask.

Back in his cocoon, he felt better. He gazed out of his win-dow at the small people walking back and forth, many of them laughing and smiling. He took some deep breaths. He was al-most free of this. He just needed to keep everything together for a couple more weeks. Kate would be buried and gone. He could see the light.

He focused his attention back to his desk and his computer. He rummaged through his office email, too much for him and most of it he forwarded to Mel. When he reached the last one, he fingers lingered over the keyboard. He didn't recognize the sender. He stopped cold when he read the subject: 'Sale on lap-top! KATwTOYS'

It was short and to the point. His face turned red and his blood pressure jumped. He picked a crystal paperweight and threw it against the far wall. The loud noise echoed around the walls. It smashed into a million splinters and made the floor look like it was covered with glitter.

The white screen with black lettering mocked him: *Used Sony laptop for sale…$200,000, price firm. Terms 48 hours. If not sold, Friday night it will be anonymously turned over to the police. Let me know if you're interested.* Two of the more revealing pictures were included.

PS- KATE SAYS HI!

"Brendan, are you all right?" Mel flew into the room. Behind her Shelly strolled in.

He felt his throat close. The elder inspected the floor across the room and looked up at the attorney sitting behind his desk. Her hands sat folded across the front of her.

Brendan threw his hands up on the screen in a reflex to hide the message. Since neither of the women could see the screen, it telegraphed the source of the problem.

"Problem with your computer?" Shelly paused. "I would like to speak with you. Let me know as soon as you are...available." She looked around again, un-amused at the sight and walked out without waiting for any response.

"Brendan, what happened?" Mel asked.

"It slipped."

Across the room? "I'll call maintenance and get someone up here to clean it. Are you sure you're okay? Your face is all red."

"I'M FINE! LEAVE ME THE HELL ALONE! I have work to do!" He took a breath and ran his hand over his short, blunt cut hair. He swallowed and spoke, sounding a bit more composed. "Take care of it later. I'm in the middle of something."

Mel followed instructions and closed the door behind her. Only last week had he told Mel about his pending divorce. She assumed something must be wrong with the "very amiable split."

"Prick..." she muttered under her breath.

Brendan was left alone again with his computer screen, his hands gripping the sides. Someone was blackmailing him! They must have Kate's laptop and somehow his office email. Shit. Luckily the police investigation should be all but over. It had to be a petty thief who poked around in his garage and got lucky. A pro would have cleaned out the house and sold the computer by now. He seethed with anger. Could they have any proof that he killed Kate? No. This was just bait; assuming that because it was in Hollis, it has something to do with the murder. Not bad. The punk is banking on the idea that Brendan did not want this info public. The attorney hated being played. He ran through his mind the option of not responding. Give no validation to this. It could work. But what did those last messages from Kate say? He had not even read them, but now an amateur put together his involvement. The police would have less trouble. The message on the screen floated. Deleting it would not make it go away. "FUCK!"

He reverted back to the oldest law tactic in the world. He hit reply. 'I'll need more time.' He sent the message.

Minutes ticked by. When would he get a response? He got up from his desk and paced his office. He recalled Shelly wanted to see him, but she would have to wait, all day if necessary. He couldn't leave his computer unattended. The attorney pulled his tie loose to help him breath. He felt constricted.

He did not have to wait long.

At the café, Ray logged back on under her bogus name and account. If she was wrong, she'd get no answer. The dead surgeon did it. But if she was right… Within minutes, she'd hit pay dirt. She read the response then sent her own.

Brendan leaped back to his desk when the signal beeped.

'Take all the time you need. Just decide by Friday 10 a.m. I will check my mail again only once at that time. YES or NO…if yes, I will tell you where to meet me on Friday at 6 p.m. If no, then it will be with the police by noon. Have a nice day.'

He looked around his desk for something else to throw. He had not come this far to be taken down by some low-life thief. Whoever this was, they were out of their league. He pounded the desk with his fist.

Ray packed up her laptop and exited the café. She had 'a live one.' A great, big smile came across her face and her green eyes sparkled.

Thirty-Four

Matt sat across from Kyle at the kitchen island. She insisted on staying in her own house, cursed as it was, and Matt insisted on checking on her.

"They'll finish up over the new couple weeks. If nothing new arises, they'll probably close the case. They like closed, solved cases," Matt reported and took deep sips of hot coffee, which he brought for both of them. Being able to meet at sunrise worked out great for Matt who was an early riser and at this point, Kyle was awake most of the time anyway.

"Have the calls stopped?"

Kyle let out a big yawn. "Sure, I unplugged all the phones. Jeffrey reaches me through my voicemail."

"What are you going to do with the house?"

"Burn it!" Kyle snapped.

"Kyle..."

"I spoke to Annie. As soon as she gets back, she's throwing her cousin's family out and I am moving in with her. A couple weeks or so. It feels like a morgue here."

"You shouldn't stay here. You know you can stay with us."

"I know, and I will if I need to. I'm not sleeping anyway. I'll just exist until Annie gets back. I can take the cat and the dog." Kyle rubbed the head of Pumpkin sitting on her lap, listening. Maggie sat below, glaring up at the overweight cat. "She even has room for Jeffrey when he's around. It will all work out."

The mention of the animals brought a smile to Matt's face.

Kyle often said his only character flaw was his dislike of anything with more legs than him. He'd patted and then pushed Maggie's head away from him more than once.

"I guess I'll sell the house. But then again, who would buy this tainted property? It would have to be some twisted devil worshipper."

"This will all settle down. People forget."

"I may not have to do anything with it. If the family of the young woman sues, I won't have to worry about what to do with the house."

"Did you call that attorney I gave you?"

"No. I will. I promise."

Kyle told Matt nothing of her hiring a private investigator. If it turned up nothing, so be it. At least she tried.

"Matt, one more thing. The accident between Jason's and this woman's car, where did it happen? I know in Hollis, but where?"

"I think the report said Pierce. But Kyle, let it be."

"Yeah," Kyle said.

The many reports lay scattered all over the desk. David folded his hands behind his head staring down at the organized mess. His eyes were tired and ached to be rubbed again. Who knew that going into criminal justice meant spending hours reading and writing paperwork? If officers realized this in making career choices many of them would have gone elsewhere. He spent most of Wednesday sifting through every inch of the case page by page. Now, a day later, and he had only more questions. It was all to be closed soon, and it bugged him. There would be no more investigation. No more leads. What bothered him most was the recurrent supporting role of Reed. He was linked to the victim and the suspect. He'd popped up fast to assist the widow and advised her to clear all information through him.

He picked up his phone. "Detective Hayden, it's David Linscot." David ran his reservations by the seasoned detective.

"Look David, lawyers bug me just as much as the next cop. I make an arrest and before I can walk to my desk to start the paperwork, the piece of shit passes me with his lawyer. They'll defend anyone who'll pay them. They're like prostitutes! Anyone with cash. But if you go accusing one, especially an expensive one, you better have some proof. And besides, Reed has accused you of being unprofessional. Says you've got the hots for the widow so you're not objective. But, if you start pointing a finger at him…all hell could break loose! I'll grant you, there are a few coincidences, but do you really think the guy killed that woman?"

"Look, I don't hate all lawyers. There are good ones and bad ones. Just like cops. This case….I don't know exactly, it's bothering me. What are the chances of me coming down and taking a look at any physical evidence you guys have?" David asked.

"I can't see how that could be a big deal. If it helps you put this to rest. I'll get it worked out. When?"

"Today."

Hayden let out a laugh. "How about tomorrow? I can be free in the morning."

"Friday morning it is."

The day dragged for David. He could not get his mind free of this case and of Kyle. Late in the day he went in to let the chief know he'd be in Boston tomorrow.

"David, I thought this case was all but solved," the gray haired man said, sitting behind his neat and orderly desk.

"I just want to take a look at more of the pictures of the victim's apartment and at some of the physical evidence."

"I think this case has become personal for you. Let's not waste our time."

"There is something wrong, Chief. I'm sure of it. We don't have a single phone call or piece of personal evidence to tie Mercer to the woman. None of his prints were found in the apartment. Just give me the morning. If nothing turns up, I'll let it go."

The chief rubbed his eyes. He saw David would not let it go. He hired this guy because of his amazing track record as an investigator and now he wanted him to lay off. "Okay, in the morning. But, you get a look and get back here. Then as far as I'm concerned this case is closed and we do not spend anymore department time on it. Clear?"

"Clear."

On his way home David followed his usual out of the way route via Kyle's house. He slowed going by, noticing every light in and outside of the house was on. He wanted to stop in just to tell her this wasn't over yet. Wait, he told himself. Maybe you'll have something tomorrow. He shouldn't be getting her hopes up over a gut feeling he couldn't prove.

He continued home.

The hard disc popped out of the computer after copying all relevant information. Ray marked it 'insurance' and tucked it into her backpack. She glanced over at Pete, stretched out on the futon, consumed with a reality television show. Pangs of guilt tugged at her gut, a feeling she barely recognized. She had a few rules she lived by, her primary one being self-preservation. Her only other code was keeping up her end of a deal. Pete trusted her with this computer and if she was going to make a big score, she should really be cutting him in. It was her warped idea of karma. It kept her waking up each day and landing on her feet after some tough scrapes.

"We have to talk about the laptop." Ray meandered over to the futon.

Pete did not respond. He was too wrapped up in watching a guy eat something that did not appear on the food pyramid. What would Rhino Beetles fall under? Protein? Starch? She gagged as she watched a man eat the insect/beast. She heard the host say, "That's the surprise. They fight back!" The hand size, black insect with a horn was a formidable opponent. She waited until the show went to a commercial. What some people would do for money.

"Pete…I've gotta tell you something. It's about the laptop."

"Oh, did you get rid of it? You said you didn't find anything else."

"That's not entirely true. I'm getting rid of it tomorrow, but I did find some stuff on it. I wasn't sure if it was anything, but now I think it is. That's why I'm telling you. I think this computer is worth money to a guy mentioned in some IM's. I think he was doing this chick and he was married. One message says she was pregnant... and then they stop."

"What makes you think it's worth money?"

"I contacted someone at that address and told him the laptop was for sale. I'm going to hear back from him tomorrow, but I think he wants it and is willing to pay."

Pete took a moment to catch up and then it hit him. "You blackmailed this guy? What did you do, threaten to go to the police?"

"Yes."

"Ray, how do you even know how to do this? What if this guy is dangerous? How do you know he's not going to find you?"

"Oh please... do you think I'm stupid? There's no way to trace me. I know what I'm doing."

"So you are going to meet him tomorrow? No way! Ray, it isn't worth it. We should bring this to the police. Maybe this guy killed the woman. Or he knows something."

"Look, I only told you because by right you should get half of the money...half of 100,000!" Okay, her karma thing only went so far. "You're like Mr. Born Again Christian. It's like you found religion or something. This is easy money. Some guy doesn't want the police questioning him about banging some young piece of ass. Or so what if he killed her? Who cares? If he wants to stay out of jail, he'll be happy to pay for this. It doesn't make any difference to us."

Pete didn't hear anything after the mention of the money. "A hundred grand? He's going to cough up that much? Ray, that's more than he doesn't want the police around. That's a get out of jail free card. This guy must be dangerous."

"Look, I copied the messages and put them on a disc in my backpack. Nothing will happen to me."

"I want to take the laptop to that woman who lost her husband...or to the police. What if her husband didn't even do it?"

"WHAT ARE YOU, NUTS? There's no fucking way we're doing that. I will hear from the guy in the morning. If he takes that bait, I'll meet him at six and I'll get paid. We are not getting involved with anyone else. That will be the end of it. Either you want your cut or you don't, but that's it! It's not our problem."

"I don't want a dime."

"Suit yourself."

"Ray..." She put her hand up in his face. She was stubborn. He would try again tomorrow, but then he would draw a line in the sand. He did not want either of them involved with this mess. He sat beside her, reminded of how she handled Chaser. With adding blackmail to her bag of tricks, Pete wondered what other surprises Ray was capable of.

Thirty-Five

Sergeant Jim Hayden returned to his office with full cups of black coffee for both of them. They were the second this morning for each. David pored over Hayden's notepad, reading his original notes from the morning that Kate's apartment was investigated. So far, he found nothing.

"So when you got there, Jim, the two attorneys were inside. And you got hair samples from both, but only one matched up...Reed's."

"Right. We matched fingerprints on both, but only found hairs that matched Reed and the victim."

"Do you have the crime scene report showing where trace evidence was found?"

"We'd have to get that from the evidence room. The actual fibers are kept with all the details," the Sergeant responded.

"Let's go."

It was close to noon before the detectives were checked into the evidence room. The room in the basement was manned twenty-four hours a day by an armed officer. Anyone who came in was logged. Courts required that evidence be closely guarded to prevent tampering. The chain of custody must be pure and documented. Harsh fluorescent lights glowed overhead as the two sat at a metal table and examined zip lock bags and a detailed report. David felt his time slipping away. He should be headed back soon. Frustrated, he held the two bags that held Reed's hair. The mismatch hit him as soon as he compared them.

"This was found in the apartment." David held up a bag with a detailed label corresponding it to the apartment. Hayden grunted. His indulgence of David was fading with each grumble of his stomach. His head still throbbed from the headache that started last night with an argument his wife. He was about to suggest they concede and head to lunch at his favorite spot for a burger and a Guinness.

"This one was collected from Reed at his office less than a month after the disappearance. One is long and almost blond at the end, and the other is light brown and short. But, they are said to be a match."

Hayden was unimpressed. And hungry. "Dave, I'm sure you know that when they collect hair from someone, they try to get the sample from someplace where it won't be noticeable, but if a hair falls out it can come from anywhere."

"Reed's hair is short. Short as mine. If it was longer and lighter, it was from *before* the sample was taken." David held up the two bags for comparison. "What was Reed's hair like when you met him for the first time?"

Hayden was tired and trying to pay attention. He studied the two bags. He weighed his answer carefully. If he was to miss his lunch he had to be sure. "I can only remember him with a crew-cut. But, I couldn't swear to it."

"What if he cut his hair to alter his appearance? Maybe to make it harder to make an ID?" David asked.

"That's not much to go on."

"Tell me you remember him having longer hair and I'll let it go."

The seasoned detective studied the bags. His eyes jumped back and forth.

"I can't," the hungry detective grumbled. "But I'm not sure this is going to get us anywhere. I guess we could question Reed about it, but even that I'll have to run by the captain."

"I don't want to talk to Reed. Even if we have something he won't tell us a thing. But, it might be a starting point to ask some other questions. How cooperative is the grandfather?"

"Very, but remember he's the head lawyer. He won't be too fond of us making accusations about a guy who works for him."

"Well maybe we can blame it on the lab. Say we just want to make sure they haven't mixed up any samples."

Hayden made a disapproving face.

"Hey, what have we got to lose? You can blame it on me. Reed hates me anyway."

"That's true. Well, just to make sure, I'll run this by the lab first." Hayden flipped open his cell phone. He navigated through several employees until he got through to the head of the lab. The two sat looking at each other while the woman retrieved the report via her computer.

David focused on his watch. It was after 1 p.m. already; this day was flying by and unless he came up with something significant, this would be the end of it. He did not find Hayden intrigued enough to carry this on without him around.

"Yes...yes...okay," Hayden said, rolling his eyes a few times. Then he finished his call and said to David, "Okay, it's like this. First of all, the lab guys—wait excuse me—the lab people, do not take kindly to us questioning their integrity. She said this sample," he paused and identified the number on the white label of the clear bag, "was found under a cushion on the couch. It was matched to the hair samples taken from Reed in his office. The characteristics of the hair all match up on the darker color. She said hair can be lightened from the sun or whatever, but underneath is the natural. It was not matched with DNA because that was not requested and it's expensive. If we want that she'll need authorization and that will take three to seven weeks. So again, that leaves us with when did Reed get a haircut?"

David returned Hayden's long stare.

"I suppose you want to go to the office now?" Hayden asked. "Dave, you know he does not have to tell us shit. And this really isn't anything."

"It's not him I want to talk to."

"Mel, I've got to go. Call me on my cell only if it's an emergency. Got it?" Brendan said. "If anyone asks I'm meeting with the guys from Mercy Hospital." Brendan threw his new tan raincoat over his arm carrying his briefcase. It was early afternoon. He would have just enough time to get to the bank, if they had everything together, and get to the mall early. He wanted to scope things out before six.

As soon as Mel saw Brendan get on the elevator, she pulled up her Law School paper on the computer screen. If Brendan could cut out early, she could tackle some homework. Mercy Hospital? Right! They just called today to postpone the meeting until next week.

The sun set earlier and earlier, fall was coming. By late afternoon the dusky clouds made the sky appear gray. Ray adjusted the tight wig, which covered her dark hair. With the contacts in place, she looked rather mousy with brown eyes and dull brown hair. Dark jeans and gray long sleeved shirt completed her look. Anonymous.

She stuffed the cheap merchandise she purchased into a trashcan. Each hand now held a shopping bag: one with the laptop, one was empty, waiting to be filled. She settled in a window table at a mall restaurant, which faced the parking lot. She had an hour to kill and watch.

At 5:15 Ray noticed a silver Mercedes pull up and park in the back of the lot near a light post. A man in shades sat in the car. Ray smiled. Her mark had followed instructions.

She sat for thirty minutes. Then, she paid for the soda and fries and went to the ladies room. The mirror reflected a young woman that only resembled Ray. The brown short hair fell into her eyebrows. The only clue was her Dingo cowboy boots. Ready.

Ray paused at the double doors of the mall entrance. The setting sun gave off little light. Shadows formed throughout the lot.

The man in the silver car now stood outside his vehicle, leaning against it. Following instructions.

The brunette hooked up with two other women exiting the mall. "Get any good buys?" Ray asked as she strolled along next to them with a big smile on her face.

The two mall rats exchanged looks. The trendily dressed teenagers assessed Ray as a social loser but responded out of pity. Not everyone could look like them. One of the highlighted heads replied to the sorry young woman, "We can always find something. We like Rave." She pointed to one of the several shopping bags they carried.

"That's a cool store. What other stores do you like?" Ray asked, glancing over to the silver car.

The two young girls provided short assessments of a few 'mandatory' stores. "I was like….and the salesgirl was like…" Ray ignored their drivel. She accompanied them to small cute car that daddy bought. She said goodbye and marched to her destination.

The young girls walking to their cars were a mere bleep on Brendan's radar. His eyes covered every direction. Tension in his body grew with each passing minute. Reluctant, he reached into the open window and pulled out the newly purchased briefcase, full of cash, following the last direction. He had no intention of parting ways with it. He barely noticed Ray walk up to him with two bags in her left hand.

"Show me the money," she addressed him.

He turned and looked at her. "What?"

"I haven't got all night. Show me the money."

A chick was shaking him down? No way. Brendan looked dumbfounded. Ray wanted the transaction over before the deer stepped out from the headlights.

"Okay, so your boyfriend's around?" Brendan scanned the lot with quick turns of his head.

"Last time. Show me the money," Ray said, annoyed at the suggestion.

Brendan smirked and patted the briefcase. Ray turned and walked away.

"Okay, wait, wait!" Brendan yelled.

Ray turned and looked at him from a few feet away. Brendan unlocked the case and peeled it open an inch, letting Ray gaze at the mounds of cash.

She took steps forward and put down her empty shopping bag. "Put the case in the bag."

"Show me the laptop," Brendan demanded, regaining his focus.

Ray slipped the thin, black computer up from one bag and returned it in the same fluid motion.

"How do I know you won't be looking for money again?"

"You'll have to trust that you never want to see me again. Put the case in the bag."

"Give me the laptop first."

She put both bags down in front of her and took a step to the side. Brendan put the case in the empty bag and stepped away also. Ray reached for the money bag with her left hand. Before she could secure her grip, Brendan's hand squeezed her wrist.

Her automatic response system activated. Her right hand swung from her pocket releasing the blade of the knife in the same motion. The knife made contact and cut deep into his upper thigh, inches away from more tender parts. Brendan's response was immediate: he yelped with pain.

Ray withdrew the knife when Brendan released her wrist. With the money bag in tow she took steps back.

"You bitch!" Brendan yelled.

"Look asshole, I'm not one of the stupid debutantes you've been dealing with."

"You cut me! Look at this." Blood stained his gray pants. His hands pressed the wound.

"Call the police." Ray responded without emotion. "Look, I keep up my end of deals. No one is going to the police. But, I will tell you that my boyfriend—my ex-boyfriend—feels compelled to go tell some woman whose husband is dead about the laptop. I don't think it will matter. Oh and trust me, you NEVER want to see me again!"

Ray walked back to the mall and entered. She went to the restrooms and lost the wig and contacts, then slipped the money into an alternate shopping bag. She exited the other end of the shopping center and got into her car. She drove home, blasting a CD by a local group rising in popularity with a mix of music somewhere between The Beatles and Black Sabbath. She yelled with satisfaction. Blood ran from between Brendan's fingers down his pants. The drips looked like candle wax overflowing from the flame. He leaned up against his car, still stunned at the course of events. A mall security scooter heading in his direction jolted him back to present time. He limped to the single shopping bag and clutched it. He hoisted himself into the Mercedes and started up the engine. With pain scorching through his left leg, he operated the vehicle and moved away.

Brendan knew where he had to go.

Pete was already there.

Thirty-Six

"Jim, you're going to take care of the warrant? I've got to get back to Hollis. I want to warn Kyle to stay away from that dirt-bag."

Sergeant Hayden nodded affirmatively while speaking into his cell. "Good work, Dave. This one would have got by me. I'll have a guy stationed here before I leave."

Dave ran from the office building to his truck. The more traffic he hit the more frantic his driving became. He reached under his seat and pulled out the seldom-used red light. Once the light was flashing and on top of his truck, some drivers yielded. Even on the highway, the volume of cars slowed his progress. He called into the station and told the duty officer to reach the chief and give him the days' events.

He directed an officer to Reed's house. He was wanted for questioning. He stopped short of sending a car to Kyle's home. She should not be in any immediate danger.

The permanent roadwork on Route 3 bottled up the traffic. An officer on duty waved him by a long strand of impatient commuters. He was just about to the New Hampshire border when his gut reeled up. He called Kyle at home. The phone rang and rang. The answering machine did not even pick up. He tried her cell. It rang into her voicemail.

Kyle where are you?

David sped up. Something was wrong.

Kyle turned down her road heading back home. She needed to eat a decent meal. Her once tight jeans, as well as most of her slacks, slipped down her hips. Maybe she could market her life as a weight loss program. The grocery store visit had gone well. Only two women turned their heads away and whispered to each other. Kyle understood. What could you say to someone whose dead husband was guilty of murder and then left the mess for his family to deal with? Next year will be better. She could only hope. On her way home, she decided on one detour via Pierce Lane.

When she reached the short road, Kyle pulled off to the side. It was not a major road in town, having been dirt until the recent paving. It was really a shortcut between two well-established roads, Silver Lake and Dove. Jason took the shortcut on his daily route. Kyle looked at the three homes on the street, set back from the road. Up towards the corner, where there were no homes and a break in the trees large enough for a vehicle to fit. She moved closer.

Pulled over into the space, she could see little of the road behind her, but the spot held a better view of the next road that it intersected with...Dove. As she admired the sand colored Contemporary home in her view through the few trees, she remembered who lived on Dove, who owned the home, the Reeds. Was it her imagination, or could this woman Kate have been spying on the Reeds from this spot in the dark? Could the accident have been just that? Then as if reading her thoughts, a cruiser pulled into the driveway of the home and parked. An officer went to the front door and rang the bell. After waiting a few moments, he returned to his vehicle and waited. With Brendan and his wife divorced, only one of them would presumably be living there and she thought Brendan mentioned staying in town. So who would the police want to speak with? And about what?

Kyle drove the short distance home. With the sun setting, streaks of light sprayed across the driveway. Once parked, she scanned the interior looking for her handbag. Then she remembered that she threw it under the pile of groceries in the back of the car. No big deal, she'd get it later. She'd call Matt, no…David, and tell him what he may already know. Mostly Kyle hoped to find out why a cruiser waited at the Reeds. With her arms full of bags, she turned and headed in.

He stood right in front of her.

Kyle's throat closed. She looked into the dark eyes of a tall, lanky young man dressed in a gray sweatshirt and jeans. And, black boots. Her heart raced. Her muscles froze. So much for being prepared. She dropped her keys and one of the bags slipped and crashed to the ground beside them.

"I need to talk to you." He saw the fear in her face. "I won't hurt you. I'm here to help." Pete bent down and picked up a couple of fallen items. He handed them to Kyle, who held them to her body with an arm.

"What?" Snap out of it, she yelled into her brain. Think! Think! Her feet woke first. She stepped backwards behind the house, feeling uneasy knowing she was heading in the direction of the pool.

"I think I know something about that woman they found in your pool."

Kyle dropped the other bags in her hands. She regretted losing the barrier but felt better with her hands free.

"I think she was having an affair with some guy who goes by BER or something. I don't think it was your husband…or maybe. I don't know. You need to read this stuff. She said she was pregnant and then she went missing. He doesn't want this stuff going to the police. Something is definitely up with this guy. I have proof." Pete reached into his sweatshirt pocket and pulled out a round disc with a white label that read 'insurance.'

Kyle heard the words but did not listen to them. The reaching into his jacket startled her and she took three giant steps back. When he looked up and noticed her movement, she halted.

"I want to help you. I would never hurt you. Honest."

The young man stood still. Kyle began to breathe again.

When her eyes returned to him, she saw again a young man, but a different one; a teenager with soiled jeans and big eyes holding out a disc. Not a weapon. His body was relaxed, not tense. In front of her was one soul trying to help another. Maybe? She remained apprehensive but not in a panic.

"What is your name?" Kyle asked.

"Pete."

"I'm Kyle."

"I know who you are, Mrs. Mercer."

That was a jolt. "Stay where you are." Kyle put her hand up to be sure a distance remained between them. "Tell me again. What is it you want me to know?"

"Well, I got this laptop…" Pete's head jumped in the direction of headlights coming up the driveway. The beams jetted across the yard, cutting through the early evening shadows. "I'm out of here. Here." He pushed the disc into her hand and vanished into the woods. Kyle stood and watched as the disc burned in her hand. The young man in the boots was gone.

The silver car squealed to a halt. Brendan stepped out, holding a dark spot on his leg. Kyle let out a deep breath and dropped her hands to her knees. Never a dull moment around here. Before he was within usual speaking distance, Kyle called out to him. "You wouldn't believe what just happened."

Brendan held his leg. He strained to walk as normal as possible, but resembled a pirate, avoiding the fallen groceries in his trail.

Kyle took notice of the struggling attorney and looked at him in a new light. "Brendan, what happened to you? Is that blood?" She bent and looked at the damage to his leg that his hand was covering. It looked like blood still oozed out. Brendan put his hand on her shoulder, guiding her to stand up. Kyle took in his face, which was pale and sweating. "Brendan, I think we should get you some help. I'll call."

"I'll be fine. Don't pay any attention to it." His eyes narrowed on her. "Tell me what happened. Did someone come here?" He spoke as slow as the adrenaline would allow. His throat was hoarse and dry.

"How did you know?" Kyle felt the disc in her hand and she looked into Brendan's eyes. They were hard, cold and looked back through her. Her heart jumped. Her stomach turned. It couldn't be. But she knew in her heart that the man she married was no killer.

"Just tell me what he said." When Kyle didn't respond he raised his voice and pressed his fingers into her shoulder. "Tell me what he said."

The force penetrated her shoulder and Kyle responded out of fear. "He gave me this." Kyle raised her hand. Brendan's focus went to the disc. As he reached for it, Kyle threw it over his shoulder. He growled something but Kyle didn't hear. She turned and ran towards the woods. The teenager, who only minutes ago terrified her, didn't seem so bad now.

"PETE!" She yelled for help. She only got one call out before Brendan jumped on her from behind. He snatched her hair, jerking her back. Kyle let out a scream but was muffled as she collapsed with him on top of her. His weight crushed her. After a tussle, she ended up pinned on her back, facing the bleeding, sweating and desperate man.

"What did he tell you?" Kyle's throat froze again. He cracked a slap to her face. Pain stung her skin. "What did he tell you? I tried to help you. I didn't want this to happen. We could've been good for each other." Brendan screamed at her. "That bitch had it coming. She wasn't pregnant. She drugged me so she could GET pregnant."

Brendan snapped into a haze of anger. It welled up and took him over. He realized what he had to do. In for a penny… His hands went around her throat. He pressed his thumbs into her neck, just as he had the others. She would be the next victim of this confusing mess. He would be long gone. This would be done. It was his only way out.

Kyle saw only his face with the darkness of the coming night all around it, like a tunnel. Gasps for air went unanswered. Her fingers clawed at Brendan's hands, but were unable to get him to even budge. It was as if in this state, he felt no pain.

Matt's voice, for years now giving her orders, came to her. He forced her to attend the Self Defense Class that he'd taught. Focus. Look for your opportunity. Look for a weakness. Think, then act.

With a fist and all the strength she could muster on no air, she punched into Brendan's left leg, getting a solid hit to his wound. He screamed and fell back. She launched onto all fours and strained to get to her feet, coughing and dizzy. Brendan came at her again. Before he reached her with his outstretched arms, a branch clocked him on the side of the head. He went down like luggage.

Kyle steadied herself next to a tree and looked into the face of her angel. It was Pete. "Are you all right?"

The red light of David's truck flashed into the yard.

"Is that the police? I have to go." He looked at Kyle and waited for her to respond.

"You go. I'll be okay now. Thanks..." Kyle whispered.

She saw the uniform running to her and fell to the ground. When she saw it was David, tears ran down her face in a steady release of pressure.

"Are you okay?" he knelt down.

"I am now."

"I'm sorry, Kyle. This is my fault. If I had done a better job, this wouldn't have happened."

"It's not your fault."

David wrapped her up in his strong, safe arms. Kyle pushed her forehead into his chest. David held her tight.

He spoke in a gentle voice. "Reed's in this murder up to his eyeballs. I don't think there's enough evidence to get him for murder yet, but we should be able to connect him."

David's head shot up, hearing a noise in the woods. After a quick glance at the injured attorney, the Officer drew his weapon.

"Police! Come out of the woods with your hands up!" he shouted and rose to his feet, pointing his gun towards the noise.

A jittery Pete crept out of the woods, keeping his distance and hands up, with his eyes glued to the gun.

"David, no! He saved me! Put your gun down." Kyle pulled herself to her feet.

David stood firm.

"Can't you just let him go? Brendan doesn't even know what hit him. If it wasn't for him..." Kyle pleaded.

David looked down at the semi-conscious lawyer on the ground and then back to the young man. He let his gun drop. "Take off."

Pete muttered some thanks and followed the order.

The attorney let out a moan. Kyle shuddered.

"Kyle, he can't hurt you now." David gave into his impulse and kissed her forehead. She was just moments from being his next victim.

He went over to the wounded man. "Looks like you have some injuries, Mr. Reed. We'll have to get you some medical attention." David opened his cuffs and secured them onto Brendan's hands behind his back, unconcerned whether the movements caused more discomfort to the man.

Brendan yelped again and again.

"What are you doing? I've been stabbed. I'm a victim. I was saving Kyle from an intruder."

"Brendan Reed, you're under arrest."

"I'll have your badge, you idiot. You have nothing on me."

"Well, to start, judging by the marks on Kyle's neck, I have attempted murder. Then, we can add obstruction of justice, conspiracy, and maybe murder of Kathleen Thompson."

"You have nothing to connect me."

"Oh, actually we do. I spent the afternoon with Shelly. You know Shelly, from your office? She was quite helpful. She said you cut your blond hair off last November. She thought it odd because your hair always looked like you highlighted it. And she hated how long it was. Then all of a sudden you made a dramatic change. She has quite a memory for detail. And then, with the help of your Tech guys, we looked at your computer. We saw enough to get a warrant. We can get more off your hard drive. And maybe your laptop."

"That's private. You had no authority."

"Again, Shelly, the office administrator was very helpful. She gave us permission to look at anything, so we didn't need a warrant. Seems she has access to everything. Oh, and Mel had a lot to say too."

David called for help, securing Reed to the ground with his foot to Brendan's shoulder. He looked back to Kyle.

Thirty-Seven

Three months later...

"I'll take care of it all when I get back," she said to the pink bikini-clad Annie. "Pass the sunscreen." The two women lay back on chaise lounges, baking in the sun. Large pink drinks sat nearby, filled with fresh fruit hanging down the sides. Annie visited here often but it was Kyle's first trip to Punta Canta, a resort in the Dominican Republic. In the distance, the waves crashed on the white sand beach, pushing a fresh breeze.

"Hey, you want to get wet? I'm hot," Annie said.

"Sounds good."

The pair walked to the enormous warm pool. It was an artistic accomplishment with blue and rust colored tiles creating a beautiful mosaic. Kyle took one look at the pool and froze. The marks on her neck were gone, but not forgotten. The body of water looked stagnant. "How about the ocean instead...that water's alive, it moves."

Annie joined her in the salt water where the predators were easily identifiable. Sharks did not pretend to be dolphins.

Back at home, Kyle stood outside the newly landscaped house. The For Sale sign sat out front. She gazed upon the extended lawn with new seed. After the demolition and removal, the backyard now held only grass and shrubs where the pool once was. Piles of new dirt and vegetation cleansed the area.

David walked up behind her and put his hand on her shoulder. "You ready to go?"

"Yes. Think you'll ever be able to charge Reed with murder?"

"There's no physical evidence tying him to the murder. He'll get some felony jail time for assaulting you among other things and be disbarred. That's not bad. Some murders go completely unsolved. The Boston PD is also looking into links between him and a young nanny found strangled two years ago."

The next morning, Kyle woke up in her new bed alone, except for Pumpkin, fast asleep against her back. Maggie snored on the floor. Kyle shot up in bed and looked around the new room. Windows behind the bed cast the morning sunlight directly in front of her, flooding the room with perky brightness. This would take some time to get used to. But the new surroundings were just what she needed. And definitely held some advantages. David emerged from the shower with only a white towel hanging from his narrow hips. Kyle smiled.

"If you're going to come out of the shower every morning looking like that, you'll be late for work….a lot!"

David smiled. "I've got all the time in the world for you. How'd you sleep?"

"Great!"

About Author Robin Beaudette

Robin Beaudette is a free lance writer residing in New Hampshire. She is the wife of a physician, the mother of two boys and enjoys the company of a loyal chocolate Labrador retriever, Mugsy, and 2 cats, Porka and Steggs. An avid animal lover, she served as a member of the Hollis Conservation Commission. She has also worked with serious youth offenders in the juvenile justice system.

Beaudette has a B.A. in Political Science, with a concentration in Psychology, from Boston College. She is a member of the Rivier College Writers'/ Critiquing Group and the New Hampshire Writer's Project. She has previously published two short stories; "Absence"- Great Mystery and Suspense Magazine 10/06 and "Dear John"- non fiction/ Friends- Stories of Friendship/ Anthology, A Measure of Words Press 5/05

Printed in the United States
220714BV00004B/10/P